Praise for *The Amate[...]*
Craig Sherborne's first nove[...]

'All women with lingering illu[...]
think should read this fast-movin[...]
shattering little thunderclap of [...]

'An engulfing, heart-stopping boo[...] [...]rmance that
dazzles the eyes and leaves the reader gasping for air.' *Age*

'Sherborne writes so well that he cannot fail to include
colour in the darkness...This is a masterful portrait.'
Sydney Morning Herald

'Fascinating, funny and unputdownable.' *Sunday Herald Sun*

'Poignant...Little can prepare us for this fine novel's
"heartwrecking puzzle".' *Weekly Times*

'Absorbing...the characters are solid and believable,
the storyline unpredictable and the rural Australian
imagery vivid.' *Books+Publishing*

Praise for *Hoi Polloi* and *Muck*,
Craig Sherborne's memoirs

'One of nature's writers.' Peter Craven

'Gruesomely honest and very, very funny.' Hilary Mantel

'Mordantly true to life...one of the most interesting
autobiographical projects on the go.' J. M. Coetzee

'He writes beautifully, especially when the material is not
beautiful at all. He can make the cruel truth poetic.' Clive James

'Riveting...Moral courage has propelled this book to the page.
Its execution is sublime.' *Scotsman*

CRAIG SHERBORNE's first novel, *The Amateur Science of Love* (2011), won the Melbourne Prize for Literature's Best Writing Award, and was shortlisted for the NSW Premier's and Victorian Premier's Literary Awards. His memoir *Hoi Polloi* (2005) was shortlisted for the Queensland Premier's and Victorian Premier's Literary Awards. The follow-up, *Muck* (2007), won the Queensland Premier's Literary Award for Non-fiction. Craig has also written two volumes of poetry, *Bullion* (1995) and *Necessary Evil* (2006), and a verse drama, *Look at Everything Twice for Me* (1999). His writing has appeared in most of Australia's literary journals and anthologies. He lives in Melbourne.

Tree Palace

CRAIG SHERBORNE

TEXT PUBLISHING
MELBOURNE AUSTRALIA

The Text Publishing Company
Swann House
22 William Street
Melbourne Victoria 3000
Australia
textpublishing.com.au

First published in 2014 by The Text Publishing Company

Cover and page design by WH Chong
Typeset in Garamond Premier Pro by J & M Typesetting
Printed and bound in Australia by Griffin Press, an Accredited ISO AS/NZS 14001:2004 Environmental Management System printer

National Library of Australia Cataloguing-in-Publication entry:
Author: Sherborne, Craig, 1962-, author.
Title: Tree palace / by Craig Sherborne.
ISBN: 9781922147325 (paperback)
ISBN: 9781922148353 (ebook)
Subjects: Rural homeless persons—Victoria—Fiction. Homeless families—Victoria—Fiction. Squatters—Victoria—Fiction.
Dewey Number: A823.4

This book is printed on paper certified against the Forest Stewardship Council® Standards. Griffin Press holds FSC chain-of-custody certification SGS-COC-005088. FSC promotes environmentally responsible, socially beneficial and economically viable management of the world's forests.

This project has been assisted by the Commonwealth Government through the Australia Council, its arts funding and advisory body.

For Gordon Glenn

And round about there is a rabble
Of the filthy, sturdy, unkillable infants of the very poor.
They shall inherit the earth.
—*Ezra Pound, 'The Garden'*

1

They tried Mansfield but it was freezing and snowed and people like them don't fit in because they don't look prosperous. One time near Yellingbo they found a church no one prayed in and they lived there and for three weeks had stained glass for windows. It was the perfect church Shane was looking for for work. They got chased out and went to Shepparton but Shane had a run-in and police said move. By then Zara was starting her problem and that worsened matters. Eventually they came back west to the Wimmera-Mallee plains because they knew the roads and home was home there though whatever relatives they'd bothered with left ages ago. Out to where trains no longer ran through the towns each day and none had passengers, just tubs of wheat and barley if those were viable that season. It didn't look prosperous which meant they didn't look out of place. There was a sense of something closing and ending with shops boarded up and mail blackening the doorways like rot. That was to their benefit and sometimes they broke in and played house till someone found them and made trouble. They could always camp in the forests. The locals shrugged off their kind as 'trants', which came from 'itinerants', because of the way they could sleep among saplings no better than camping. They weren't blacks or anything, they just lived that way. Typical trants. A little caravan of blue pine board for their travelling abode. At dark they built fire between stumps of stone and sat round that like night round the moon. They had Shane and his brains and that was their meal ticket. Most trants had been driven out of the life but they remained, the last of their kind.

Then they came upon the place off Loop Road, away from the highway on the outskirts of the town of Barleyville, a better town by the plains' standards, population almost twelve hundred. A place that may or may not have belonged to anyone but clearly wasn't at the forefront of people's thoughts. Up a rise beside a dirt track through a tree-screen of skinny ironbarks. It had no fence or gate. They set up a letterbox—a bucket turned side-on and mounted on a star picket, a mouth cut out for mail. The mail was only from the government but that was worth it. The clay ground had broken away in ruts from a long-ago storm. Tussocky grasses held it together in clumps and when the wind blew the ground seemed to move in the distance from the grey sway and chafing of it all. Not the kind of land worth ten cents to farmers. Quartz stones were sharp on the feet but intriguing to peer at, dusty white with tan patterns. Bits of bark and leaves blew everywhere or crackled like footfalls from the heavy sun.

The best thing was the house. When they first saw it it no longer looked liveable because grass sprouted in the roof and pushed up through the floor. That could be dealt with. It was old with a wrinkled feel the way the weatherboards had peeled and twisted. From the front it looked like a face with its open door hanging wide from the hinges and either side a window for eyes. Tattered blinds fluttered like eyelids and when birds flew out of the broken glass the window could have been blinking. It was time to stop moving and having nowhere for their anchor and always the expense of keeping the caravan roadworthy. This was something more normal that came free.

They parked the caravan beside the house, at a right angle to it so the L-shape blocked the west winds and a lot of the hard west sun. This meant the canvas that usually formed the caravan's porch could go over the house and serve that same purpose. Shane used nails with flat heads to make it stay up permanently. The metal buttons that clicked it together were tough to push in which made it good and tough to pull apart once united. It sagged like the house had a hat brim.

Shane and Moira slept in the house and Rory and Midge had the caravan. For Zara a tent was tied on the end of the caravan. Shane got it from the new bloke he was dealing with in town. The tent was green with a plastic window and a flap-door for privacy and was well pegged down but had stones for extra weight around the bottoms to block draughts and snakes. She originally slept on her mattress in the house but it only had one bedroom and the kitchen was hot and cramped for sleeping. She'd got irritated and demanded a room of her own.

They rolled a stump into the centre of the L for a table and ashtray, got rocks from all around for a barbeque arrangement and spread themselves out with their paraphernalia: old deckchairs and a sofa they'd taken from the side of the road somewhere which was synthetic enough to withstand weather. They put up their kero lamps for night light and strung a cord that had bulbs plugged to it around the porch for when they got a generator to replace the dead one.

Shane's new bloke had some pot plants at the back of his shop and he let Shane have them. Moira loved this and put them under the porch for decoration where she could move them in and out of the shade and sprinkle on some water. Water was a problem because the shallow hollow they called the dam, which Shane and Midge had dug by hand, hadn't filled due to the dry. When it eventually did it would be brown and salty anyway. The house came with a rain tank off to the side but it was empty and not likely to hold the merest moisture. Holes were everywhere and the bigger holes wore long, droopy moustaches of rust. Shane kept his eye out for a better one on his work trips and got lucky at a woolshed in West Paradise. A tank in sound condition, not too big or awkward to transport. He emptied what water was in it, roped it down in the car trailer and brought it home. He also took some of the guttering, which was in good shape compared with theirs. The tank stand was solid too so he dismantled that for their using. Shane and Midge rigged it to the house—new tank, new guttering, new stand. Now all they had to do was wait for rain.

In the meantime they drove to the Barleyville trotting track for water. It was only ten ks every second day and it was fresh town

4

water from the taps at the horse stalls. They filled three jerry cans and had a wash and used the toilets, a break from the long-drop Shane had dug with Midge on barrow duty carting away the dirt and helping bang together some roof iron for a screen. Rory and Zara went to school for a little of last year and used the facilities there, though it was summer holidays at the moment.

On one water run, about a k from the trotting track a tiny dog, a fox terrier type with ginger markings, ran after the car. Shane noticed it in the mirror and felt sorry for the creature and stopped to shoo it away. The dog wouldn't go and had a limp like Midge, as if hit by a car once or born that way. A dog seemed like a good idea so when it wouldn't go they adopted it on the spot as a watchdog and family mascot. He lived on scraps and kangaroo shit and they called him Limpy. He could detect cars far off on the highway and scurried about yapping until they faded from hearing.

There was a car turning off the highway this minute, coming straight for them, but Limpy didn't bark. His tail went stiff and shook because it was their car, the silvery old Falcon station wagon with chugging V8 and squeaking suspension. They shortened 'wagon' to 'wag' for its name. The dust sprayed up behind it and swirled like a funnel. Limpy trotted to greet it. Moira was driving and Zara was in the passenger side. Limpy ran from side to side to greet them equally and wouldn't stop when Moira told him not to jump up.

'Rory,' she called. 'Rory. Come here.'

Rory heard and wasn't ignoring her but he had his two throwing knives from Shane for Christmas—soft blue handles and nicely weighted blades—and hadn't finished practising. He'd ridden to the Mockorange Road turnoff and played dragons with himself but that got scary, so he came home. He knelt behind a rock among the ironbarks just up from a hare he was aiming at and let fly with a knife. He missed by a long way and the hare scampered. Rory liked the way it pulled back its big ears for running and hunched as he himself did when he rode his bike. But that wouldn't stop him trying to get it. He walked to where the knife landed and flicked it to the ground for practise. Moira was still calling but he practised twice more before he gave in to her. He wondered whether his skinny arms would get some meat on them if he practised throwing enough. His shoulders too. He had an excuse for walking slow because of his flat feet, but that didn't apply to puny shoulders.

Moira called him again and took two bags of groceries from the car and put them on the ground. She went to Zara's side of the vehicle and said, 'Come on, out you come, sweetie.' She clapped her hands softly in a bossy fashion. Bossy but smiling and enjoying herself. She reached to the back seat and said, 'All right there, baby?' She unbuckled a baby capsule, slid it onto her thigh and lifted it out. 'Not too hot, little man?'

She puckered her lips and blew air into the capsule, which to her sounded an inhuman name for a baby thing. She preferred 'the little bed'. 'Zara, sweetie, I think you should carry the wee man and say to him, Here we are home. He's sleeping but he'll feel your voice.'

Rory tucked his knives into the drawstring of his trackie pants and scuffed up to the car. His runners trapped little stones in their tread and always made his scuffing louder. Moira nodded at the bags of groceries. 'Use your muscles on those.'

Saying something like that—'Use your muscles'—to Rory would normally make Zara snigger. He saw she wasn't sniggering. She was staying in the car, staring directly ahead as if still travelling.

Moira nudged him. 'Go on. Carry the groceries.'

He took a bag in each hand and groaned about them being too heavy. Moira said not to be a sook and just carry them. 'When you've done that there's a pram in the back. Take it out and put it in the tent.'

Rory groaned again. He shuffled past Zara making a heaving noise, hoisting the bags up like barbells for her amusement. She usually shook her head in mockery at him but didn't bother this time, which made him shuffle faster to be funnier.

Moira lifted the baby from the little bed and held it so its head nestled her jaw and her fingers could keep its neck straight. She backed away from the car and rocked on each foot, saying, 'There's the boy.' A spinning top of dust swept by in a gust and she held the baby closer till it passed. The smell of smoke was in the gust. It was bushfire season, but this smelled far enough off. She rocked slowly towards Zara. 'Can't just sit there, sweetie. Out you come. Come on, out.'

Zara did as she was told—she got out and closed the car door. She put her thumbs in her belt loops above her hind pockets, looked down at the ground and fidgeted her toes in her thongs to stop the tiny stones from catching under them.

Moira cradled the baby's furry skull in her palm. She smelled it and said, 'So milky and clean, eh, Zara? About as clean as anyone ever gets.' She leant forward and held out her elbows, directing Zara to take the baby.

Rory bustled past them to the back of the car. He manoeuvred a green pram, like a mini tent with wheels, out onto the ground. It was folded up and he couldn't get it to wheel without unfolding it. Unfolding it was like trying to unclench pincers, so he dragged it as it was.

'Don't drag it,' Moira said. 'You'll rip it. Here, leave it. You're as useless...I'll do it.' She wanted to yell at him but not near the baby. She yanked the pram upright into position and told Rory to wheel it gently to the tent. 'I said, gently.'

The boy scuffed his feet with extra slowness which to him equated to gently and he decided that Zara looked like she always did, not any older for having a baby. Moira had her hand on Zara's shoulder, telling her to walk towards the porch to avoid the heat. 'Don't keep his face covered,' she said, fingering the rug the baby was swaddled in. 'Got to let him breathe.'

She was trying to get Zara to smile but instead it looked like she might cry again. She'd cried in the car and her eyes had the runs from make-up. Moira reached under and around the baby and took the weight and Zara let go.

'Ho, ho, what a load, aren't you, wee man? A nice big boy.'

She kissed the baby on the face which was puffed and pouted in sleep. 'So, sweetie, we've decided on the Mathew name once and for all, no going back?'

Zara nodded.

'Good. No going back. You know I like Mathew. It's got a touch of the old-fashioned and everyone's making up names now... Saxxon, Braython, you know?'

Zara nodded.

'Mathew, say hello to your uncle Rory. Rory, come here and say hello to your wee nephew. And don't shorten it to Mat. Mat's a thing you wipe your feet on. It's *Mathew*. Rory, come here and say hello.'

Rory peeped into the swaddling and said hello and how you doing. He started laughing at the bald amount of hair on the skull.

'I'm going to put him out of the sun,' Moira said.

She went towards the tent and stopped and made a flicking motion with her head to signal for Zara to follow. 'You coming, Zara?'

Zara nodded that she was but not this second. In a minute she'd come. Moira took a slow breath and let it out as a sigh.

'Moody mums, eh, Mathew? I'm going to put you down in the tent. It's hot but not too hot in there, wee man. Come with Nana.'

The tent's flap was tied open like a triangular door. It was dark inside but not blinding dark because the plastic side window was open.

Rory said, 'You going back to school when it starts up, Zar?'

'What?'

'Only a few weeks off. You'll probably get out of going back. You wanted to leave anyway?'

'Hadn't decided.'

'Soon as you could, you said. School could go fuck itself. Fuck waiting till you're seventeen.'

He started speaking in that way he did with no commas and no thoughts in a clear order. An excitable jumble about an idea he had: If he did so bad at school they'd have to kick him out, wouldn't they? 'Do they kick you out, Zara? I want to do bad so they got to kick me out.'

9

He celebrated getting kicked out by pretending to throw his knives at her. She flinched and swore at him. He complained that he was joking and didn't deserve swearing.

Moira came out of the tent and told him to stop being a pest.

'I wasn't.'

She asked him where Shane was.

Rory said he was off somewhere and Midge was off somewhere with him. He said they were making a storage shed in the bush for their business instead of leaving it under a tarp. Ten minutes' walk over the rise.

'Zara, sweetie. It's nice and comfy in there. You can go in. I'm going to get Shane's dry-cleaning from the car. You go in, lie down.'

She walked over to the car and fiddled getting the coat hanger off the hook above the back seat. Zara sat under the porch and lit a cigarette.

'Was hospital good?' asked Rory. 'Getting waitered on and stuff?'

Zara dragged on her cigarette and didn't reply.

Moira came back with the dry-cleaning in cellophane. Shane's coat from Shepparton when they got him for those Masonic Hall doors. Coats work in courtrooms—coat, tie and a shave. Moira cut his hair and he looked perfect and got his sentence suspended and no fine. He spilt beer over the coat during celebrations. Always got to have a clean coat and tie ready, that was Shane's motto.

'Zara, go lay down will you while Mathew's sleeping. Might as well while he's quiet.'

'Is she going back to school?' Rory asked.

'Forget about that now.'

'Reckon she'd cop some shit.'

'I said forget it. And watch your mouth.'

'Well she would. And some of those chicks at school gave her shit when she swelled up.'

Moira took a few steps his way with her hand out like she'd belt him. 'Go away, Rory.'

'I didn't mean nothing.'

'Find something to do. Go ask Shane for something to do.'

He did as she ordered, scuffing and mumbling down the side of the house. Then he turned around and stood with his hands on his head like Simon Says. 'Is she going back to school? I only mean it's better if she don't. Let me handle the shit alone. I can handle it better if she's not there. People expect you to stand up for your sister.'

Moira had her back to him and kept it that way. She knew he was pretending to throw a knife at her or giving the finger but she didn't react. She ignored him, which was the best way with Rory. She took a pack of cigarettes from her pocket. The pockets were big in this dress—the one with flowers patterns, her favourite—and the lighter always got lost down the bottom. She dug around for it and lit up and sat on the deckchair next to Zara.

'You've fed Mathew, haven't you? Of course you've fed him or he'd be crying. He'll be awake soon and bawling so you better keep your liquids up. You want a cup of something?'

Zara stubbed out her cigarette in the dirt beside her feet. 'I want another ciggie.' She pushed her hand down her jean pocket and pulled out a crumpled pack.

'How many you had today?'

'Not many.'

'Well, keep count.'

Zara opened the crumpled lid but the only cigarette left was broken at the filter. She said shit to it and threw it to the ground. Moira bent over and picked it up and placed it in the ashtray on the stump. It was really an old chipped dinner plate but it was good for butts.

'You know what I think?' said Moira. 'I think Mathew is the best name in the world. Not too different and not too ordinary. You know what I felt when I was picking you up? I felt excited.'

'Can I bludge a smoke?'

'I've got used to the idea of having a little Mathew around. Shane's settling down to the idea too. I say to him, You'll be a sort of granddad, Shane. He don't flare up. He don't go all gooey either. But he don't flare up. Good sign.'

Zara held out her hand and snapped her fingers impatiently for a cigarette. Moira reached into her pocket.

'How many you had today?'

'Not many.'

'Your limit's meant to be five. Nurse said not at all, but if you have to, five.'

She took one from her pack and lit it for her.

'That's number two. Nurse said I got to mother the mother.'

Zara crossed an arm over her knees and rested her head there.

'You all right in the heat, sweetie?'

'Just tired.'

'That nurse woman. She didn't ask too many questions, did she?'

'Yeah.'

'What questions?'

'You know, how we were set up. Money and stuff.'

'Asked me the same. I'm only thinking of the baby's welfare, she said. Know what I said? I said, Oh, can the baby go on welfare too? That shut her up quick smart. You know what I told her? I told her we'd just absorb little Mathew into the family. They can sneer all they like, her type, but that's what we are, close enough anyway. Family.'

She leant over and rubbed Zara's back. 'You're home now. We take care of our own.'

She kissed Zara's hair, which had the mint smell of hospital soap. 'You sure you don't need some liquids?'

'I need sleep,' Zara mumbled into her knees. 'I'm dizzy.'

'Probably the smokes.'

'I got to sleep off this sickness.'

'You're not sick—you're a mum.'

'It's a sickness.'

'It's not a sickness. Don't talk sickness.'

Moira stood up and squashed her smoke into the ashtray plate. 'You better eat plenty, that's the secret. You're starting to thin back to normal and you need your energy. You don't want to end up too thin. Not with Mathew needing you to feed from. I'm going to get you some liquids.'

The house had the blue look that floated inside when the falling sun spread out along the horizon like a blast of light. It caught the edge of the caravan and shone up under the porch and in the windows. It was a buckled blue nearest the kitchen section because

Shane had not yet found glass to fit that window. He'd got glass for the other one and puttied it in place himself but the kitchen window made do with two layers of glad wrap taped together in patchwork style. If the wind came up the layers blew out and Moira fastened the shutter Shane had made from slats of wood left over from building the tank stand. In calm weather the caravan's blue was reflected inside as now. It bent and rippled in the patchwork and made watery patterns on the wall. It was so blue on clear days that the flame from the camp cooker mingled with it and couldn't be seen. You could forget it was on and waste a whole gas cylinder.

The jerry cans were translucent plastic but the blueness coloured them as well, darkening the water within and making it look pleasantly cooler. They didn't keep ice so that had to do them—imagining coolness as they pushed the rubber tap top and poured. Moira poured a glass for Zara, mixed with orange cordial to hide any plastic taste. She cocked her head in the direction of the door but didn't take her eyes off the pouring in case she spilt a drop.

She took a biscuit from the stack of tins on the bench that served as cupboards. A ginger nut and a sticky one with lemon cream. One of the flies buzzing around the tins flew up and hit her lip. She puffed it aside and waved others from the biscuits, then ignored them when they settled straight back. She was used to flies till they weren't flies anymore, just part of the air.

She came out the door and there was Zara doubled over and retching. Moira put the glass on the doorstep but rotten dips in the timber made it tip over. The biscuits got crushed in the effort to catch it.

'What's wrong? You want something to be sick in?'

Zara shook her head. 'I need to sleep.'

She held the cigarette out for Moira to take and get rid of. Moira stubbed it and knelt and rubbed Zara's back, up and down the knobby ridge the girl's spine made from bending so far forward. 'I did a session at the laundromat with your sheets. They're nice and ready for you.'

'Don't rub my back. Don't want to be touched.'

'Let's go and get you in the tent.'

'No.'

'If you want sleep then that's the place for you.'

'No.'

'It's nice and ready.'

'I mean by myself. Somewhere to sleep by myself.'

'There's only Mathew in there with you.'

'By myself.'

There was guttural force in her tone. She jabbed her elbow up to make Moira's hand stop rubbing.

'I've arranged things in there for you, Zara. It's clean and comfy.'

'It's all over now. My body's back to normal like it never happened.'

'Never happened? That's silly talk.'

There was a bulge showing under Zara's blouse, a loose bit of skin from her stomach that was obvious when she didn't sit up straight. Up straight it couldn't be noticed. Zara sat very straight and patted her stomach and put her fingers under the blouse to test the looseness. She made a face, a disgusted look, when she felt the spongy texture of herself. She smiled when she took her fingers out of her blouse and patted her stomach and pushed it smooth.

'Listen, girl. You got a baby now. Sleeping's good for the baby to do. You go have a lie down if you want and that's fine. But silly talk and pretending it never happened, that's good for nothing.'

Moira rubbed her forearm where Zara's elbow had connected. She put her hand in her pocket for a cigarette but thought that would make Zara want one. The girl would just sit there smoking and talking silly talk. Moira clenched her jaw, bit hard as she always did when angered. She winced at the electric shock it caused in her gum where a back tooth was missing. 'You're in your tent with Mathew where I've made it nice. You can go have a lie down and look after him. I'll put the groceries away.'

She waited a moment for Zara to nod or say something or make a move to the tent. The girl did nothing, just sat there. Standing around watching wasn't going to shift her so Moira went into the house where the blue glow was dimming and brightening according to the clouds moving across the sun. She picked items from the plastic shopping bags—margarine, instant coffee, canned sausages in spaghetti, bread, toilet paper, potatoes, corn chips, tubs of instant noodles, Coke, dish cloths. The margarine had leaked. She sucked it from her fingers. She left the Nescafé to one side because she wanted a cup. She lit the cooker for the water and refilled Zara's spilt glass with cordial and took it to her.

The girl hadn't moved. Moira put the glass at her feet, screwing its base into the pebbly sand so it wouldn't tilt. 'You want some chicken noodles, sweetie? I got water on.'

No, Zara indicated by shaking her head. Her eyes were closed. Her mouth was closed and smiling. Not a full smile, more a dreamy turn of lip.

It was late enough in the day for a carpet of sun to spread out in front of the porch, squeezing through a gap between the L of the house and caravan. Clouds took it away and put it back again like sleight of hand. It was a pleasant effect, the simplest magic, and always left Moira cheered. Maybe it had cheered Zara too, she thought. Had put that smile on her face. It was not something she would risk asking in case it broke the girl's spell.

Life was measured in being cheered one minute and not the next but trying to stretch that good minute out longer. When she got new underwear for Zara for hospital she herself was cheered because it was so sensible. She was cheered at having the idea to use pantyhose for Zara's Christmas stocking. Hanging from her ward bed full of underwear and chocolate, it would make the biggest sourpuss laugh. She had a reserve of coins to wash baby clothes. That cheered her. Zara's smiling cheered her. She decided she better urge the girl into the tent before the smiling passed.

No good. Zara held her elbows in a ready position and would not be urged to her feet. She scratched at her breasts, at the sides and underneath them. She squirmed, as if getting bitten.

'What's wrong?' Moira asked, kneeling down to her.

Zara kept scratching her breasts and then punched them. Three blows.

Moira tried getting her arms past the elbows and fists, saying, 'Stop,' using her bigger weight to hug the girl. Her own breasts and belly were hefty enough to smother Zara's arms and keep her pressed close despite the wriggling and fury and the guttural sound.

'Shh. Stop. Shh. Don't. Shh. What are you doing to yourself! Shane and Midge'll be here soon. You don't want them seeing this.'

Zara was sobbing now.

'Look up at me. Look in my face. You got a baby now. You got to love it. I'll help you.'

'I don't want it.'

'Well, you got it.'

'Take it away.'

'We're not taking it nowhere. This is his home. It's not hospital, all unnatural and cold. It's home.'

'Nurse said it must be a shame.'

'What shame?'

'At my age, having a kid.'

'You forget about a stupid nurse. They're meant to be educated, that lot. But she must be stupid. You know what she said to me? She said, Oh yes, it was an easy birth. No problems at all. Nature's perfect age, fifteen. Okay?'

Zara nodded, okay.

'When I had you I weren't much older, so they can stick their shame.'

Mathew started crying in the tent. A little engine of crying that sputtered at first then got its rhythm.

'There you go,' said Moira. 'Come on, he wants his mum. He wants you. You're wanted. That's a good thing.'

She took Zara's wrists in a soft grip and made her lower her guard. Told her to put her hands at her sides and tilt her head

18

back and let nature work on her body. She undid the buttons on Zara's white blouse, bought from the Barleyville Salvos for this very purpose. It opened easily and had a sash of white lace that was dignified. T-shirts were not dignified when you had to hoist the entire front up to get at the nipples. The blouse splayed enough to let a breast come through but didn't gape and ruin privacy. The bra was Zara's normal one because she never was big in that department and didn't need much extra size for baby feeding.

'Your milk should be coming down, so just relax yourself.'

Zara started doing the buttons up. Moira touched her arm and tapped on it as an instruction for the buttons to be undone. Zara kept buttoning them.

'No. Don't, sweetie.'

She directed Zara to stand and come with her to the tent. She fended Zara's hands from the blouse to prevent more buttoning.

They got to the flap of the door and stepped inside. There was gold-green dimness in there, of dark canvas and sunlight peering in through the back wall, exposing slits in the weave. Bubbles of sweat had formed beneath the clear plastic laid over the ground for a rug. The old canvas smelled like wet soil. Moira had burned an incense stick for a freshener that morning but the aroma was gone. It didn't matter, she thought, as she walked Zara in. The tent was as spruced up as she could make it, with Zara's bed folded down in a welcoming way and sprigs from the waxy red pot plants decorating the pillow.

Mathew was on his back on the bed. He was crying, one long breath of crying. Just as soon as Zara was settled Moira intended to bring the pram in and jam its wheels between two wooden boxes. That would have to do for a cot for now. She'd bought the biggest pack of nappies the supermarket had and wished she had a cupboard for them but leaving them in the wrapping would probably be cleanest. They'd be handiest beside the pram with a plastic bag of Salvos baby clothes.

'Where are my posters?' said Zara.

'You don't want posters.'

Pop-star posters. Handsome boys with sneers and sulky frowns.

'Where are they?'

'I put them in a box. And I put your CDs in a box.'

'I want them.'

'Forget them and feed Mathew.'

'Where are they?'

'Under your bed.'

Zara got on her knees and looked under the bed and pulled out a cardboard box. It jammed on the low metal base but she kept pulling despite the box tearing at a corner. The bed lifted, its frame lurched. Mathew tipped this way and that and Moira hurried and got him.

'You don't need posters and kids' stuff like that. Sit down and feed him.'

Zara had the posters out and was unfolding them and smoothing them on her knees for hanging. There was tape on their edges but it was bent over, stuck down. She tried to peel a corner free. The corner tore.

'Sit on the bed.'

Another corner tore.

'I said, sit on the bed.'

'I want them on my wall.'

'Sit down.'

'No.'

'Take Mathew and feed him.'

'No.'

'Yes.'

'There is no baby.'

Moira put Mathew in the pram and kicked the box away from Zara's reach. She scooped up a poster and another poster and ripped them in half and then in half again. Zara snatched at one but Moira kept ripping and clenched her jaw, turning her shoulder to barge Zara away if it came to that. If the girl wanted trouble then let her have it. She was going to sit down whether she liked it or not. Moira's arm muscles were starting to sag these days but they were still strong enough to deal with Zara. She took hold of her in a barging embrace and then softened her grip because the girl was tearful and shaking like a frightened thing. She kissed her head. She told her to sit down and do what Mathew needed doing.

She picked up the baby and made Zara take him across her lap. She unbuttoned and loosened the girl's bra so a breast was free. A breast that had never seen the sun as the V of her neckline had been stained by it. It was transparent white even in this light. Moira lifted the breast with her fingertips and Mathew latched on and sucked. She stroked its underside and gave gentle squeezes to help Zara's milk come down.

'That's right, sweetie. Close your eyes. Lean back and let it happen all natural.'

2

Midge wished they had thinner tape but they only had packing tape so he fixed the posters with that. A rough job—he couldn't get the boy faces joined flush—but he did his best. He did it needing only one candle and no lamps because the night was so clear it was like a version of day with the moon a silver sun and so many stars crowded above you you couldn't stare at them for long or you'd go star-blind. A typical summer night out their way: the sky's electrics.

Moira said it was Zara who tore them and he was not to listen if the girl denied it. She didn't want to seem mean for tearing them and thought it made Zara sound mature—tearing up posters that shouldn't interest mothers. She thanked Midge. Said Zara did not need posters: she was a grown-up now.

He taped them anyway, just in case. He had no decent present for Zara and her baby but if she wanted some decoration she at least had these to fall back on. He used the fold-out Formica table in the caravan for the job and kept the hair from his eyes with his old jockey helmet. It made his scalp sweat, which he liked because wet hair stopped the grey from showing. Zara might not call him an old fart so much if he kept his hair wetted. Just as she stopped calling him chicken legs once he took to wearing long jeans instead of the knees cut off. He kept his front false tooth in all the time so she didn't call him gummy.

Shane thought about the poster issue and nodded that Zara must be growing some common sense: if you're old enough to have babies you leave childhood behind. He nodded again like an authority then stopped being so clever, expecting Moira would say, 'What would *you* know?'

He sat on a deckchair and rolled a cigarette and lit it. There was a fizz from the flame singeing his goatee. He rubbed at it. The whiskers had got too long, he'd have to snip them back—his top lip was too bushy for safe smoking. 'So, she set to sleep right past tea?'

'I thought I'd leave her,' said Moira. 'Mathew woke up before. He didn't get enough to drink. I'll have to give him some formula.'

'What formula?'

'Stuff you buy.'

'Expensive?'

'Not very.'

'It is when he can get it from her for free.'

'Just give her time. She's still getting used to everything. Formula's good. Lots of vitamins.'

There was a gargle noise, an infant cough from in the tent. Moira went over and lifted the door flap so the sky shone in.

The noise stopped and in she crept to make sure Mathew's blanket wasn't hot and bunched around him. He was fine, and Zara was breathing a slow, quiet snore.

Out she went.

'You get the Tatts numbers in, babe?' Shane asked.

Moira said yes and rubbed her hands together as if giving Shane some good news. 'And I thought up a beaut new syndicate name.'

'You what?'

'Just for a treat.'

'You don't change the syndicate name. It's bad luck.'

'Did you ever win with the old one?'

'That's not the point. You don't change the name Midge and me been using for years. *Brothers SM*. Shane and Midge. It's tradition.'

'I wanted to include Mathew. It might be lucky. I got the lady behind the counter to write down the first bits of all our names for our Tatts card: *Momaza Shami*.'

'What?'

'That's all the first bits of our names squashed up.'

'You didn't change the numbers, did you?'

'No.'

'Give us the change. Should be five bucks fifty.'

Moira rubbed her hands again. 'I spent it.'

'Half that belongs to Midge.'

'Midge, you won't mind?'

Midge was still patching posters in the caravan but always had his ear cocked and put his face in the doorway and said no, he didn't mind, in his co-operative manner.

'I spent it on a raffle ticket. Bought it for Zara before I

25

picked her up. It was one them ladies' stalls.'

Shane flopped back in his chair and groaned and laughed in the one breath. 'Ladies' stalls.'

'It was a whim.'

'Like mother, like daughter. She has a whim and gets potted from it. You have a whim and buy tickets in some Mickey Mouse raffle.'

'The Ladies' League.'

'Mickey Mouse.'

'You get a crockery set and a fifty-dollar voucher to use in shops around town.'

That made Shane sit up and stop his mocking. He took the rollie from his mouth and let the smoke curl from his nose.

'Fifty bucks,' he said, pinching his lip hair and rolling a dag of it in contemplation.

'And a crockery set.'

'Fifty bucks. Not bad.'

'I bought eleven tickets at fifty cents each.'

'You've covered the field then. Probably only a dozen tickets in the draw in a Mickey Mouse raffle. Fifty bucks—not a bad divvy for five-buck-fifty invest.'

'It'd be in vouchers. The crockery set looked lovely. If we win it how about you get fined for every chip or breakage you cause.'

'Says who?'

'Says me. Come on, that's fair. It'd be fun.'

Moira fished in her pocket for a cigarette, lit it and had a deep draw to quell the excitement of winning crockery. She had the idea of winning already in her, which was stupid until you actually knew you'd won. Midge came out of the caravan and she said, 'It'd be fun, eh, Midge? Getting fined?'

'Yeah, yeah, sure,' he said. He'd combed his wet hair back and it made a ducktail from being too long for combing neatly. He shook his asthma puffer and made its canister rattle. He sucked a deep breath of it, and another one, and held the breath. Then he coughed to get his gluey windpipe clear.

Quiet, Moira indicated by holding her finger to her lips. Midge coughed with his mouth closed. He coughed through his nose, a snorting, then spoke, whisper-low, with the spluttering halting him between words. 'Be good to get a peek at Mat.'

'Mathew,' said Moira. 'Don't shorten it. It's Mathew.'

'That girl can sleep,' Shane said. 'She'll sleep right through tea at this rate.'

'She's a bit off-colour,' said Moira.

Midge stopped coughing. 'What, sick?'

'She's just had a baby. The body has to change and sort itself out.'

Midge nodded. 'Too right.'

Shane got his sarcastic tone back. 'What you mean, too right? You had a baby you not told me about?'

'Nah, just imagining it.'

'Soon as it dawns on her that it's Friday night she'll be trying to con one of us into dropping her off at the town hall.'

'What would she want at the town hall?' Moira said.

'The disco.'

If Shane seriously thought a girl just out of hospital wanted a disco she wouldn't waste her breath on him.

'Better not let her go into town or in nine months' time there might be another Mathew.'

'No more of that. We had that out,' Moira said, with her eyes narrowed for arguing.

Even as she said it she knew it was foolish. They hadn't had it out, not to Shane's satisfaction. If he had his way he'd drive Zara crazy with his 'Who's the father?' questions. Which led to a worse commotion: how could the girl be six months' pregnant before Moira knew she was? Before Zara herself even knew? Moira was the girl's mother and she didn't pick something like that up. Just thought she was getting chubby. Shane's favourite question was, 'Didn't you teach her nothing?' Which was not a real question, just a dig at Moira.

He went into the house, taking a long, angry stride over the doorstep. He flicked open the esky in the kitchen corner and got out the bourbon. The bottle was warm but that was the advantage of drinking spirits over beer. Spirits were naturally hot. He fixed himself a glassful, bourbon with some Coke, and sipped it and took a bigger gulp and came outside.

She decided to get in first, moving close to Shane to help keep her voice down.

'Before you start, I'll tell you again: she knew. She had to know. It's common sense. She just wouldn't admit it to herself.'

'Didn't you teach her nothing?'

'What do you care—she's not your daughter.'

That was the first time she'd used that line. Shane had to sip his drink and think of something clever. 'That's not the point, Moira. Since we been together, Zara and Rory are under my roof.'

'Roof? Some roof.'

Shane had no answer for an insult like that. He mumbled a few sentences about how if she didn't like it she and her kids could bugger off and go their own way. Him and Midge would turn this place into a nice little property.

'Property!' Moira scoffed. But she didn't want the fight to go further. She wasn't about to take the kids and go her own way. She was Shane's wife, or as good as that, and had been for five years. The longest marriage of her life. The other two she'd had weren't like marriages at all. They were boyfriends, though from them had come Zara and Rory. One day Shane would have a child with her—that was what he promised. Then he said it would be too crowded. Some days she wondered if he really didn't love her and was waiting to have a baby with someone better.

Midge didn't like cross words. He didn't like them between himself and others. And he hated cross words between Shane and Moira. The world didn't work properly when it happened. His policy was to pretend he had a chore to do and go off somewhere so he couldn't hear it.

'Did you say the car was running funny, Moira?'

'What?'

'Thought you said the car was making noises.'

'Just normal.'

'I better look anyway.'

Whenever he tried to walk fast his hip locked because of a race fall years ago. His left leg dragged and he had to slow down. It dragged now but he skipped it forward so as to keep up the pace.

Limpy jumped out of a hole under the house and followed him, excited by the prospect of the car starting and wheels to run after. He barked and Moira shut him up with the threat of throwing a stone. Rory's head popped up behind the wheel of the car, or rather his silhouette. The boy liked the car for its better radio reception, and providing he didn't run the battery down it was allowable.

Shane's drink hadn't lasted long and he got another, making this one not so strong in case it sharpened his tongue too far. He said, 'Yeah, well, still questions and no answers.'

'Please give up, Shane.'

'All right. All right.'

Not a man to be trusted when he did that—gave in easily. The giving-in usually lasted less than a minute. He couldn't help himself and he'd have one more say: 'Let me just finish by saying this' or 'I'll say one last thing.'

He sat on a deckchair and sipped his glass. 'Let me just finish by saying this. Whoever that baby's father is, he's got a responsibility or two. Tip in some cash. Pay his way.'

The father could have been anybody—she was always running off to parties. Too drunk to know was probably the truth. Her fantasy was that the poster boys did it.

3

Dinner was a quiet affair. Because of the heat Moira brought the gas cooker outside and propped it between the barbeque stones. Shane lit two kero lamps for her to work by. He suspended them from a limb of ironbark in the collection of trees around the L-shape. Half of them were crooked and almost leafless, with trunks no thicker than their stringy branches. The largest were as tall as any tree and had a mop-top of leaves pale and wet-looking under the moon. These were best for hanging lamps—putting them high up helped to cast the light a fair distance. The crooked trunks looked like people spying from the shadows, or kangaroos bent forward for peeping. A high lamp, combined with the heavens and their star show, kept the unnerving sight of them at bay.

Sausages in spaghetti. Moira got Shane to open the cans instead of just sitting there. She stirred the contents in the pot on the cooker for serving with bread and runny margarine. One can each, including Zara's for when she woke. Moira and Shane were still arguing though it was a silent grudge and weaker the more the food filled them and the cricket noise shut off, started again, shut off. Silence got so much that when the crickets stopped you heard yourself breathe and the person next to you. The very earth breathed among the trees and across the grasses. You could imagine your feet were hurting it as you stood.

Shane finished eating with his usual wipe of bread around his plate. On a Friday his habit was to drive to town with Midge for a few drinks. The pub had a TAB out the back and they watched the week's gallops replays and the night's trots and dogs.

He put the plate beside his feet and told Midge to wolf his meal. 'We'll be off, Moira. You go to the bank?'

Moira nodded that she had and went into the house for her shoulder bag. She took cash from the zip pocket and gave it to Shane.

He kept his hand held out as if weighing the cash. 'Bit light on, in't it?'

'I paid for the pram.'

'And how is Alfie?'

Alfie was Shane's new bloke, provider of the pot plants.

'He took ten per cent off the pram.'

'He's generous. Antiques racket must be thriving. He sold those brass door knobs I gave him?'

'Sent them to Melbourne.'

That was Shane's work, thieving old stuff from the once grand places now closed up, abandoned. Not here so much, but an hour or two south-west where the fields had been sold to companies who farmed from overseas and the homesteads around them, colonial and stubborn, stood orphaned in weeds. He thieved from

32

pretty churches fenced off in paddocks. Schools on forgotten gravel roads and community halls and dusty, bookless libraries. Cedar wall shelves sold for three thousand dollars in the high streets of Melbourne. Press metal ceilings, Victorian fireplaces, rose windows, fancy cornices, brass light fittings, floorboards of the thickest and darkest kind. Alfie of Barleyville Second-Hand shifted it to dealers once a fortnight on his truck. Shane's fee was the best he'd had in this business: forty per cent of the wholesale price. They'd done three loads together, though it was getting harder because the best places had already been stripped.

'Did you tell him I got another load for him?'

Moira rubbed her forehead. 'I meant to tell you. He said for you to hold on to it. He doesn't want it at his place at the moment. He said the shire had sent heritage people sniffing around and it'd be safer with you.'

'For how long?'

'Just a wee while.'

'Don't like goods lying round forever. We stripped that homestead next to the state forest clean, eh, Midge?'

'Yip. Good load.'

'Verandah lacework—be a hundred and twenty years old. Iron as good as the day it was cast.'

'Nice tongue-in-groove wall,' said Midge.

'And a massive mantelpiece. Carved wood. No white ants.'

Moira said she was sorry but that was what Alfie told her.

Shane shrugged that she had nothing to be sorry for.

She picked up the plates and put them in the wash bucket in the kitchen. There was no water in it yet. They could wait till tomorrow. Tonight she wanted to get Zara out of bed and eating. She asked Shane if he wanted a jacket for town. The air was starting to shift around and stir up streams of chill from somewhere in the night. The flat country to the west, most likely: it always took a few hours to cool off after night arrived and the sky's fallen orange ball had disappeared completely. Then it got coldest of all the region.

Shane didn't need a jacket. He asked Midge, 'You want one? Don't forget your asthma puffer.'

He's like a father to him, Moira always thought, more than a brother. Proof he had fatherhood in him, for all his bluster.

Rory asked if he could go with them. He always asked. He always got told no. Still he gave a whine as if grown-up and entitled to be out with the men. He hopped on his bike and raced level with the driver's door all the way to the sealed road. Then he cut across a paddock where the fences were down and if he didn't tire he could catch the car up where the road looped back on itself and connected with the highway. Limpy kept with him as far as the sealed road but couldn't maintain his yappy scampering any further.

Moira wondered if she should wake Zara, if Limpy's racket already hadn't. Or fix some formula for when Mathew woke in case the girl refused to be roused. She decided on fixing formula. It was years since she'd done this but that hospital nurse and her had talked: the particular brand to buy, the mix and measurements, the degree of warmth to the touch. Just in case it was needed.

First, the feeding bottle Moira bought would need boiling in water. She put a pot on the cooker and had a cigarette while the bottle bobbled and steamed. Then she placed it on a clean tea towel

34

to dry while she boiled another potful to mix with the formula. When that had churned long enough and shrouded the pot in mist she used the tea towel to grip the pot handle and lift the water onto the barbeque's brick ledge to cool. The coolest air would be among the trees, too far out of the lamplight to see clearly. If she carried the pot there she might trip and scald herself. She had to be content with the brick ledge. She wanted several trial runs at making mixtures. She dipped her finger until the water felt body-warm. She poured it into the bottle, three-quarters full, and peeled back the ring lid on the can.

The powder was like yellowy flour and had a faint vegetable smell—potatoes. A measuring scoop was in there. She tipped one scoop into the bottle, closed the teat-top and shook. She tested the taste on the back of her hand, another few drops on her wrist, then her palm. The flavour was awful—watery milk with a metal tang. She wondered where the potatoness had gone. Potato at least had an appetising odour. She had prepared everything as told and presumed this batch was as it was meant to be. Breast milk was watery but this was watery and sour. Moira poured it out.

Her second try was no better and she poured that out too. Then she heard Mathew splutter into tears, like crow noise if it wasn't so soft. She went into the tent and stood still until her eyes adjusted to the dark. She pushed the door flap as wide as she could. Enough natural light to see Mathew fidgeting his tiny fingers. Zara was not stirring. Mathew must be in good working order, she thought: she could smell him needing changing.

'I think it's feeding time, Zara.'

Still no stirring.

'He needs a change. How about I do that while you get ready to feed him?'

She reached in and lifted the baby.

'Come on, Zara. The men have gone. It's their night out. We can have a quiet time of it. Come on.'

It wasn't likely that Zara was sleeping through Mathew's crying. She was lying there awake with her back to the racket. Moira wasn't going to start a row, not with Mathew bawling in her ear. She decided to change him and then try the formula on him.

She took the child to the porch and set him down on a deckchair directly under lamplight. She went back to the tent and tore open the pack of nappies. Then back to Mathew to change him. She'd forgotten to buy tissues to wipe him with but the cleaner edges of his dirty nappy would do for now. Holding legs so small was a kind of farming. She thought of lamb's legs, newborn the way you see them in roadside paddocks. They take their weight straight away on this earth. Baby legs can't even kick away your fingers. She spoke to Mathew as she worked, telling him she had formula all ready to mix and that his crying good and loud showed a decent pair of lungs.

There was cooled water left over from her practice goes. She scooped in powder, shook the bottle and was ready to start. She lifted Mathew up, sat down on the deckchair and placed him on her lap with the bottle angled across her breast to feign the real thing. She let a few drops dribble onto his lips and used her forefinger to smear it around and tease him into sucking. He sucked the tip of her finger, and she slipped the teat forward between his lips and he sucked that. It took a while for him to suck as hard as

36

she thought he should. But his hands did curl eventually, a pawing reflex of pleasure.

Zara came from the tent wearing her black T-shirt. It never looked comfortable given its tightness, but she wore it anyway for going out. She had black knickers on. They rode up at the back and she picked at them. And pantyhose with the seat cut out. Only the legs remaining, sagging thigh-high, black and too big for her.

'Take those stupid things off, girl.'

'I can hold them up with some elastic. Or a rubber band.'

'They're your Christmas stockings. They weren't meant for wearing.'

'Haven't been laddered. Except there.'

She pointed to a place above her left knee.

'Take them off.'

'A bit of nail polish'll fix it.'

'Since when did you become an expert on pantyhose?'

'Where is it?'

'Where's what?'

'Nail polish.'

'We don't have nail polish.'

'Do I look good in them?'

She took a few steps and showed her legs off with a slow turn.

'You look stupid. But it's good to see you cheery. That'll relax you for milk coming down. I've started him off with this stuff but now you take over.'

Zara wasn't listening. 'What date is it?' she said.

'I don't know.'

'When's New Year's Eve?'

'I don't know. A day or two.'

'There'll be parties in town.'

'Come and sit down.'

'No bastard's given me an invite.'

'It's not important. Sit down and do some feeding.'

'I want to pull a skirt over these pantyhose and see how I look.'

'Afterwards.'

'No. Now.'

'Deal with Mathew and then we can go for a walk. Beautiful night like this. Let's take the pram and look at the stars. All the shapes they make.'

'We got no nail polish?'

'I told you, no.'

'I'll walk to town and get some.'

'You will not. Stop this nonsense, please. Get it into that head of yours that Mathew is your son. You take him and you feed him like you was shown, and stop this walking-into-town nonsense.'

Zara rammed her fists down on her knees. She screamed no and rammed her fists again. It made Moira flinch and take a tighter hold of the baby, a sudden, snatching action that caused the bottle to fall loose from his mouth. She took a long breath to control her voice. 'Take him and feed him.'

'I don't want to look at him.' Then Zara said it again with slow, gritted gaps between the words. 'I. Don't. Want. To. Look.'

The baby started crying and Moira told him, 'Shh, baby. It's all right. It's all right.'

Zara went to the tent, swearing at the stones hurting her feet but stamping harder as if wanting to be hurt. The stockings bunched around her ankles. She stamped into the tent and flicked the door flap down.

Moira flicked the flap up. She had Mathew tucked along her right arm in a football grip. The bottle fell from her left hand as she swung at the flap angrily to let herself through. Inside was stuffy dark with only the outlines of the few furnishings to gain her bearings. Zara was by the bed, in silhouette. Her shape disappeared into the darkness of the corner. She was on the other side of the bed now. She slumped between it and the tent wall.

The bottle was on the ground somewhere but Moira wasn't going to feel around on her hands and knees. She put the baby in his pram and told him everything was fine, though that wouldn't quieten him. Zara was talking in a babbling, sobbing way. The words were lost in Mathew's crying. Moira knelt on the bed to hear better.

'I weren't strong enough,' Zara said. 'Weren't strong enough in my arm to do it.'

'Do what?'

'I couldn't look at him and do it.'

'What are going on about?'

'In the hospital. When nobody was around I tried to do it but I couldn't look at him. It made me not strong enough if I looked.'

'Do what?'

'I closed my eyes and I put the blankets over his face and I pushed down and down so he wouldn't breathe and he would just die and go away. But I opened my eyes and I couldn't keep pushing. And he opened his eyes and he saw me trying to do it.'

Moira wanted to lift Zara from where she was wedged. The girl would not be touched.

'You're frightening me now. This is one of your lies. Say it's one of your lies. You made it up and you're frightening me.'

'Didn't make it up.'

She grabbed Zara by the back of her T-shirt and shook her.

'Say you made it up.'

Zara let herself be shaken, her head going side to side as if a doll neck.

'Zara?'

'I'm off to town.' She stood up.

'Answer me, girl.'

'I'll borrow Rory's bike.'

'Get out, then. Go. Get out.'

Zara ran past her, out of the tent.

'Come back, Zara. Please.'

In among the saplings Zara ran. She was holding the cut pantyhose up over her knees. She kept going further, where the trees were shadows of themselves and huddled together and breezy. They closed behind her and spoke in their leaf-whisper.

Where's the bottle? I'll have to wash it, Moira thought. Mathew will just have to bawl while I wash it and make a new mixture. Rory was arriving on his bike and Limpy with him. The dog would be sniffing around the bottle in a second if she didn't get it off the ground.

'Rory, come over here—I need your eyes. Help find Mathew's bottle, there's a good boy.'

'I saw Zara running through the trees.'

'That's none of your business.'

'Did she eat dinner? Cause if she didn't eat it, can I have it for her? I'm still starved.'

4

Lying in bed listening to the dark plays tricks with sounds. Moira was sure she heard Zara treading over leaf litter three times before she finally looked through the house's good eye and saw her for certain. The girl was going into the tent. She hadn't walked into town. That would have taken hours in bare feet, or stocking feet which were as good as bare feet, and it hadn't been hours since that horrible business. Not even Zara would go into town without more clothes.

Moira didn't want to speak to her. What would she say? Better to let it blow over till tomorrow. Though her stomach felt cold and churning thinking about what Zara had told her. When you have to take your own daughter's baby and keep it by your side, keep it by your bed. When you fear harm might come to it—its own mother doing the harming—your stomach is cold and churning and you want Shane to come home soon and be with you for safety.

When he finally did she'd got Mathew back to sleep after a feed from the bottle and a change. She'd tried sleeping herself but could not do more than shut her eyes for a minute like a long blink. Mathew was in his little bed on the floor an arm reach away but still she had closed the house door, something she wouldn't usually do on a hot night. There was a bolt on the frame, rusted and sticking. By giving the door a shove you could shift it across. She did this and felt better. But she still preferred Shane to be there.

She pushed the door wide open for him in case he was tipsy and waited on the step while the car was parked under the low-limbed sugar gum they called the garage. She saw that Midge was driving, so Shane must have tied one on. He got out of the car and bent over, hands on knees, as if vomiting. Yet he wasn't drunk in that way. He wasn't even drunk. You could tell by the clear-tongued voice he was greeting Limpy with. Midge tried to help him along by holding his elbow. Shane pulled his arm away and stood upright and walked. He was rubbing his side. He told Midge to leave him and turn the lamps off and go to bed. Moira asked if anything was wrong and Midge was about to answer but Shane waved for him to go to bed rather than speak on his behalf. 'I'm fine,' he said. Which Moira knew meant he wasn't. It was useless to badger him. If something was wrong Shane didn't tell you until he was ready. You could badger all you like, he'd say nothing.

When he got in the house he went straight to the bedroom ready to drop and sleep. He didn't need to feel his way in the dark. He lurched towards the bed with habit for his eyesight. Moira tried to warn him about the little bed being there but he was deaf from tiredness and clipped its edge and fell over. Not to the floor but onto the big bed, shunting the casters against the wall. He let out some swearing into the bedding and lay face down holding his side. Moira slid the little bed back from where Shane's toe had budged it.

'You in pain?'

'No.'

'You want a Panadol?'

'Yeah.'

Shane raised himself on one elbow. 'What's that?'

'It's Mathew.'

'Why's he in here with us?'

'I'm looking after him.'

'Why?'

'Letting Zara have a night off.'

Moira rifled in the kitchen for the biscuit tin they used for chemist things. She pressed two pills from the blister pack and gave them to Shane, and water. He gulped them and flopped down again. Even in the dimness there was blood easy to see, a snot of it dried where it had dribbled beneath his nose. His nostrils were black. There was a cut under his eye, about an inch long. The space between the bottom lid and the cut was swelling.

It was a while since this kind of trouble. Shane wasn't a fighter. He wasn't tall enough to have reach. He had strong arms for lifting homestead booty but he had no wish to lift people. People trouble got you injured. And the jail time was longer. It was better if you lost the fight: you looked the victim. Moira hoped Shane had lost. She was angry at him for fighting but hoped he lost for their sake and wasn't too wounded.

He fell asleep. She took off his boots and his pants. She left his shirt on in case she touched his sore side. Then lifted his head onto the pillow. She wanted to clean his face but that would wake him. Mathew would be hungry soon and that would also wake him. She decided to stay up all night and have the bottle washed and filled with formula. When Mathew woke he'd have the teat right there at his mouth. There'd be no hunger-crying. Just normal silence.

The swelling hadn't closed his eye but thankfully his eye white was bloodshot and the top of his cheek was shiny as if it might go purple. Under the morning sun Shane looked enough like he was the loser, which Moira was grateful for, though she'd never tell him. He'd lost some skin off his knuckles and his ribcage was red and risen near his armpit but his face looked the worst, as if he'd lost easily. Shane wouldn't let her fuss with soapy water. He was acting brave, which Moira knew meant embarrassed. She was giving him sour looks, her lips pursed, disapproving of him, but he didn't give her any. He usually would—he had no time for sour looks punishing him. She relaxed her lips to let him know she was nearing the end of punishing him.

'So you're not going tell me what happened?' she said.

He shook his head and said, 'Why's the baby sleeping with us?'

'He didn't make a sound. And you slept good. Tell me what happened to you. Did it involve police?'

'Nah.' He shook his head again.

The sun was the colour of glass. Hot glass spilled from it, or so the light seemed. It poured through or over any obstacle in its path—scrub and tree tops. The trees pointed the way along the ground. The porch held no shade against it, not at this early hour.

It would take till midday to form a line of shelter. Until then the house might as well be in the sky given the heat. The tent and the caravan might as well be in the sky in the afternoon when the sun faced their direction. For now, it was the house.

Shane sipped coffee on the theory that the warmer you were on the inside the cooler you felt outside. It took a full cupful to work and in the meantime you sweated but it was worth the discomfort till then. He strolled off around the side of the house to visit the toilet and sit there with his coffee air-conditioning.

Moira took a cup to the caravan for Midge and called for him to come out and have a word, please. 'What happened?' she said.

'Fan belt broke on the way home last night.'

'I'm not talking about fan belts. I mean Shane. He's beaten up.'

Midge straightened his shoulders. 'Not beaten up. He stood his ground good, Moira. He don't go too bad when he's had a few. Mind you, someone makes you mad enough.'

'The other person. Did they get hurt?'

'No.'

'Property?'

'They kept away from big breakables.'

'Police?'

'Nope.'

'What was the fight about?'

'Nothing much really.'

He was shuffling about, uncomfortable with the topic.

'Didn't you try and stop it?'

'Me? I keep out of scraps. Too small. Get done. I'll watch the trots, thank you very much. You know they got four TV screens at the pub now?'

'I'm not interested in TV screens. Who was this fight with?'

'Jim Tubbs.'

'What?'

Tubbsy was a friend of Shane's. Moira had a soft spot for him because she met Shane through Tubbsy, at the Horsham Tractor Pull festival where Shane was drinking with mates. Moira was there with a boyfriend who peddled stolen diesel. Tubbsy said that was a sleazy business. Come meet a friend of mine who's in antiques. Tubbsy could get over-friendly with the drink under his belt, put his hand on your backside and give a rub and squeeze. But he came from trant stock and lived in Barleyville these days. There was a trant bond between them.

Tubbsy did farrier work and had arms thick as anvils. Nobody took on Tubbsy who didn't have anvil arms of their own.

'What made them have a falling out?'

'Best if Shane tells you himself. Zara still asleep? You reckon I could peep in on the little fellow?'

'No. Tell me what happened. Now.'

Midge got his asthma spray out and took a puff and shifted his weight from leg to leg.

'I missed the lead-up. That Jim Tubbs, he's a real mongrel sometimes. Filthy minded. No wonder his missus shot through.'

'Keep going.'

'Jim went too far. He's got a mouth. It was just a joke but he said, "Come on, Shane. Be honest. Zara probably dropped your son, eh? You been having her on the side." Shane did his block.'

'I hope he did. I hope Shane did a job on him. The pig.'

'Shane and Tubbsy are mates, Moira. It'll blow over. Shane says we're not going to that pub again. But it'll blow over. Hope so. Four TV screens. A whole wall.'

'Shut up about TV screens. He's saying my Shane and my daughter, and all you think about is TV screens.'

'Sorry, Moira. Tubbsy's not a bad sort. It'll blow over, that's all I mean.'

She could have cuffed Midge, the fool. She walked off instead. Into the house to get her smokes. It looked like only half the amount in the pack was there that should be. Rory—he must have stolen a fistful this time. He tears a strip from the flint side of the matchbox to light his matches and sneaks off smoking like he's the master thief of Barleyville. She'd deal with him later.

Midge was wary to go near her but wanted to let her know he meant no insult.

'No sense in being bitter, that's all I'm saying,' he said, stepping into the house. 'You're right, Tubbsy's a pig. But no sense in being bitter.'

He thought he'd try steering her away from the subject of Tubbsy. 'Moira, you and me is step-relations, yeah?'

'Yeah.'

'And that means Zara is too. And now Mathew.'

'Yip.'

'Family. Close as you can get. So I was wondering. Can I watch Zara feed the baby?'

'What?'

'Not now. I mean sometime. When she's settled back home.'

'No. What kind of question's that? It's a private time.'

'I'm just interested because I never seen people do it. Seen heaps of animals—foals, lambs. Not people.'

'What are you, a perv?'

'No, no, course not.'

'You will not watch Zara feeding Mathew.'

He said he was sorry for asking and that she didn't have to use a word like 'perv'. He waited for her to say she was sorry.

Midge sat at the kitchen table. It was a table meant for class-rooms—Shane took it from a school near Avoca that was closed up. You could lift the top and put your valuables there. Only Midge did. He kept an envelope of photos from his jockey days. And the write-up he'd got in the Swan Hill press when he won by three lengths on Horsequake. It was his only write-up and his only winner but more than Moira had ever done, he brooded. You think you're true family with someone and they won't even say they're sorry for calling you a perv.

Then he noticed Mathew through the bedroom door. A miniature bed beside the big bed. Which made him laugh, as if the little bed was the bigger bed's young. And he saw Mathew was in it and he said sorry to Moira for laughing too loudly. He whispered sorry twice more and asked if he could go take a look. Moira nodded and led him into the bedroom. 'This is Midge,' she said, smoothing a wisp of silk hair on the baby's crown. 'Midge is part of the family too.'

Midge's face crinkled with smiling. His whiskered skin folded upwards and inwards in deep rows. His brown buckled teeth were all on show. Moira's introduction had taken the wind from him.

He needed his puffer. His puffer was in the caravan and he wasn't about to go and get it. He grinned, short of breath and pink in the eyes from happiness. He was sorry he'd ever had a brooding thought about Moira.

'Tell you what, you can have a hold. You want a hold?' she said.

Midge shook his head. 'No, no. He looks too—peaceful. I might drop him.' He was wheezing and coughed into his sleeve.

Moira slid her fingers under Mathew and lifted him to be against her neck. She took a step towards Midge and he stepped away, then he stepped forward as Moira reassured him that he wouldn't drop the baby. All he had to do was make a cradle of his arms and be gentle. He made the cradle and whispered that he would. He took the baby's weight and said, 'I've got him. I'm holding him. Am I doing it right?'

'Yip,' Moira nodded. 'How's he feel?'

There were no words in him to make a sentence. This kind of holding was beyond language. He stood as if connected to the world's holy scheme.

'Tubbsy? You took on Tubbsy?' Rory said, walking backwards in front of Shane while Shane was walking from the toilet. Rory had wanted to sit on the toilet and was waiting for Shane to finish but that urge disappeared on seeing Shane's face. The boy's mouth was wide open with awe and Shane slowed his pace so Rory didn't trip and stop talking. He was enjoying the admiration. Just a boy's admiration, but that was the best kind, he thought, because boys don't hide it. When they made you a hero they made it obvious.

'Hey, Mum, Shane took on Tubbsy.'

'I know, I know,' she said, with her eyes closed, and a shake of her head. The anger was false, for Rory's sake, so that he didn't think she praised fighting. She really wanted to kiss Shane for this fight, a fight for family honour. A fight that told Jim Tubbs and anyone else that they may not be angels but they had standards.

Then she did kiss him. She took his hand as he walked past her and lightly kissed his knuckles, their sticky wounds. She pulled a deckchair into a strip of shade shaped like a long trapdoor in the ground by the side of the caravan. The trapdoor was getting shorter by the minute but it would last for breakfast, then twist into other shapes around the back of the caravan, branch-fingers by the dozens, twig-toes.

She told Rory to come into the house with her and get some corn flakes. He complained about the long-life milk not tasting like proper milk, as he did every morning. On this morning Moira asked him to consider Mathew and not wake him with whining complaints. She told him to be more generous with the sugar to sweeten the milk flavour and go outside, quietly.

She prepared corn flakes for Shane and put on some extra sugar for him. He never complained about the milk, but Moira wanted to spoil him. She took the bowl out and stood looking at his face before she handed it over. His left cheek looked so painful she felt an urge to kneel close and spoon the corn flakes up to his mouth. Instead she said, 'I'm going to clean you up.'

She asked Midge to go to the barbeque and light the cooker. He was still in a dreamy state and she had to ask him twice before he jolted himself into stride. She went into the house for a saucepan of water. The jerry-can water was tepid but Moira wanted it hotter. And wanted something to put in it for those wounds. All they had was the methylated spirits they used for cleaning the glass in leadlight windows. That would be good enough, she decided. The smell would be awful, and the stinging too, but Shane would pride himself on not wincing, especially with Rory watching.

When the water had boiled she dipped a metal mixing bowl in and filled it to half, and into that she poured the metho, two splashes of it. She stirred the metho around with a rag, the water burning her fingers. She carried this to Shane and began dabbing and wiping his face in between his mouthfuls. He sucked air through his teeth when the metho stung, but did so grinning at Rory as if performing pain rather than feeling it. When Rory asked what the fight was about Shane said it was over nothing. 'Just piss-talk.'

Saying 'piss-talk' made him wince as if truly suffering the metho. He said, 'Sorry, Moira,' and winked at Rory. She hated swearing. If someone swore around her they'd given up caring about her, that was her view. She wasn't worth respectful language to them. She was too low a person to be bothered with. 'Piss-talk' was down the rung on the scale of swearing but she said thanks for the apology as if it were higher.

Shane held up his hand for her to stop dabbing. He watched Zara walk from the tent and stand in the blaring sun. She rubbed her waking face and yawned. She had on her T-shirt and knickers. Her thin white legs still had sleep in them and were slow and shaky in making steps. Rory said to her, 'A fight,' to explain Shane's face. Midge was at the barbeque stirring a teabag in a cup of water.

He wished he'd put his helmet on this morning. He'd been so dreamy he'd forgotten about his greyness. He used his fingers for a comb and said, 'Morning, Zara. I seen Mathew. I went in and held him. He's a fine fellow, that one. How you doing?'

Moira told him not to rush at her with so much chatter. She put down her rag and bowl. 'Put on your dressing gown, Zara.'

The girl yawned, rubbed her eyes and didn't move. Moira went into the tent and got the dressing gown from the broken suitcase at the end of the bed that did for a set of drawers.

She put the gown over Zara's shoulders. It was Moira's old one, pale blue and fraying flannel, too big for Zara and more like a blanket hanging from her. Moira told her to put her arms in the sleeves but didn't help her do it. She was fussing around Zara but not looking in her eyes. She made herself smile but only so Shane could see it and not start asking if something was wrong. She told Zara to pull a deckchair into the piece of shade near Shane and she would get her breakfast.

'I'm not hungry.'

'Yes, you are.'

'I'm not.'

'You must be.'

'I'm not.'

'If you're not hungry, fine, forget breakfast.'

It was difficult keeping smiling. Moira remarked on the sun being strong today. Sun-talk was preferable to trying to smile and communicate with Zara. She asked what the men had planned this morning.

Refining the shed design, Shane said. Rory could make himself useful by helping to cart stones from around the place to weigh down the shed's tin roof. With Alfie scared of moving a load to Melbourne they might have to store goods for a few weeks. It never rained. But just say it did. There could be water damage that hurt value.

'Car's free then? I'd like to go into town,' Moira said.

Car was free, Shane nodded.

Midge chimed in. There was the fan-belt problem. He had to use his trouser belt to stop the engine cooking last night. 'Belts don't work too well. They slip,' he said. 'If you can lend me a strip of stretchy material I can rig something better up, just temporary, but it's still risky driving with it.'

'I need to go into town. What kind of stretchy material?'

Midge shrugged. 'Dunno.'

'Bra strap?' Moira said.

'Bra strap?' Shane laughed.

Rory mimicked Shane. 'Bra strap?'

'I don't think a bra strap would work,' said Midge.

'Well, I need to go into town. What about pantyhose, the legs of them? Nice and stretchy.'

He considered it a moment. 'Pantyhose. They'd work good.'

She held her palms out, inviting Zara to offer those tatty Christmas stockings. 'Zara? The Christmas stockings? Sweetie, you want to get them, please? I need to drive into town. Come on.'

'The stockings? They're mine.'

'They're not for wearing, sweetie.'

'I'm going to fix them up.'

'You can't wear those.'

'I'll fix them.'

Shane laughed, a low note in his belly. 'Fix Christmas stockings? What for? Next Christmas? Might not be a next Christmas. World might blow up. That'd stuff Santa Claus up.'

'I want to wear them,' said Zara, her mouth clenched, determined.

'Wear them?' said Shane. 'What, over your head? You going to rob a bank? I was going to rob a bank once. Till I found out the fuckers didn't hide the key under the doormat. Whoops, sorry, Moira.'

Rory giggled and Midge had to chew his lip to stop giggling with him.

'I'll put nail polish on them. I'm using them. They're mine.'

Her voice went up high, almost yelling when she said, 'They're mine.' She gripped the dressing gown tight to her throat as if cold and jog-walked to the tent and flicked the flap down behind herself as she went in.

'What's the story with her?' said Shane.

'You shouldn't have mocked her,' Moira replied.

'That wasn't mocking.' He stood up and went over to the tent. 'Hey, Zara. That wasn't mocking.'

He waited for a response, bent forward, his ear against the flap.

'I said, that wasn't mocking.'

Moira pulled on his sleeve to make him come away but he wouldn't.

'Listen, girl. If you're under my roof you pull your weight. Share things. If the car needs a stocking you hand it over.' He waited. 'You hear me? Don't bloody well ignore me.'

'Leave her,' said Moira, tugging on him.

'Okay. Okay. But I'll say one last thing. If you're old enough to have babies you're old enough to pull your weight.'

After taking a wheezy cough Midge said, 'I'll buy her a new lot. Zara, I'll buy new pantyhose to replace them.'

He took a fold of notes from his back pocket. Flicked off the rubber band that bound it and counted out twenty dollars in five-dollar bills. 'That enough, Moira?'

'That's good,' she said. 'That's very decent.'

'Here's some more. If you go to Brogan's garage and ask for a fan belt I'll fit it when you get home. Don't let Brogan do it. He'll slug you twenty dollars.'

'You're a gem.'

The compliment must have made Shane jealous for one. Moira saw him hang his head down then jerk it up with an idea. 'I'll tell you what,' he said. 'We get the fan-belt issue sorted out and maybe we can go on an outing somewhere. What do you say, Zara?'

'You serious?' said Moira.

'Yeah, I'm serious.'

'All of us go, you mean? Like a proper family?'

'Yeah.'

She smiled at him and put her hand on his shoulder. 'What you reckon, Zara? Shane says we'll go on an outing.'

'As a family, Zara,' Midge said.

Zara pushed aside the door flap. 'Where?'

She'd taken off the dressing gown and put on the pantyhose legs. They concertinaed over her knees like shedding skin. Shane was about to mock but Moira fixed him with a fierce gaze. It demanded his silence, then it weakened into pleading for him to behave.

'Ask Shane,' she said. 'It was his idea.'

'Can we go to the pool?'

Shane shook his head. 'They don't want us at the pool.'

'He's right. I don't know about the pool, sweetie.'

'Please. The pool.'

The pool was somewhere they were not welcome anymore. A wristwatch and money stuffed down a shoe in the change room had been stolen while Rory was there. He said he didn't do it and Moira was inclined to believe him. Shane was as well. It was the way the boy protested, so genuine, with real tears and loud crying, so unlike his usual lying. Then he switched and claimed he *had* done the stealing, which they figured was just Rory trying to impress.

That was two months ago and the pool had been off limits since. They'd used the horse pool at the trotting track a few times. Trainers were finished with it by five each evening and the brick wall was low enough to scale if you took a ladder. Zara hated the thought of swimming where animals swam. Moira was on her side because who knows what germs might get up inside you when you're pregnant. Midge explained that horses were cleaner than humans, but he failed to convince her.

'Please. The pool. The real pool. With people there and I can be social.'

'Come on, Shane. We can give it a go,' said Midge.

Shane nodded. 'I suppose we can think up a way.'

'We are going then?' Zara stood up on her toes, excited. 'I better get ready.'

'We're not going now, sweetie.'

'I better get ready anyway.'

'Don't forget those stockings,' Moira said, holding out her hand, snapping her fingers. Zara pulled the stockings from her feet and stared at her shins and the backs of her legs.

'I need to get some sun on me. I'm white all over.'

She passed the stockings to Moira, who gave them to Midge— one leg for installing now, one to stash in the glove box as a spare. He said it was best if she watched how he tied them on. The knot he used was just a normal bow, a double bow, but the tension was the important part. She best learn the correct tension in case there was trouble.

She'd just started walking to get the instruction when the baby began crying in the house. Zara froze at the sound, rubbed her hand over her shins and ran off through the trees to find sun for her legs.

'Where's she going?' Shane said. 'Looked like she just shat herself, if you'll pardon my language.'

'I won't. The girl's fine.'

'Doesn't look it. Better do something about that crying.'

Moira told him to get busy with his shed if he didn't like the crying. Unless he wanted to help clean the bottle and boil it. There was formula to mix too. He said he would go to the shed. And he'd appreciate it if she could have the car back by early afternoon. He wanted to go make up with Tubbsy. He said it would be Tubbsy's shout, given his cuts and bruises.

'You're not going to drink with him. What about last night? The things he said, Shane. He insults you and my daughter and you'll drink with him?'

'Things blow over, Moira.'

She stared at him and he had to turn away. She gave a flick of her hand and went into the house to leave him with his shame.

5

There was squealing in the engine where the stockings were slipping on the cogs, but the temperature gauge stayed steady at just under half.

The blue walls of sky closed in as Moira drove. The ceiling of the sky was just above the car roof. The road ahead rippled as if melted and the heat blew like the very air was blowing away. Breathing dried her throat. She could believe the sky wall up ahead had turned to hot liquid and she was about to drive straight through it, right through to the other side where there was nothing but outer space and she'd be lost and alone.

Not entirely alone. There would be Mathew, lying in the back, the seatbelt at full stretch around his little bed. A towel was wound up in the right window against the sun's aim. The other window was open like a drumming fan. She'd fed him, though he didn't take the teat well. She'd washed him over the kitchen sink, cupped water where he lay in the crook of her arm. He was clean and content as far as she could tell. Perfect for having a nurse check him.

She knew her rights and knew she didn't have to do this. No government people could poke their nose in unless the baby was officially in danger. Mathew was not in danger. Not now. But she wanted to check he hadn't been damaged by Zara. Some inner injury that could get worse and make him suffer or not live long. She had put her cunning hat on and was ready for them.

The maternity centre was attached to the hospital, a room off to the side with a row of floppy agapanthus for a green path. She rang a buzzer and waited and when a person came she apologised for not having an appointment. She was in town on business, she said. Just thought it would be nice to have the little fellow call in and say hello and give thanks to everybody for helping bring him into the world. And while he was here have a check-up, though it was plain to see he was as healthy as spring grass.

The person at the door wasn't the right one for check-ups but if Moira wanted to wait a nurse would be along soon. She said she would wait in the lovely air-conditioning and sat with Mathew sleeping in her arms. Everything so clean—floors, walls, surfaces. And the smell so freshly sterile there must be someone mopping every minute of the day, she thought.

What if a nurse found damage in Mathew? How could cunning help her then? She would have to say that Zara was to blame. No. She wished she'd never come here. It was asking for trouble. Police would get involved. Mathew and Zara would be taken away.

The nurse was a chubby woman with grey-brown hair cut short like a man's and wearing black slacks and shirt. She was bossy too. Moira wanted to keep up a cheerful banter about Zara being such a good around-the-clock mother and that was the reason she'd stayed home today, to catch up on lost sleep. The nurse was more interested in files and documents. She said check-ups were for the benefit of baby and mother. Without mum there wasn't much point. To which Moira answered, 'Thought I was doing the right thing.' She said it in a tone of meek apology. 'Didn't mean to waste your time. We'll come back when we can. Don't know when that would be. We live out of town and we're always away on business.'

'Oh, since you're here. Don't rush away.'

Her flabby, freckly arms reached out like a tray and Moira trusted the baby to them. The nurse wasn't an affectionate baby-holder, no cooing and kissing or compliments about beauty. But Moira could see she was working to a system. She peeled back the little sheet he wore for swaddling and said he looked healthy enough to her, peering professionally at where the cord was cut at his navel. She said, 'Good,' and 'Good' again when she looked into his mouth. Then his eyes. She weighed him on scales, laying him in a plastic bowl. She smiled and said, 'Fine.' She measured him with a tailor's tape. She put a stethoscope in her ears and put the other end on his chest. After she'd listened for a moment in frowning concentration she said, 'Good. All in working order.' She handed Mathew back. She even smiled.

Moira flared her nostrils in relief but didn't let any extra emotion show.

Not until she got back to the car. There she strapped Mathew in and sat behind the steering wheel and let herself weep.

She got a fan belt from Brogan's, and wouldn't let him fit it, just like Midge told her. Her cunning hat was still on and she was so thrilled to have a healthy Mathew that she thought she'd try to get the men at Brogans to work for nothing. They didn't come at it but she had fun trying. She said, 'So much for community spirit,' and, 'If I break down in the hot sun and die it'll be on your head.' They laughed but didn't budge.

The newsagent lady scanned the Tatts numbers for winnings. None. Moira had her change the Momaza Shami syndicate name back to the original so that Shane had nothing to complain about in future.

The crockery raffle was announced that morning. The organisers pinned the results to the community notice board. Moira wanted to delay knowing because that way she could pretend she'd won. She couldn't pretend forever. She carried Mathew to the town hall, where the board was, and waited for someone to walk by, someone she could ask to read the names out, claim she was blind without her glasses. An old man on a walking stick did it. He had half a nose and only one ear, the way they cut cancer away. Her name wasn't on the glory list but she didn't care like she'd thought she would. She had a fit and well Mathew.

There was rubbish in the boot to dump. Two places to do it— the supermarket dumpsters or the trotting track bins. She didn't need to shop today, and had a jerry can to fill, so the trotting track it was. That meant driving in a homeward direction with the sun now to her left. She changed the window towel to the other side. She waited for the stocking to stop squealing and grip the right parts of the engine. Once it did she accelerated gently, wishing she didn't have to drive off. It would be lovely to wander in town with Mathew and not have to face Zara. What should she do with Zara? Nothing, maybe. Let the girl sleep away her life and forget she had a son. Or help her into loving it, make her love it. Hold her hand and be gentle, or force her with a savage tongue.

Morning training was over and Moira had the track's car park to herself. She got rid of the rubbish. The bins were full of feed sacks and dung and she had to use the sacks like gloves to push hard and make a space for her plastic bags. A cloud of flies blew into her hair as she did it. The smell of horse dung was usually a pleasant, garden kind of odour. Squashed down within its juices among flies and sacks it stank like any other rubbish.

She washed her hands in the ladies', a good lathering of wall soap, and went to the toilet. Washed her hands again and filled the jerry can. Then washed her hands again and took Mathew into the toilet with her, laying him on the bench you pulled out from the wall for changing. He was awake and hungry and starting to bawl. She changed him and gave herself a quick wash under the arms and between her legs and put Mathew in the car for hurrying home. 'You hang on, little man. I'll have you fed in no time.'

Not a good moment for the stocking not to grip, she thought aloud. But it did grip and off she went over the shuddering rail crossing, past the silos that soared high like the enormous chimneys of an underground town. Above those flew an air-town of pigeons and above them clouds arched and spread like smoke. She sped up towards the open road. The wind was strong enough to bunt the car and tug at the steering wheel. Dust was lifting from the paddocks and crossing in front of her like dirty drizzle. At the bridge that was supposed to go over water but instead went over saltpan she turned left onto the highway and headed for home.

The siren went just once but was piercing and caused her to flinch and tap on the brakes in panic and say sorry to Mathew for the braking, all in one heartbeat. Her rear-vision mirror flickered blue and red. Moira pulled to the gravel verge, stopped the car and turned the engine off.

Her cunning hat knew what to do. She had Mathew to help her. She'd use his presence to get sympathy for whatever it was she had done. The policeman was a young fellow. Curly blond with perfect muscle in the weightlifting way. His hands rested on the weaponry on his waist. The young ones were nastier, Shane always reckoned. The older ones had more of a worldly style, were more lenient and polite, knowing more about life. The younger ones liked to prove they were better than you.

'Hello, officer. Sorry if I did wrong.'

'Driver's licence, please.'

'I got it in my purse, I think.'

She reached across to the passenger floor and pulled up her bag. She had a feel around inside. 'Don't seem to be here. I was in a rush. I had to take my grandson to hospital. He's okay, thank God.'

'What was wrong?'

'He's just been born. I panicked and needed him checked.'

As if on cue Mathew let out a hunger sob and followed it up with solid crying.

Moira put her arm over the seat and stroked him. 'Easy, darling.'

She put on a worried face and thought about sniffing, as if close to tears. She stayed with the worried face for the meantime. 'He needs to get home and be fed and put to bed. It's been a big day for him. Big day for us both. Have you got children?'

'I need to see your licence.'

'It's not in my bag.'

He put on a blue cap and pinched the peak as if gesturing goodbye. It was no goodbye. It was suspicion.

'Was I speeding, sir?' asked Moira.

He was slow answering. If he said yes she knew to say sorry at least three times. Make police feel they're standing over you, in charge, superior, that's the rule. If they feel superior they feel they've dealt with you and might let you go.

'No. Been some roadside fires. We're stopping cars at random. You local?'

'Yes.'

'Seen nothing unusual?'

'No.'

He took a black flip-pad from his breast pocket and asked for her name and where she lived. 'Just off Loop Road,' she said. He asked for her phone number and she said they didn't have one. He jotted down the rego and took a stroll around the car, bending to assess the state of the tyre tread and muffler. He asked to see the headlights on, and the indicators. Then he went to his car, sat in it with one leg out the door. Through the mirror Moira saw him talking on his equipment as if to himself. She reached to Mathew and let him suckle the tip of her finger for fake feeding. He was fooled for a second, then continued crying.

The policeman got out of his car. 'I've got no matches for a licence under your name,' he said.

'That's strange.' Moira knew not to smile or hold eye contact for too long when you're being cunning. Better to put her wrist over the steering wheel and give a casual flop of the hand.

'I'll need you to bring in your licence to the station for sighting. We'll expect to see it by, ah, week's end, yeah?'

'No worries.'

He nodded and stood there, staring at her. He put on his sunglasses. He wanted to say more, she was sure of it. He had a quip or question he was keeping to himself.

He walked to his car. Moira waited for him to leave before she started the engine.

6

Shane was in a bad mood so Moira didn't tell him. She'd been stopped before in other towns and simply ignored it. That was a benefit of the travelling life over settling. If she was told to present her licence at a police station they were usually on the road in a few days and she didn't bother. Because they were settled now she would have to tell him, wouldn't she? Maybe not. If she ignored it like always the problem might ignore her. She had to the end of the week to decide.

Shane's mood was about Rory. You try to take the boy under your wing and he turns his back on you. He'd rather complain he was bored, go off on his own instead of contributing labour. Instead of learning the difference between Victorian-era goods and cheap modern he preferred to slink away saying he wanted to be a dragon. Of all the fantasies you could have in the world, he chooses something so far-fetched as a dragon.

The pool business was solved, though. Shane had an idea and was delaying telling Moira because while the idea stayed in him unspoken it glowed in his insides. He had no interest in going swimming at the pool, but his plan would keep him in Moira's good books. It was a humming pleasure to know he would be in Moira's good books the moment he let the words go from his mouth. He would wait until she'd tended to the baby and he had her full attention instead of competing with baby feeding. He sat under the porch doing his paperwork and could hear her in the house singing in a lullaby mumble. He couldn't make out the words but the tune sounded like 'Michael Row the Boat Ashore'.

'You know how to spell "proprietor", Moira?' He knew very well she couldn't spell it but he thought asking would get her attention focused on him. It didn't work. Her lullabying didn't break breath. He wrote the word on the form, spelling it out to himself: *Looked for bar work. Spoke to P-r-o-p-r-i-a-t-e-r.* At which point Moira came out of the house, saying, 'Little fella's off like a light,' and Shane saw his moment, put down his pen and rubbed his hands together.

'This pool business. I worked it out. Sit down and I'll tell you.'

'The pool business? Oh, the pool business.'

'What we do is this: I take my bolt-cutters and we wait until the night session, nice and dark outside of the floodlights. And I cut a hole in the boundary fence wire and Zara slips through and has a swim and does any socialising she wants.'

'That'd be great, Shane.'

'Problem solved.'

'You're very clever.'

She leant forward and put her hand on his hand, on the sticky knuckles she was careful not to hurt.

Shane's glow got warmer. He said, 'Rory could probably slip through too and they wouldn't notice him if he kept his head down. And you could slip through for a swim and then you can all slip back out the hole when you're finished and we head off home.'

'Oh, I won't be going swimming. I'll mind Mathew.'

'Mathew.' He sighed. 'Mathew. How come you're getting landed with all the work with him?'

'I don't mind. I'm enjoying it.'

'He wakes me up at night I'll kill him.'

'Don't you say that! Don't you ever say that!'

Moira pulled her hand from his with a deliberate chafe over his wounds.

He flicked his sore hand and sucked on the knuckle. 'It's only a saying. Jesus.'

'I don't like it.' She composed herself. 'Let him sleep with us for a while, Shane. Please, honey.'

'Why? What's wrong with him sleeping with his mother? She shirking her duties?'

'No.'

'The kid got something wrong with him?'

'No. The doctor said for me to help. He said it'll take the pressure off Zara. She's young and her body and her mind need time to cope. You know nothing about women.'

Moira's particular habit if she was lying was that her neck stiffened and got longer and her chin pushed against her throat. The strain of it stopped any uncertain fidgetiness in her face. She had to be careful if doing it with Shane because he knew all her secrets and would be looking for her traits. She lifted her chin up to make sure he saw her throat and saw no stiffening. She concentrated on making her face remain steady. She fought against her chin dipping down.

Shane shrugged and sighed again and said, 'If a doctor says so, I suppose you better do it.'

He folded his form neatly in half, then thought of something and flattened it back out on his knee. 'Am I supposed to include Zara on our form or does she get her own? Might complicate *our* form having her included with a baby. Might get asked in for questioning.'

Questioning was always a concern. A few years ago Midge got questioned about his form and they checked up whether he'd been looking for work as stated. They kicked him off welfare and he had to wait to apply again. Ever since, Shane had rotated it with Midge. Midge went on for a few months and then went off and Shane applied. Then Shane went off and Midge went back on. When Shane went back on Moira was included as his dependant. Zara and Rory too, which meant more money, but still they stuck to the rotation system. Better to be safe rotating than risk being banned from applying at all. Shane called it 'flying under the radar'.

Yet, in Zara's case the rotation system might be worth revising. With a dependant of her own she'd get good money if she applied. If she went on their rotation system it could be profitable.

'I'll look into it,' said Shane. 'I'll get the forms. Weigh the ins and outs.'

He folded his form into his pocket. 'You go tell Zara about the pool.'

Moira went to the tent door and peeped under the closed flap and gave a soft call. 'Zara, sweetie? Sweetie, I got good news. Shane's got a plan for the pool.'

She ducked through the flap into the tent, sunlight coming in with her like a fog with dust and insects in it. 'I said, Shane's got a plan for the pool. He'll get his bolt cutters and we'll go in through the fence.'

For all the smell of canvas and plastic she could smell Zara's hair needed washing, the mustiness of it, and the damp odour of her sleeping body. All of which would be solved by a good swim. 'Sweetie, come on, wake up.'

She knelt by the bed. Zara moved her legs under the sheet.

'You said you wanted to go to the pool, so let's go tonight.'

'I don't want to.'

'But you said you wanted to.'

'Don't want to see nobody.'

'But you wanted to.'

'No.'

Shane put his head under the flap. 'All good in here?'

Moira ordered him gone. She strode over and put her hands on his chest and said, 'Out.'

She stood in front of him and walked him backwards outside. She said Zara wanted to thank him very much for the pool plan and was looking forward to a swim as soon as she felt up to it. Her neck stiffened, her chin closed over her throat and she smiled and touched Shane's bruised cheek lightly and he accepted her word.

She waited until Shane and Midge had driven off—'I got a bone to pick with Alfie in town,' Shane said—and then went back into the tent, hooking up the flap to let the day in. She crouched on the plastic beside Zara and stroked her hair and shoulder. 'This is no good. We can't just go on like this,' she said. 'You can't just lie there.'

She might as well have been talking to herself. Zara was awake and listening, her eyelids were moving, but she was silent.

'If you're not going to speak, if I'm going to talk to myself, I might as well say what I'm thinking.'

Moira knelt, straight-backed, her hands clasped against her chin like prayer. 'What I'm thinking is, I get someone to help you if you're like this. There'll be someone at the hospital, maybe. Come to the hospital with me.'

'No.'

'You don't want help?'

'No.'

'What, then? What do you want?'

'To go. I want to go somewhere out of here.'

'Where would you go?'

'I don't know. Somewhere better.'

'You got no money. Where can you go with no money?'

'I don't know.'

Moira's hands cracked in the knuckle joints because she was clenching so tightly. Angry and pitying at once.

Hospital. There was a worry with hospital, she realised. It would not be as simple as giving Zara medicine. There would be questioning. And if they found out what Zara did they'd be on the phone, you could bet on that. Next thing the police would be doing the questioning and Zara would be a murderous mother in their eyes and Mathew taken away.

She didn't say this to Zara. She said, 'We don't want to bother with hospitals. We take care of ourselves. No one else sticking their nose in. No one saying: If the girl doesn't want the baby we should take him away.'

'I want him taken away.'

Moira gripped the girl's shoulder and squeezed but didn't shake those words out of her like she wanted to. Instead she said, 'You do not want him taken away,' and let her head drop and her voice drop. Her breathing was shuddery.

Zara's breathing was shuddery too and there was a faint whistle in her nose.

'You don't want him taken away. Sounds good now but what about ten, twenty years. You'd be the woman who wanted her baby taken. Let me help you. I can take care of Mathew and you can get better in the meantime.'

7

Alfie wasn't at his shop, it was a wasted trip, so they drove straight home. Normally they'd have gone off and had a drink at the pub but not today—Tubbsy might be there. Shane made it clear to Moira that his loyalty was with her. He'd had a good think about it and decided some things shouldn't blow over. Not straight away. Maybe sometime in the future, but not at the moment. She kissed him for that. Just on the cheek, which was more meaningful than the lips because the lips can be mistaken for sexual, not heartfelt thanks.

Wind had lowered itself along the ground instead of staying up higher and blowing clouds into thinner clouds. It had come down fast like a dry storm with dust for rain. Hotter than you'd think air could be without coming from heaters. If a magpie tried to fly against it it was ripped away and forced to land. The short trees whipped forward. The bigger trees twisted and hissed. Dead branches snapped. A gale that had hours to go before it tired. The flat earth gave it a clear run.

Best thing to do was stay inside and suffer the heat with the slats closed across the tearing glad-wrap window. If you went outside you needed the house or the caravan for a windbreak. There was a spray bottle that Moira half filled with water. You sprayed it on your skin and the wind cooled you, but only for seconds. She put Mathew on the kitchen table and sprayed him over but he didn't like it and cried. Shane was on the bed having a sleep. She heard him turn over—squeaks of the bedsprings. He didn't rouse from the baby's noises, but even so she took Mathew outside, a shield of tea towel for his face. She didn't last two strides before the wind made her go back.

Rory was outside. Moira didn't notice. He saw her and didn't want her seeing him so he crouched behind Zara's tent, the canvas cheeks puffing from gusts. When Moira had gone back inside he pushed through the flap. 'Hey, Zara. Wake up, Zara,' he said. Even when she swore at him to fuck off and leave her alone he persisted and asked for a lend of her make-up. 'Where's your make-up bag?' And sunglasses. He wanted a lend of sunglasses. She had the airline pilot sort that she'd thieved or traded or something. He said he wasn't leaving her alone until she lent them.

Typical Rory, thought Moira when he leant against the doorframe for dinner, sunglasses on, baseball cap pulled down like a snub to her. Typical Rory, said Shane. Sunglasses and cap, trying to be a tough guy.

The boy ate outside, saying that inside smelled of babies. The gas was lit for Mathew's feeding and it doubled the heat.

Midge joined him, though Rory moved off to be alone as if brooding over his bowl.

Moira took a serve of instant noodles to Zara and left it by her bed with advice to blow on it and sip or it would burn her tongue. She didn't know what else to do but feed her. Keep up a ration of connection.

When night came it was starless dark and so windy the trees sounded like rapids. There was no point sleeping outside as you normally did when the nights sweltered. Who could sleep in that wind? Yet there being no stars meant the wind would soon change. The north-travelling clouds were thickening way up there out of sight. South-west clouds were doing the same and were ready to clash. Limpy slunk off under the house for cover.

It happened after midnight. A southerly snap of coolness that caused the house's timbers to flinch. The tree rapids became wilder and thunder rolled above them. Lightning twitched among storm clouds. A few fat raindrops spattered on the roof but that was all. No rainy smell for the nostrils, let alone anything to fill the tank. The stars came out and bats flew white beneath them. You could see all the way to the moon again. Rory slept through the change and Zara must have too. Moira and Shane didn't. They went outside so the air could tingle their skin. Midge came out and did the same, holding up his arms to let the jolting cold in.

The air was still cool at morning and it worked through the flesh, bringing good spirits to everyone. Not Zara—her spirits were too closed over to receive fresh weather. Rory was persisting with his tough-guy look but took off after a feed of Weet-Bix to lift stones onto the shed's tarp fringe. He wasn't told to, he just offered. Shane put it down to the weather or a spurt of good-boy hormones.

The day's priority was to get into town and catch Alfie. Get in early when he was sure to be in his office. Moira said she'd come too. There were groceries to buy, and washing to do, and they might as well all go in together. That was true but she was also mindful of police. Better to have Shane driving and not draw attention to herself just a day after getting stopped. She sat in the back seat with Mathew and two plastic bag loads of washing. The window down an inch for the breeze. No need for a towel to keep the sun out. The sun lacked bite today. It was up there in plain view but uncompetitive against the coolness.

Front of Alfie's shop was for the ancient implements: hoes and scythes of the Grim Reaper kind. Ploughshares and pitchforks with red-rusty prongs. Bridles and a horse harness with straw bursting from the stitching. Like a dusty museum of the plains. But in this museum everything was for sale, though not much ever sold to Barleyvillers. Not the meat scales and pump organ. Old tonic bottles dug up from cottage gardens. Sewing machines and top hats, polo sticks, fur stoles, lace doilies and mounted ram horns. Lace bed linen and table cloths, sun-yellowed but heavy with grace. All of them popular in city junk stores.

Locals preferred the middle section of the store where more practical goods could be picked through for bargains. Egg beaters and egg poachers. Pottery bowls and jars with *Sugar* painted on them. Cutlery, carving knives and steels laid out on metal shelves. There was fancy crockery—not a full set but odd cups and plates.

Moira couldn't bring herself to like just one cup and saucer, however pretty and floral and only five dollars instead of a fortune. She'd had her heart fixed on a full, gleaming complement. She didn't know why exactly. Some ladylike fantasy of being a better person in better times. Settling for one cup would ruin the fantasy and make her resent needing fantasies. Fantasies were just another way of saying your own life won't do.

Yet she would have slipped a cup and saucer into the folds of Mathew's pram if Alfie wasn't important to Shane. She was tempted anyway but saw Alfie looking over Shane's shoulder, suspicious, which offended her. She picked up a cup and held it to the light, shook her head dismissively and put the cup down in its saucer with a forceful clink.

The good stuff, the hefty period-feature items, was out the rear through the sliding door into the backyard and converted hayloft. The loft took up most of the yard and had crumbly timber walls patched with fibro and lengths of tin. Its padlocked door was a big modern kind tall enough to take vehicles. This was where Shane and Midge were used to doing business. They would lift their load from their trailer in through the door and Alfie would give each item a wipe with his chamois as they set it down. He would give them an estimate of what it might fetch in Melbourne and he would make some calls and arrange buyers. Men who had first names that sounded like last names—Sinclair and Godfrey.

Today was different. The loft was empty and Alfie wanted to keep it that way. He stood in the yard, his hand visoring the sun from his eyes, and complained about do-gooders. Historical Society snobs who called abandoned homesteads 'heritage' and wanted them protected by the state as if we were England. 'I'm sorry, Shane, but they're clamping down on illegal stripping of places.'

'I got prime iron lace work.'

'Sounds lovely. However—'

'Hand-carved mantelpiece.'

'Superb.'

'That place near the state forest.'

'A splendid homestead.'

'I took some of the walls. Cedar panels, Alfie.'

'Outstanding. But I can't take it at the moment. All these do-gooders.'

Alfie wore his watch on a chain not his wrist and flicked the lid open when he was thinking business. Flicked it open then shut again, slid it into his trousers and took it straight out and flicked some more. A gold lid that made a click. Open, shut, open. He was flicking it now, which made Shane fancy that he could be talked around. He was also smoothing his bald head thoughtfully— another business habit. And pushing his tongue into the gap in his front teeth.

Shane kissed his fingertips as if praising a meal. 'Cedar panels and hand-carved mantelpiece. Beautiful, aren't they, Midge?'

'Too right.'

'Show him how wide.'

Midge took three strides, stopped and considered the distance, and took another stride. 'This wide,' he said, looking down.

'We almost had to split it in half at the joins.'

Alfie's watch lid clicked faster. 'That's all very well but I've got to be careful. Truth is, as well as the do-gooders I've got police asking if I sold a rifle. I don't have a licence to sell a rifle.'

'Did you sell a rifle?' asked Shane.

'That's not the point. I can't conduct the homestead-stripping side of my business as normal with do-gooders and interfering police.'

He said he was sorry. If it was any compensation he'd put his hands on a generator. 'You wanted a generator, if I recall?'

'We do,' said Shane.

'We really do,' said Moira, wheeling the pram into the yard.

'Well, I've come across a nice diesel one. Weighs only seventy-eight kilos and powers 240-volt bulbs easy. Nice red colour, missus. It'll be here in my shop next Tuesday.'

'Price?' said Shane.

'Let you have it for four hundred.'

'Four hundred!' Shane waved his hand as if fending off flies.

Midge did the same.

'We wanted a second-hand one,' said Shane.

'This is a second-hand one,' Alfie said, giving his watch lid some quicker clicking. 'I can let you have it for three hundred. As a favour. Can't be fairer.'

'Still steep,' said Shane. 'Especially when you're saying you won't take my goods.'

The watch lid went quiet. Alfie patted his bald crown. The watch lid started clicking slowly. 'Carved mantelpiece, you said?'

'Yip.'

'Lacework in good nick?'

'Perfect nick.'

'How many trailer loads you got stored?'

'Two trailer loads.'

'Yours is not a big trailer. That's hardly worth the risk for me if you've only got two trailer loads. Two trailer loads won't fill up my truck. By the time you add petrol, the profit is—' He gave a shrug to indicate minimal profit. 'Tell you what. You heard of Bonham Estate?'

Shane looked at Midge and they both shook their heads. Moira too.

'Down near Mortlake. Big farm the Chinese bought last year. The whole homestead is just sitting there, empty, of no interest to the current managers. I've seen photos of the place in its heyday. It's got these old leadlight doors and windows through the place. They'd be very fragile but very saleable. And the old-style pressed metal ceilings. And those little fireplaces in the bedrooms. The little black ones like arches. You interested?'

'Sure,' said Shane.

Midge stepped out a rectangle of strides and squinted as he counted the measurements. 'Doors would stack in the trailer easy, but no more than six, I reckon.'

'Six would be fine,' said Alfie.

'And three fireplaces could fit in the car, if they're little ones and we put the seat down.'

'If three's what you can fit, then three it is.'

Shane held up his hand. 'Wait a sec. What happens then? You say you don't want stuff lying around here. That means *we* got to store it?'

Alfie shook his head and gave Shane a matey tap on the chest. 'I'll hire you my big truck and you can do the transporting to Melbourne. Nothing to do with me what you use the truck for. That's your business. I'm just hiring it out.' He held up his hands innocently and laughed.

'What's the hire fee?'

Alfie grinned. 'I get sixty-five per cent of the profit.'

They haggled a moment. Shane wanted the generator included for nothing. He got Alfie down to $150. Moira leant close to Shane and asked him to ask Alfie for a floral cup and saucer for nothing. Alfie said she had good taste and wrapped them in newspaper.

8

The welfare office was open but empty of clients so Shane didn't go in. If you went in and you were the only person you were the centre of attention and could not be discreet. He wanted to thumb through forms on the racks and choose the right one relating to Zara and hand his own form in. On one occasion when it was his turn to go on the welfare rotation they wouldn't let him just thumb through the racks and hand in the forms. They made him sit down and said it was new policy to discuss retraining.

He got an hour-long lecture and had to pretend he was engrossed. They asked him what skills he had and he wanted say thief, but of course he couldn't. Not that he was ashamed of thieving. He was proud that he could take a crowbar, screwdriver and wooden wedges and ease a window away from the frame without wrecking it. He took care when chiselling out ceiling roses. They could be a hundred years old but they were safe with him. He was more a recycler than burglar, that was his view. He stole from other people the things they didn't seem to be using.

He was his own man. Worked his own hours. He liked the feel of being an outsider. Midge had been trained once, to ride a horse, and where had that got him—a Swan Hill winner and a buggered hip.

So, no, he wouldn't go in when it was empty.

Instead they drove to the laundromat and parked out front under shade. Moira told Midge to watch Mathew and to give her a yell if he stirred. She took the washing in and divided it into two loads.

She put in the coins—three dollars a load—and picked the soggy fluff out of the machines from the people before her. Why they couldn't clean up after themselves, she didn't know. All they had to do was look inside once the machine was emptied and there it was. It made her disgusted to do it for them. Blue fluff like a cat's fur ball mixed in with shredded tissues.

She added detergent from the dispenser on the wall. It gave complimentary powder, not a fragrant brand but it was free.

She pushed the buttons for go.

Next stop was the supermarket.

The sun was still blowing a sweet breeze. Shane and Midge stayed in the car to receive it, their elbows resting across their wound-down windows. A sheet of warm light over their laps. On hot days they went inside for the air-conditioning but this was perfect.

Moira usually took a trolley but today she had the pram. There was a metal basket welded in under the pram's frame, not big enough for major shopping but plenty of room for a tray of sausages and tubs of instant noodles. Two cans of chilli beans, three bottles of Coke. She put two containers of baby formula in the space around Mathew's feet. Bulky enough that no one could accuse her of trying to hide them by using baby feet.

It was tempting to do it, hide things, in these newer-style supermarkets. In the older ones with a single cash register the person serving you took time to look you in the eye, glance for any unusual bulges in your clothing. A smiling game of interrogation. In these newer places with three checkouts with beeping scanners the girls were young and hardly looked up. They passed the goods across the infrared and said, 'How's your day been?' You could have pockets full of chocolate and they wouldn't twig.

The owner was an Indian fellow Barleyvillers called Mr Dixchit, his surname, instead of Habil, his first. You couldn't use his colour or mention *curry muncher* for a nickname, not to his face, but his surname sounded as rude and he answered to it with a polite bow of his head. He must be doing well for himself to put in scanners, people nattered. Two new aisles and a wall-long refrigerator unit. And fresh linoleum. The butchers and grocers had closed down for miles around and he'd got the benefit. Calling him Mr Dixchit was a kind of revenge. If he was struggling they would have used Habil.

The girl who served Moira was the tall, black-haired one with braces on her teeth. The fastest to scan your purchases and pack them into plastic bags. She spoke so softy you often missed her greeting. You had to say, 'Pardon?' so she'd repeat it. But today she was louder, not so stooped in the shoulders to shrink her embarrassing height. When Moira said, 'You're chirpy today,' the girl grinned so wide Moira saw all her rubber bands and wires.

This was her last day working here, she said. She was off for a holiday before school starts. 'There's a bunch of us,' the girl said. 'We're doing VCE this year and we're quitting work.'

'Good for you,' said Moira, and then joked, 'Who'll do the serving?'

'Don't know. New girls, I guess. I think he's doing interviews, Mr Dixchit.'

Moira stood there a moment, midway between taking baby formula from the pram and placing it beside the scanner. 'You need anything special to be a new girl?'

The girl tipped money into Moira's palm. 'Just what I'm doing. Pack the bags. Count the change.'

The girl said Mr Dixchit did not have an office so much as a storeroom with a table and chair and he wasn't in there much. You had to catch him while he was ticking off deliveries or stock-taking shelves. Moira couldn't find him but spoke to an Indian woman she presumed was his wife. Dressed in a drapery way—shiny orange cloth tossed over the shoulder. A dot of red on her forehead. Her halted, foreign way of speaking made her words sound exaggerated but proper. Better than most people sounded in Barleyville.

Moira felt terrible standing there in her grimy frock before drapery and good speaking and yellow-gold bracelets and neck-laces. The only decoration she had was an eagle tattoo across her shoulder blades, and time had blurred that old thing hazy and creased. This lady's hair was plaited perfectly, a black and grey rope of it tied with a ribbon of blue. Moira's hair was not even brushed and was itchy at the scalp and this was no time to scratch. She tried to compensate by copying the lady's speaking. She sucked the edges of her lips in against her teeth and dropped her register a notch to be more plummy. 'I have a daughter, you see. And I think she's at that age when work is calling her.'

The lady smiled and suggested Moira provide a résumé. Moira didn't know what a résumé was but she nodded as if she did know and asked what else should be done. 'I expect you'd want to speak to her. She's a very well-spoken girl. She's not like you get round here. Not, you know, rough.'

Mrs Dixchit said there'd be interviews next Tuesday at 11 a.m. If the girl would like to be in attendance she'd be more than welcome.

By the time Moira got back to the car park she was wheeling the pram so quickly from excitement Shane thought she was being chased. He sprung out to get beside her and ward off any threat. She waved him away and told him to help with groceries. Fold the pram. Lift the seatbelt up—it was hanging over the little bed. She lowered Mathew in and settled herself next to him. But even as Shane started the car and asked, 'What's the excitement?' Moira was having second thoughts. *She* might be excited but what about Zara? A job was nothing but a harebrained scheme.

She didn't answer Shane until they'd gone past the silos and the swirling pigeons. Out onto the open road between wheat-stubble fields and cockatoos walking the roadside as if they'd lost something.

'I was thinking,' she said. 'Zara's fifteen now. I thought maybe she should try and get a job. Get herself out and active.'

There was no response from the front seat so Moira said, 'You know, a job?'

Shane and Midge gave each other a look, their bottom lips floppy with puzzlement.

'We heard what you said. What sort of job? Not much of them round here,' Shane replied.

'The supermarket.'

Midge shook his head once. 'That's aiming pretty high.'

'Hold it minute,' Shane said. 'You serious, Moira?'

'Yeah,' she said, unsurely.

'Her bring in her own money?'

'Yeah.'

Shane put his elbow out the window so he could hold his chin and consider. 'We leave her off our forms it makes things straightforward with the government. We just stick to the old rotation system.'

'Wait on,' said Midge. 'What about Mathew? How's he get fed and watered? I bet she wouldn't earn enough for two.'

'I'd take care of him, wouldn't I, Mathew?'

She reached into the little bed and touched him. Skin so pearly smooth it felt more like water than flesh. As if her hand would scoop some up if she wasn't careful. His fingers and toes small enough to still be in the womb, pre-human.

'You reckon she'd go for it, a job?' said Shane.

Moira shrugged. 'Don't know.' She flicked a fly from Mathew's nose. The damn thing kept coming back and she wound the window down more and patted and pushed at it to climb up the glass and get out.

More of those cockatoos bobbing this way and that as if they'd dropped money. And seeing them reminded her—the laundry!

Shane turned the car around and just for a second Moira was distracted by the petty dilemma she always had with the laundry. Does she leave her soggy fluff in the machines to teach a lesson to people who leave theirs in? Or take it out as an example to them? She always took it out but no one learnt.

9

Those fake sort of clouds had come. The ones that looked like someone drew the shapes—head-and-shoulder pictures by the dozen. They lurched eastward and fell down behind the back of the world. The air following them was gaining heat but not like northerly furnace air. It burnt into you pleasantly, not cruel.

Moira hung the washing on the line of wire between the house and an ironbark. She didn't rush to finish and get the sun off her neck and arms. The stinging was going through her system nicely. She would rather have that sensation than an argument with Zara. An argument was more likely than a thank you and a kiss, a hoot of excitement. It was probably best to forget the job idea completely. Yet what then for Zara?

Enough sun-stinging and putting it off. Shane and Midge had gone to get a new tyre for the trailer for the Mortlake trip and Rory's bike was gone. She had privacy. Mathew was asleep in the house.

She ordered herself to put up the last pegs and go have the conversation this minute. Boil up some tea, add lots of sugar and take it into Zara in the new cup and saucer—so prettily gold around the rim and delicate and red with painted flowers.

She ducked through the flap, eyes closed in dread as she said, 'Sweetie, look what I've got. Brought you some tea and look what I brought it in.'

The girl was not in bed. There was green-tinged light circulating with dust and motes. The window flap on the swaying back wall was open. A breeze flowed through. Zara was on the ground, hunched over a mirror and snipping at her hair with scissors. She had cut it to boy-style shortness. Chopped, uneven. She was kneeling in the offcuts.

'Zara, don't!'

She didn't listen and kept cutting. Moira put the tea down, spilling it, and again told Zara to stop cutting but she kept going.

'Your lovely hair. Now look at it.'

'I want new hair.'

'You got lovely hair.'

'I hate it. It's dirty.'

'A wash would have done.'

The mirror was the shaving mirror Shane used to get tidy— plain glass on the one side, magnified on the other.

'You went through Shane's things?'

'Just a lend.'

'Sweetie, please. Let me do it. You made it a mess.'

Zara's fingers wouldn't easily slip free of the scissor handles, the narrow loops. A knuckle got caught. But she let Moira take over. She straightened her back and held the mirror up to watch the scissoring.

Moira wasn't ready to start. She wanted to show off the crockery and relay her good news. 'Look at this. This is real classy,' she said, lifting the cup out of the saucer dripping tea, a plop on the plastic floor. 'Nice, eh? Now have a sip and you'll be sipping from something classy. Go on. It's got plenty of sweetness.'

Zara drank with a slurp.

'Don't do it in that way, sweetie. Hold the cup like this, between this finger and your thumb, and press like this and up and sip without all that noise. There you go. That's proper. Good. Like a lady.'

They both sat on their heels while Zara sipped. The girl was pale and looked ill or sad. Moira couldn't tell which. Probably sad because she had appetite enough for drinking tea with hungry sipping. Emptying the cup and holding it out requesting more.

'That's a good sign,' Moira said. 'I'll bring more after I've told you the news. I want you to listen and keep quiet and not get upset or argue. All right? Promise?'

She recounted the conversation with the tall girl and the Indian woman—such a grand lady with all that drapery and jewellery. Such an unusual people, Indians: the middle of summer and they dress in drapery like it was winter.

Then the main news. 'I'm not saying it's a certainty. I'm saying it's a chance at doing something. An interview at a supermarket. That doesn't come along every day. A chance for a job and earning money.'

Zara shook her head: no, it doesn't. Then shook it again to reject the idea.

'Why not, sweetie?'

'Why would they want me?'

'Why wouldn't they want you? You're too smart to lie around doing nothing all day. You need something and this is something.'

She moved close to Zara to speak at a whisper. She wanted to say how working at a job might put her in the right spirits to love Mathew. Instead she used her cunning hat. 'You told me you want to leave. Well, here's the way to get money to do it.'

'You think?'

'We put our heads together we can give it a red-hot go. We'll have to fix this hair, though. Can't have hair like this for an interview.'

She budged Zara's shoulders to position her more into the light. She rose up on her knees and began cutting the jagged edges even.

10

Shane and Midge knew what a résumé was. They'd shared the same one for years for their rotation. There was nothing on it but made-up stablehand work and casual labour but it kept the government happy.

'How can you have a résumé when you're fifteen? You've done nothing. Got born. Got pregnant,' said Shane.

Moira glared at him and he said, 'I'm just saying.'

They were eating lunch at the kitchen table. A loaf of white bread with the fresh sticky feel still in it. A slice of cheese and a shaving of raw onion between two slices. Moira drank tea from her new cup and put peanut butter on bread for Rory for whenever he showed up. Midge hardly ate his slices. He'd got out of the habit as a jockey and to watch him you'd think he was still wasting for rides: he removed the cheese and onion and ate them with the bread only picked at.

'When she comes out don't say nothing about her hair.'

'Why not?' said Shane. 'What's wrong with it?'

'Nothing's wrong with it. It was just an accident. So don't say nothing.'

Shane spoke with his mouth full. 'She'd be able to pay her way with a job. My advice is *cash*. See if they pay cash. Keeps everything off the records if it's cash. That's my advice.'

'She hasn't got the job yet. But we'll work a line on them. I was thinking we'd take Mathew with us and I'd stand there with him and it makes us look, you know, family people.'

Midge nodded. 'Indians have big families.'

'How do you know?' mumbled Shane.

''Cause there's millions of them.'

'Taking the baby could make her look slutty.'

'Shane, shut up.'

'I'm just seeing through their eyes.'

Midge said, 'Might see a baby as a steadying thing.'

'Thank you. There's one gentleman here.'

Moira saw Zara and went *shh* to Shane in case he spoke. The girl was outside and didn't enter when Moira called, 'Come in, sweetie.'

She'd lit a cigarette and was standing in the sun, the smoke like steam coming off her. Midge stared through the glad-wrap pane and thought he was looking at a stranger. A boy, not Zara. He stood up and went to the doorway. He shook his head at how short hair changed a person so. Left them still pretty but more serious-looking in their features, and harder. He could wear his jockey helmet twenty-four hours a day to slick his mop and he'd still be the same Midge. He liked the idea of being someone else.

'You cut her hair, Moira?' he said.

'Most of it.'

'Good job. Could you do me?'

'I'd be happy to. Just make an appointment. Can I get you some noodles, sweetie?'

Zara nodded with an uttering of smoke.

Moira lit the gas, put water on and peeled the lid off a tub of noodles. She bit the corner from its sachet of spices and patted them on. She sensed Shane was about to offer a hair comment, never mind her request not to. His chewing had slowed from having to mind his face bruises. His swallowing was slow and squelching. He leant back in his chair until the front legs lifted up and he could crane and get a better view outside.

'Shh,' Moira said.

'Didn't say a thing yet.'

'Good.'

'I was going to say congratulations to Zara, that's all.'

'You can do that.'

'Congratulations, Zara. You never know, they might give you free groceries. Or you might be able to sneak some out. See if they'll pay you cash, that's my advice.'

Zara stubbed out her cigarette in the ash plate and lifted her chin for a long exhaling. When her breath was clear of smoke she smiled. 'I'd have a uniform, wouldn't I? And I'd have money.'

For this situation Zara's age should go up to seventeen, Moira said. Seventeen sounded adult-like. What's more, seventeen was the limit for leaving school. If you can say to the Indians you've left school then you can say you're all theirs and not distracted by school commitments.

'You think we'd get away with seventeen, sweetie? I think so. You think so, Midge?'

'That short hair makes her sort of, what's the word, tougher.'

'Tougher's good. That's like older.'

'No more school?' Zara said.

Moira shook her head. 'You always skipped it anyway. They come after you, we say we're only travelling through.'

'No one's bothered so far,' said Shane.

'That's right. Seventeen it is, then. And we'll have to spruce her up nice and all clean and well dressed?'

Zara said she had no good clothes. She'd go check but she had nothing that was up to scratch. It was a supermarket job, Shane quipped. Not a beauty contest.

She went into her tent anyway. She left the flap up for more light and pulled out the cardboard boxes of her clothes and chewed her lip at them. When Moira came in with noodles and tea Zara took the noodles and slurped a mouthful in an absentminded way while concentrating on her clothing. She removed her T-shirt to try on a top that was meant to be white but was grey from so much washing. Her pasty skin had pinkened. Her cheeks had flame in them now and her eyes were wide and bright.

Such a strong, rare moment, thought Moira. A moment like this, when your idea had led to something, was a moment when you felt the world was *your* world. That it spoke your name for once and gave you its full attention. Moira wanted to thank it as she would thank a person. How do you thank the world? She said thank you silently, mouthing the words. Her idea might not lead anywhere but her daughter was out of bed and had the beginnings of a smile.

Yet there were matters to be raised. Moira realised she was afraid of Zara. One wrong word and that smile would vanish. She must choose her words cleverly. Not too firm a touch to them. Not too soft. Look at the ribs on the girl. She was thin, her stomach sunken. She had breasts but they might as well not have been breasts. So small. Not the breasts of a mother.

'Do they hurt at all?'

'What?'

'Those.'

'No.'

'Are they hard? Cause you don't want them hard from the milk going bad.'

'They're not hard.'

'Let me check.'

'Don't.'

Afraid or not, she pressed on: 'Don't you have an urge in you? Just to hold him?'

'What?'

'Your son.'

'No.'

'But if you held him.'

'No.'

'If you fed him.'

'No.'

'Just tried to.'

'Go away.'

'You better think about something, then. You better think about the next time you open your legs.'

She took a rectangular packet from her pocket. She slid the contents out. A blister pack of pills. She tossed them onto the bed.

'These are mine but I don't want them. When you run out we'll get you more. I can only handle one of your babies at a time.'

Moira wished she'd not said all that. She wanted to go back into the tent and erase the last two minutes. Bring back the pleasant job dream. But she was standing in for Mathew, that was how she saw it. Babies don't know what's happening to them. You have to feel their feelings for them. Be angry and hurt and bitter on their behalf. She cried on his behalf. He wasn't much of a crier. He cried when hungry and when that was over he slept with perfect peace. She cried the tears she thought he would have cried if he knew his mother had rejected him and much worse.

She did it behind the house, among the washing which was already dry and sun-rough. She could cry there in secret as if pretending to collect clothes. When no tears were left she unpegged all she could hold over her shoulder and went into the house to sort them. Shane was there but he was plotting a map route with Midge: how to get to Mortlake fastest and stay off the policed main roads. She dropped the washing on the big bed and lifted Mathew from the little one. He was fidgeting his way out of sleep. Mouth and eyes trying to work themselves open. Moira kissed him and held him close, the creamy smell of his body and sour nappy odour. She laid him among the washing, stepped into the kitchen and lit the gas. She changed him while his bottle boiled. She wiped him clean with jerry-can water and dusted on some talc.

He cried while his milk was getting ready and Moira let him cry instead of her usual hurry to stop him. He had a right to do it. It was only the hunger crying but she told him he had a right and should cry like hell and no one could blame him. Shane complained—'He's got a set of lungs on him'—and she ignored the comment.

When the formula was mixed she sat on the bed and cradled Mathew, letting the teat drip onto his lips to give him a taste for it. He didn't latch on and suckle straight away. He began to, then stopped and grizzled. He'd got into the habit of spitting the teat away and taking a while to be restarted. She reached out with her foot and swept the door as shut as it would go. Its bottom jammed on the floor and never fully closed but there was privacy enough to put Mathew on the bed and unzip the back of her dress. Moira let it fall forward over her arms and onto her waist. She sat and unclipped her bra and lifted it up so her breasts came out and she could settle the baby into position with his mouth under her left nipple. She dripped formula onto the nipple and tilted his head so he could be teased into feeling it against his lips and want to take it. 'Come on,' she whispered.

When she felt him suck hard enough she leant back and replaced her nipple with the bottle.

11

A few hours later the north heat was blowing again. The tree rapids sped up and flung away unwanted bark. The sun reached a low-enough angle to begin reflecting blueness off the caravan. The wind made the caravan quiver, which made the blueness quiver as it entered the house. Moira closed the shutter across the glad-wrap window and put a brick against the open door to stop it swinging and banging. She heard Limpy barking in his pipsqueak yap. It was wilder than usual. She expected Rory was exciting him with a ball or lizard carcass. She yelled out the door, 'That you, Rory?'

He'd not been sociable for a couple of days and stayed behind his cap grunting *yip* or *nup*, probably jealous of no attention being paid to him. Second fiddle to Mathew and Zara. She decided to treat him with a packet of salt and vinegar chips she was saving. And a Mars bar that was squashy in the wrapper from melting but he preferred it that way and liked to lick the lining till it was clean. 'Rory, come here, I got something for you.'

The barking was furious now and not playful. She'd have got

Shane to hush it but he and Midge were at their shed pulling any nails from their stashed goods and polishing brass from a box of fancy wall fixtures. 'Rory?'

He was under the sugar-gum garage listening to the car radio, stretched along the front seat, his feet out the window. His head had bobbed up but the shade was dark and Moira couldn't see him. What she could see was a police car, the white and blue check stripes, driving up the dirt road, its dust tail raised high behind. Limpy raced onto the road, challenging the car with barking, then veered off to the side and let it through.

Moira wished she could kick the brick away and close the door to fool them that no one was home. No point with Rory right there. Besides, it would encourage them to snoop around and wander into the bush and find the shed, Shane and Midge with hammer and Brasso in hand. Best to greet them politely and be hospitable and wave as they pulled up. Then comment on the blazing weather.

The car parked on the fringe of the sugar-gum shade and Rory slid out of the wag and took some backward steps, springing up and down on his toes. Moira called for him not to do that, spring up and down as if goading them. She told him to come to her at once, and repeated, 'Don't spring like that.' He had on board shorts that hung below his knees. There weren't pockets for shoving his hands in and pretend to be casual. He tugged his cap down instead, tucking his ear tips into it and pulling the peak lower.

The young blond one from the other day got out of the passenger side. He lifted his chin on seeing Moira and bent down and said something to the person in the driver's side. Then he stood straight and looked about the place with his sunglasses off. He put them back on and walked a few steps, wary of Limpy who was trotting in an arc around him and growling.

From the driver's side came an older officer, tall and heavy across the midriff. He wore a blue Akubra, which almost blew off as he crouched and snapped his fingers for Limpy to have a sniff of him. Limpy crept near but had second thoughts and barked and retreated.

'Afternoon. I'm Senior Sergeant Fowler. This is Constable Dench,' he said, walking to the house.

Moira went to meet them. 'Afternoon. Hot enough for you?'

'It is indeed.'

He took his hat off and fanned his face. Put the hat back on.

'Can I get you some water?'

'We'll be fine, thank you.'

He nodded hello to Rory. 'What's your name?'

'He's Rory,' said Moira.

'Afternoon, Rory.'

Rory turned, nodded, staring at the ground.

'How old are you, Rory?'

'He's fourteen.'

'Lots of space out here for riding a bike. You ride a bike, Rory?'

'He's got a bike. He loves riding.'

'And you are?'

'I'm Moira.'

'You know there's been four days of total fire ban in the past week?'

'Not surprised. Always fire bans in this heat.'

'Exactly. Which is why it staggers me that people still play with fire.'

A bead of sweat fell down his temple and he flicked it away with a finger. He took off his hat and wiped the inside band. His short grey hair had a wet crease around it.

'What colour's your bike, Rory?'

'Why?' said Moira.

'You play dragons, son?'

'Nup.'

Moira tapped the boy to stand up straight and not say *Nup*, say *No, officer*.

'He don't know much,' she joked. 'But he's a good boy, eh, Rory?'

'Yip.'

'Would you like a cup of tea, you two gentlemen?'

The sergeant shook his head and put his hat on and strolled about the L-shape. 'Not exactly the Hilton, this place. How many of you live here, Rory? That's a maths question.'

Moira didn't like that tone but knew to accept it with no back-chat or change in her expression. She gritted her teeth and kept silent.

'There's me and mum. Shane and Midge. And my sister Zara.'

'She's in the tent resting. She just had a baby,' said Moira, making a performance of hushing her voice.

'Is that so? Funny in this day and age how you lot do the breeding and the better of kind of people avoid it.'

He glanced at the blond one and they exchanged grins.

'What colour's your bike, Rory?'

The boy shrugged.

'Where is it?

'Dunno.'

'Rory, tell the officer. Sorry, officer, but he gets all shy.'

Constable Dench sauntered towards the side of the house and said, 'It's right here,' and pulled the bike into view. A small one with handle bars that rose high in a U shape.

'Your bike's red,' said the sergeant. He sounded disappointed.

He moved closer to the boy. His underarms were dark blue with sweat. On his back and his chest blots of damp were showing through.

Rory stepped towards Moira and behind her.

Dench let the bike fall to the ground and knelt to inspect it just as Shane walked through the trees by the caravan. Midge followed. They were out of breath, Midge especially, and were trying to keep their breathing slow and innocent. Midge coughed and bent over to spit.

'Is there a problem, officer?' asked Shane. He made sure to smile and not make the question belligerent.

'You are?' said the sergeant.

'Shane.'

'Shane,' he said, chewing his bottom lip thoughtfully. 'I'm new to Barleyville and can't put faces to names. But I see you've got war wounds on your face. You the Shane who had a tangle with a Jim Tubbs the other night?'

'Nah. Tubbsy's a mate. It was just mucking round.'

The sergeant laughed quietly to himself. He took off his hat to wipe the inside again. He patted his forehead and neck with his handkerchief. 'Tell me. Any of you know anything about fires being lit about three ks south of here?'

Shane shook his head. Moira too.

'Roadside grass went up. Leapt into farmland and burnt out a hay shed and a mile of fencing.'

'That's terrible,' said Shane.

'A kid on a silver pushbike, says a witness. Probably playing dragons. That's the new thing they do in town nowadays to relieve boredom. They hold a cigarette lighter up to an aerosol can and whoosh, they've got a flame thrower, much to their delight.'

'Stupid bastards.'

'Exactly. You don't have a silver bike as well as your red one, Rory?'

'Can't afford two bikes,' said Shane. 'And we keep the boy out of any nonsense.'

'Sensible.'

The sergeant strolled a few paces. 'You own this place?'

'Nah, just using it,' said Shane.

'Squatting?'

'We're just travelling through.'

'Trants?'

'Yeah.'

The sergeant took a black pad from his rear pocket. A pen from his chest pocket. The blond one did the same.

'Can I have your names?'

'I'm Shane.'

'Last name.'

'Whittaker.'

'And you're Moira Whittaker?'

'No, Duggan.'

'And he's Rory Whittaker?'

'No. Spinks.'

'His sister is?'

'Zara.'

'Spinks?'

'Bunce. Different fathers.'

'And who are you?'

'I'm Midge. Shane's brother.'

'Midge Whittaker?'

'No, Flynn. Half brothers.'

The sergeant shook his head. He shut the pad and lifted his hat to rub the sweat off in the crook of his arm. Dench whispered something to him and the sergeant said, 'Ah, yeah,' and looked at Moira. He narrowed his eyes and took a step her way.

'You're not driving without a licence, are you?'

Moira swallowed and didn't answer because this was no time to lie. The tree rapids surged and bustled while she said nothing. Leaves came loose, airborne as insects.

'You were meant to present your licence at the station. Why haven't you?'

Shane interrupted. 'Sorry, officer. She doesn't have a licence. I've said to her over and over don't drive without a licence. But sometimes she thinks to herself, I'm only going up the road. How about we say it won't happen again and leave it at that?'

'You get one warning and one warning only.'

'Understood. No worries,' Shane said.

He nudged for Moira to speak and she muttered, 'Sorry. Thank you.'

The sergeant turned and walked to the tree-garage, picking his wet shirt from where it stuck to him. Dench reached the car first and pinched away twigs from the windscreen.

Rory was starting to snigger. Shane told him to shut up and grabbed his wrist to stop him swaggering off. 'Don't you move.'

When the police car was invisible behind dust he let the boy go but wouldn't let him run off. 'Look at me, boy. I said, look at me. You doing this dragons shit?'

'No.'

No wasn't good enough for Shane. 'You had nothing to do with that road fire?'

'No.'

'No, you had nothing to do with it? Or no, you had something to do with it?'

'No. I mean yeah, it wasn't me.'

'You play dragons?'

'No.'

'Bullshit. Your bike's usually silver but now you've got a red one. How come?

'I don't know.'

'You pinched the red one?'

'No. I swapped it.'

'Who with?'

'I don't know. I saw it in town and liked it better.'

'So you swapped it?'

'Yeah.' Rory grinned.

'Because people saw you lighting fires.'

'I didn't light no fires.'

'You start fires and we'll have cops down on us, big time.'

'I didn't start no fires.'

He stomped his foot, hating not being believed. His cap slipped back off his face and Shane saw something beneath the peak he wanted a closer look at. Rory pressed the cap onto his head with both hands but Shane wrenched it off and pulled the boy's hands away from blocking his sight.

A bald patch in the fringe and frizzled hair around it, pubic-short from being burnt. The scalp was red at the hairline and the eyebrows singed and made to look normal with a touch-up of mascara and gingery pencil. Shane smeared it with his thumb and Rory squealed that it was painful to be touched there.

'I didn't start no fires. It was an accident. I was playing dragons and the flames got away. I burnt myself and some grass and it was an accident.'

Shane hit him—only a cuff across the hair but Rory fell down and yelled that he was sorry. Moira grabbed Shane's arm and he yanked it free and said her son was a dumb, useless piece of shit who didn't have brains enough to know fires meant major jail time. Like murder. Not under the radar like normal.

He strode to the caravan and skipped up into it and yelled, 'Where is it? Where's the stuff, Rory? Come here. I said, come here! Where you hiding it?'

Rory started crying and stood up and held onto Moira's waist. He hid his face in the small of her back. She put her arm under his arm and patted him.

In the caravan there was crashing and thumping. Shane was lifting up the wall seat that was Rory's bed and the stretcher bed Midge used. 'Where the fuck is it, Rory?' he was yelling. He slammed the cupboard door beneath the tiny Formica bench and kicked the leg from the foldout table. Moira told Midge to go stop him but there was no chance he'd try that.

Zara put her head out of the tent and babbled about the police. Had they come for her, to question her? Midge told her to go back inside and avoid seeing Shane's temper.

'It was just general inquiries,' he said. 'Why would they want to question you?'

The crashing stopped and Shane jumped from the caravan with two cans of fly spray and a lighter. He threw them on the ground and swore at Rory to come out from behind Moira and take the hiding he deserved. He told Moira to stand aside and stop mothering the idiot who started fires and needed a lesson taught to him. She said she'd do it herself but Shane kept coming towards her saying she was too soft for teaching lessons. Starting fires called for a hiding not a talking-to.

Moira held out her hands, shepherding Rory to stay behind her, but the boy had a temper of his own. He elbowed her aside and pulled his two throwing knives from the holster he'd made that fitted inside the back of his shorts. A wedge of cardboard bound with packing tape and a belt of binding twine taped to that. He held the knives out like he would stab Shane if he had to. One step closer and he'd aim at Shane's ribs. His face was screwed up with panic and forced-back weeping. The knives were shaking in his hands. Spit blew out of his mouth and spattered onto his chin.

Shane stood still and looked at the knives and the shaking and considered them a comic play-act. Rory performing rage rather than the real thing. He kept going closer and laughed. 'Look what we have here. What knife you going to use first, boy?'

'Rory, don't do that,' Midge said. 'You'll make big trouble.'

'Put those down,' Moira demanded. 'Please put them down. Do as I say.'

There was no laughing from Shane now. He was narrow-eyed, had a gravel-growl for a voice. 'Which knife's first? Come on, then. Do it. Have a go. Come on. Have a go.'

There was rage in the boy but not malice enough for knifing Shane. He dropped the knives and sprinted off. Shane went to grab him as he dashed by but Midge reached and took a handful of his shirt. He said, 'Leave him, Shane,' and wouldn't let the shirt go which made Shane lash out with his arm and collect him in the stomach. Midge buckled over and lay folded up in the dirt. He couldn't take a breath. He made a choking attempt and stuck his tongue out.

'Jesus—sorry, Midge,' Shane said, kneeling and stroking Midge's shoulder. 'Sorry, sorry. You need your puffer?'

Midge nodded. His face was purple and there was water running from the corners of his clenched eyes.

'See what your idiot son made me do?'

Shane ran to the caravan and got the puffer from Midge's box of toilet things and hurried it to him.

'There you go. Steady, Midge. Slow breaths. Slow breaths. I'm sorry. Don't worry about Rory. I'll patch things up. Slow breaths.'

When the breathing became regular Shane helped Midge up and offered him his hand to shake. 'Come on, say we're sweet. Go on, squeeze a bit. You got to mean it. That's better.'

12

Shane never thought he could feel close to a child that was not his own blood. He and Zara had never clicked in that way, which he was glad about. For him step-fathering was more natural man to boy than man to girl. Showing affection to a girl could be taken the wrong way. Man to boy there wasn't any danger. Rory had never once said to him, 'You're not my father.' Never once said, 'I'm not your son.' Threatened with a hiding you'd think the boy would say it. They'd become close as blood, as if really related.

That meant getting in the wag and going after him where he'd bolted up the dirt road, north where the wind came from. No boy would get far in that wind. It pushed you back like a hand pushes. It reached out of the sky and would not let you pass. He found him in the disused school bus shelter where Loop Road dipped across Curdle Creek, which was a creek only in name.

He stretched over and wound the passenger window down and said, 'Come on, mate. Hop in,' but Rory refused to look at him. He wiped his eyes and stood up and walked along the road edge towards town. Shane eased the car up alongside.

'Come on. I was only saying I'd give you a hiding to scare you. I wasn't going to give you a hiding. I was bluffing. You got to learn about bluffing. Bluffing is where you get what you want without actually going through with the threat.'

There was no break in Rory's stride.

'Come on. When have I ever given you a serious hiding? You was holding a knife on me, Rory. Come on. If you're bored and looking to play this crazy dragons crap then let's think of something else for you to do.'

Rory halted. 'I don't want to go back to school. I'm shit at it and I hate it.'

'Sounds good to me.'

'Yeah?'

'Yeah. Fuck school. What do you want to do instead?'

A shrug was the only answer that Shane expected. He did not expect what came next.

'I want to be like you.'

He frowned at first and thought Rory was playing. If it was snideness a sneer or smirk would break out on the boy's face. But there was no smirk or sneer.

'You want to be like me?'

Rory nodded.

A jolt came low down in Shane's chest. A missed heartbeat. Pride and the thrill of responsibility.

'That would be good,' he said, palming the door open for Rory to climb in. 'You could be my apprentice. You like that?'

'What's an apprentice?'

'Someone training with someone. My trade is the future, Rory. There's an old saying, and I can't remember exactly, but it's about how you'll have one man who owns this stuff he doesn't give a shit about. And there's another man, and to him that stuff it's like treasure to him. You understand? The more the old ways die out here, the more we'll do well.'

Shane took Rory's hands and turned them in his own for inspection. Thin scarless fingers, pink on the underside compared to his own grainy, rough ones. Those hands would have to change.

'Strong hands are very important in our game. All the lifting. And they've got to be gentle too. Because when you're dealing with brittle things like leadlight and finicky bits of wood you need gentle hands to work with. How about I start showing you? You come on the Mortlake trip and we'll start you learning.'

'Promise?'

'Promise. You feel better now? Had a good cry?'

'I wasn't crying.'

'Why are your eyes red?'

'You promise I can go thieving with you?'

'Promise. Shake on it.'

They shook hands and held on a long time with Shane squeezing harder by degrees and Rory trying not to flinch. Then flinching and laughing and asking to try again.

They were still trying when they got back home. Moira and Midge were pleased to see them bantering but they were in an exchange of their own that wasn't quite settled. Midge had said, 'Why would Zara think those cops wanted to speak to her?' Moira had answered, 'Who knows?' And Midge said, 'She's done nothing bad, has she?' Moira waved the question away. Midge thought that was strange. A wave instead of plain no.

With Shane and Rory arriving he didn't bother asking further. They were handshaking and twisting arms up each other's spines. Shane was letting Rory have a couple of victories. They were giggling but Midge was wary in case the horseplay went awry.

'See, Midge? Me and dragon boy here are best of friends. My best mate next to you.'

He held out his hand for Midge to shake it but Midge didn't want his arm bent and fingers squeezed hard.

'I won't do nothing,' said Shane.

Midge gave in and straight away he winced and dropped to one knee.

'You fell for that, brother.'

Moments like this he wanted to rail against Shane and make *him* the feel the brunt of teasing. But he accepted his lot and pretended to laugh.

Cutting Rory's hair was Moira's priority. The car licence problem was more important but she could see no way to solve it. Cutting Rory's hair was something she could control. She sat him under the porch in the least line of wind and got the scissors and a comb. She shaped the length to match up with his burnt fringe. Dabbing his scalp with water where flames had left a red patch. A rash more than a wound. He didn't moan too much when she touched it.

Shane said a haircut would make him manlier than having messy hair long and curly. 'You'll look like you mean business.'

That made the boy sit still and take the haircut as if being initiated into a special apprentice look. The first step of his working life.

'I'm going to Mortlake. Our trade's the future.'

'I want to keep him out of trouble,' Shane said to Moira. 'Teach him to pinch proper.'

Saying the word trouble prompted him to make a rule about Moira and the car.

'You'll just have to stop driving. Simple as that.'

'I can take the back roads.'

'You'll get caught again. They're on to you. Didn't matter when we kept on the move. But we're not on the move no more.'

The problem came down to reading and writing. Moira could do neither. Words got jumbled since she was a girl. They made no sense and she couldn't spell them. She grew to hate their humiliating letters. Spent her life faking understanding them but she could not fake reading the driver test. She tried it once and put her ticks in all the wrong boxes. Even trants could do reading and writing, but not her. She called it her blank spot. Her blank bonehead.

She pulled Rory's ear down to cut the hair behind it and he complained she was pulling too much.

'I'll be able to go nowhere. I'll be trapped,' she said.

She had to stop trimming because her eyes were welling.

'You won't be trapped. I'll be your chauffeur,' said Shane.

'Me too,' said Midge.

'But I won't go by *myself*. And if Zara gets that job I'd drive her.'

'She probably won't get the job,' said Shane.

'She has to. She needs to get out and be doing something.'

'I'll drive her,' Midge said.

Shane gave a single clap of his hands. 'There you go. Solved.'

The haircut resumed despite Moira's bonehead feeling heavy and inclined to hang. Blank, ignorant head, she said to herself. The wind parted Rory's hair at the side. She'd left that side too long and had to cut more. Blank bonehead. Ignorant moron Moira.

When Rory was done Midge praised the result and asked if her talents could make him tidier, please. She was grateful for his compliment and his manners and sat him down. She did her best to sculpt his greasy strands. He got splinters of hair down his back and itched and wriggled through the procedure. Bush flies flitted around his face like snips of darker hair. They bit his bare arms.

When he saw his reflection in the house window he said he felt ten years younger. He called her a miracle worker.

Shane agreed—a miracle. He sat and asked for her wonder treatment on him. She was smiling by now and said, 'Since you asked nice.'

They didn't notice Zara come out of the tent and stand in the gusty sunshine wearing a black shirt she'd fished out and was ironing smooth with the flat of her hand. She wore her best jeans which also were black and had minimal fading down the leg fronts. Her shoes were slip-ons, too tight from being outgrown but brown and only scuffed at the toe tips. She had make-up on, a powdery pallid layer. Eyelids blue when she blinked and her lips shiny purple. She held out her hands like a model showing off to get attention. She said, 'This good for the interview?'

Shane and Rory only nodded but Midge and Moira said, 'Wow.'

13

A character reference was desirable, Midge said, if Zara's résumé was to look official. But who would provide it—Midge himself? He had no community standing. Shane suggested Alfie might do it.

In Midge's opinion a résumé should be typed. School was closed so Zara could not use the computers there. Would Alfie let her use the one in his office?

Next day they drove into town, Zara in the front seat with Rory and Shane to her sides. Moira was in the back 'doing the honours', as she called feeding Mathew. Midge tightened up the straps on the little bed and sat the other side of it and sang 'Old McDonald Had a Farm' badly and with wheezing between words, but it hardly mattered given the baby's slumbering.

Alfie agreed to let Zara sit at his desk and type if she was quick. As for a character reference, he thought it best to decline. He hardly knew the girl and it was wise to keep a professional distance. They decided to use Midge's name after all and refer to him not as a former jockey but something impressive—thorough-bred industry consultant.

Moira was keen for Zara to be turned out extra-clean. Given the shiny state of that Indian lady she needed to be clean and classy in presentation. In Alfie's office, along the window-wall that faced out to the shop floor, there was a glass cabinet displaying earrings and finger rings with diamonds and rubies set in silver and gold. Necklaces and brooches of intricate filigree.

'Can I ask the prices on these?'

Alfie smiled and shook his head. 'Those are expensive. That diamond ring is almost five hundred dollars. That gold necklace is four hundred and so is the bracelet. They're estate jewellery.'

'What's estate jewellery?'

'When someone has died.'

'Five hundred dollars for something someone died with on their body?'

She shivered at the notion of slipping the rings off corpses. Selling them for big money seemed cold and wrong. And yet how important they looked, like treasures families hand down to prove their good breeding. Which you could join your-self up to if you could only afford them. Hold your head higher as if superior.

'I was wondering,' said Moira. 'That lovely gold necklace there with the thick chain and locket at the end? And that bracelet there with the red stones in it. Would you rent them out?'

'Rent them?' Alfie laughed. Then his brow furrowed with thinking. He started doing his watch-lid clicking. 'Never thought of renting.'

'How much to rent them?'

Shane took her elbow and tugged her towards him. 'What you doing?'

'Zara would look so good in them.'

The watch stopped clicking. Alfie's brow twisted and a fringe of sweat appeared. 'You mean *you* rent them?'

'Yeah.'

'I thought you meant generally as an idea.'

'What price to rent them?' said Moira.

He put his hand on the cabinet glass and patted it. 'I wouldn't rent them.'

'To us, you mean.'

'I didn't say that.'

'You'd get them back if that's what you're worried about. We'd only want them for an hour or so.'

Shane tugged her again. 'We don't want to rent them.'

'They'd make Zara look so special.'

'They're not for rent,' Alfie said.

'I'm not going to take off with them.'

'I'm sure you wouldn't. It's just that—'

'You don't trust us.'

'Sorry about this, Alfie,' said Shane, standing in front of Moira and turning her towards the front door.

'You'll rent us a vehicle but not these?' she said.

'Jewellery's different.'

'How?'

'Um—well, no number plates, for one thing.'

'Ask him as a favour, Shane.'

The word 'favour' made Alfie hold up his hands and close his eyes. He spoke before Shane had a chance. 'Like I was saying with the referee issue, it's good to keep a professional distance. Not blur the line and get too, what's the word, informal and complicated.'

'Understood,' Shane said. He used his eyebrows and a jerk of his head to motion for Moira to keep quiet. 'Thanks for letting the girl type her thing, Alfie. Cheers and all the best.'

He took Moira's wrist, attached her hand to the pram handle and urged her to go. He looked around for Rory to make sure he was following. He glanced for any unusual bulges on the boy, just in case. He told Midge not to stand about reading Zara's résumé page. He could do that out in the street. Zara said she'd made a typo spelling *thoroughbread*. Shane said too bad, they'd used up enough of Alfie's generosity.

As soon as they were out through the shop door Moira cursed, 'Arsehole,' through her teeth. She directed it at Alfie's name on the sandwich board on the footpath. 'Arsehole,' she repeated to double the disrespect to him.

Rory gasped. 'Mum swore.'

'Shut up,' Shane said.

The pram's wheels squeaked from the brisk pace of Moira's pushing. Her left thong came off and she jabbed her foot back into it as if she were kicking something.

The Barleyville town wind was different from the Barleyville out-of-town wind. Out of town the wind flowed at you and however powerful it had a natural ebb to it, a personality of sorts. One minute tearing about in a temper, the next stroking the grass across paddocks. The in-town wind came from all directions. It squeezed between buildings and side streets, disorderly and whistling. It came out of the concrete with extra heat on its breath and had nowhere to go but around.

Moira grabbed her frock from being blown over her hips and put a skip in her walk to get across the intersection. Once you got under the verandahs in the old part of town you at least had the sun out of your eyes. Barleyville's old part was only eight buildings long but they were the taller places—the council offices and two hotels. The new part had the supermarket, the service station and farm supplies. Shops like Alfie's and the land agent. The laundromat and takeaway. But the old part had the bull-nose verandahs. It had the stately guise you think of as history. Shane wished he could pinch it all, brick by brick, but you'd need a fleet of Kenworths.

Behind the council offices the brown lawn sloped to the public library. Along from that the disabled ramp curved up to the op-shop. It was a meeting hall but the Salvos used it these days—a dozen clothes racks and boxes of CDs and paperbacks. Kettles and toys. Brogue shoes with the heels worn away. Coils of belts creased along the holes. The place smelled musty and of old people. Like a wardrobe not opened for years.

Moira liked being here. She called the smell 'homely'. She could imagine the calibre of women who once wore the dresses. Scoff at the types who'd wear an orange muumuu that could fit two people. Envy the hips of anyone who slid into a long, skinny evening dress without splitting it. The sequins were like ice hair to the touch.

Shane and Midge let her have her fun. They walked down for a smoke under the peppercorn at the bottom of the lawn. Rory went to the toy box and started pulling the trigger of a cap gun over and over so it clacked with dream bullets. The noise made Zara flinch and step away from him in between clothes racks.

Jewellery hung from coat hangers. If you could call it jewellery after seeing Alfie's cabinet. This was tin and plastic and hardly rated as second best. More fifth or sixth best, Moira thought. The paint designs were chipped. The chain links were roughly pliered together where they'd broken.

'Come here, sweetie,' she said.

She held necklaces against Zara's neck and none of them suited. Their metal could have been cut from aluminium cans. And they were long and would need to be looped like rope to fit. Moira had Zara read out the prices and they were so cheap—one dollar, two— you wouldn't let a dog wear them. The ten-dollar coat hanger had a better class of chains but they had crucifixes attached and Moira didn't know if Indians had a snitcher on anything Christian.

On another hanger there was necklace of red stones that Moira admired and made Zara try on and it sat snugly against her collarbones. A matching bangle fitted her wrist if you gave a good push. But they had to be hung back up and forgotten about. At thirty dollars for the necklace and ten for the bangle the purchase was out of the question.

The lady behind the counter had a ball of wool in her lap, knitting. Moira calculated she was seventy at least going by her wavy mauve hair, the arthritic knobs of her knuckles. There was a radio playing clarinets and trumpets. If Moira was thinking of thieving she'd have the benefit of that lulling radio and an elderly lady in charge with her head down knitting.

There was another customer fingering through the racks. Fat as females get, Moira mumbled. Zara agreed and sniggered. Why fatties wear tight leggings, Moira could never understand. She called the look the 'porridge bottom'. This particular porridge bottom was too engrossed in the clothing to be a witness.

Moira whispered for Zara to take the necklace and bangle and in one casual movement slip them into the pram. Then pretend to be hanging them on the hanger and say, 'I don't like these. They don't work on me.'

As Zara did that Moira nonchalantly covered them with a blanket. She took a chain from the one-dollar hanger and said, 'I think this is the one. Let's buy this.'

She went to the counter and handed over a dollar. 'What are you knitting?'

'My grandson's jumper. You like it? It's Angora.'

'Oh, I do. I think it's lovely. It's beautiful and very clever of you.'

As she turned the pram towards the door she told Rory to put the gun back in the box and said, 'Good boy' as he did, pitched loudly so the old dear would think they were respectable.

She was so pleased with herself she didn't stop striding when her problem left thong slid loose again. She flicked it from her toes to her fingers and kept pushing the pram down the main street to get to the wag. Moira had never had the burning inside her that the normal world called ambition. She was having it now for the sake of her daughter's cause.

14

Here was the plan for the next four days: the Tuesday interview was the same day their new generator would be ready for carting. Shane decided that he, Midge and Rory would set off in the wag for Mortlake tomorrow, Saturday, and be back by Sunday lunchtime. They would then load up Alfie's vehicle and head to Melbourne on Monday afternoon with the gettings. Midge would not go to Melbourne with him. He should stay home and use the wag for driving Moira around, getting Zara to her interview and fetching the generator home. Rory would accompany Shane to Melbourne. It was about time the boy saw the city.

Moira packed a biscuit tin with three meals for them. Sandwiches more than meals—cheese and onion because they wouldn't go off in the heat. Three Coke bottles of water and three bags of Twisties. They'd get burgers on the road if they needed. She kissed Shane goodbye on the lips and he returned it. She kissed Rory on the forehead and he didn't return it. She tried giving him an extra kiss and sustained hug but he slid away and her kiss grazed his hair.

As she waved them off, and Limpy barked them off, she wished she'd grabbed Rory and made him hug her back. This was the boy's big moment, his first work trip with the men and she hadn't said much, hadn't made enough fuss. Boys don't like affection once they're no longer babies. But they need to learn a sense of occasion. She'd make the most of hugging Mathew while he was prone to it.

There were times when Moira was glad to be away from Shane. Not because she was tired of him—she loved him. Love needs its rest, though. Aloneness freshens you. Makes you listen and look at the world properly without distraction. The wind sounds louder. Sometimes the sky has a moon all day and you remember to notice it. It can scare you, aloneness. If you start looking inside yourself for company you may not like the companion you find. Moira was glad she wasn't a drinker. Drink turned aloneness into a curse. Everyone knew that. Makes you feel like the centre of the world and demand it answers to you. There are better measures you can take if aloneness got too much.

Moira's favourite measure was talking to herself. It had been so long since it rained she couldn't remember if it rained clear or white, she would say, and saunter along the roadside dreaming up a curtain of rain ahead. She would step into it and shiver. When Barleyville was prosperous all those years ago there must have been sheep on all the pastures and rose gardens around the homesteads. Gentry rode horses and well-bred ladies wore lace dresses down to their feet. People like her were housemaid material or less. Bowing and scraping. The gentry were all gone now and this was her home, she muttered to the breezes. 'I'm the lady of the land here, so good riddance to them.'

She didn't need to talk to herself with Mathew under her watch. She had him for an audience. And though babies can't understand things she gave him a lesson in the family history. How there was the good side and the bad side. The bad side was her mother's side. They all had tempers and held up milk bars and servos. It's said Uncle Reggie sold a daughter to a rich couple in Sydney. That was the kind of people on the female line. They had no scruples to them. No ounce of decency. She worried this had come out in Zara.

The good side was her father's. He died young of lung cancer and that was that. Moira went from stepfather to stepfather, none of whom smiled much or said a kind word. She promised to smile and make Mathew belong. 'We're not bad people,' she said. 'We've got the shine off us, that's all.'

Besides, there were World War soldiers on her father's side, which was as high as you get. 'If someone ever puts you down you look them straight in the eye and you say, I had family die for this country, and that shuts people up. I hope your daddy came from the good side in his family. I hope that comes out in you, whoever he was.'

The job cause meant she did not want to upset Zara. She was still scared of the girl and kept bolting the front door at bedtime. They didn't eat together—Zara was too absorbed in herself. Moira served her in the tent. Toast, noodles and tin of stockpot. A glass of Coke and a ginger nut. She put these on an even section of the plastic floor. They had one brief exchange about the complexities of gluing heels. The rubber had come off Zara's good black shoes and wouldn't stay on with super-gluing. Moira found two nails, a thin variety used for chair legs. She hammered and hammered and got the heels stable.

The other topic of conversation was the problem of sunbathing and freckles. Did Moira know how to sunbathe so your shoulders stay one colour? Freckles came out everywhere on Zara at the slightest sunray. Moira said no, she didn't know a solution. They were the curse of having Irish in you, freckles. Then she did remember a method with baby oil and vinegar. They make a mixture that helps turn your skin brown. It might have the benefit of looking more coloured for the Indians.

Moira stirred some into a rinsed-out noodle tub. She applied it to Zara's shoulders. The girl smeared it over the rest of her body and went off to lie under the sky. She took the small transistor Midge kept by his bed for listening to races. The batteries were fading and the station she found for music distorted but she didn't care. It would do to fill her aloneness.

Moira told Mathew that the bad side of the family also thought they were God's gift. Aunty Dot had two wobbly chins and she clipped you if you mentioned them. And wore a beanie to cover her balding head, as if that looked better. Zara had the vain strand coming through in her. 'I don't see a single thing wrong with freckles,' Moira said. 'They're quite pretty things, freckles.'

When the air went still and dust sifted downward from the blown heights the baby bottle took on a meaty smell as it bobbled in the pot. The smell hung in the air while the bottle dried and then blended with the powder's potatoness. Like a grown-up meal had been cooking on the gas. Maybe that was the problem getting Mathew to feed—he disliked the grown-up smell. He hated being cradled and having the teat pointed at him while you walked around. He preferred Moira reclined on her bed with her dress down and him lying between her breasts, regardless of the heat from them both. Their skins stuck together and Moira used a length of cardboard as a fan. Mathew cried and wriggled hungrily and sucked on her.

Her nipples were sunken flat in the folds of themselves but as he pressed into them they rose out and went into his mouth. He was satisfied with that for a second and then cried at sucking and getting nothing. She pushed the bottle into her breast as if part of it and he was tricked and sucked on the teat without crying. He fed that way without stopping.

15

When the men reached Mortlake the evening was red with low sun and their mouths had dried out from car wind on the sides of their faces. They felt their cheeks were cracking. Rory had never seen this part of the state. It was humpy with smooth hills and windbreak hedges, willows for trees instead of ratty gums. There were fences made of stacked stones and the fields had a green tinge to them as if rain paid visits here it wouldn't bother paying to Barleyville. Dams actually had water in them. Houses were set further back from the road than in Barleyville. You couldn't see a roof or wall half the time—trees surrounded them as if bunched in a vase.

They avoided driving through town—there was no point in making themselves obvious. They skirted around it by minor roads and found the turnoff that led to the Bonham Estate. It was a skinny tarsealed road with potholes. Shane was driving with Midge in the front and Rory behind. He put both hands on the steering wheel and made Rory sit up straight and listen to wisdom: 'You can't drive too slow on these back roads. It's a giveaway.

You look like you're trouble. Keep a steady speed. And we don't ever stop outside the place we've targeted. Just drive right by it like we're about to do now. This is basic stuff, Rory. Remember it.'

The estate's drive was not as grand as expected. The entrance was shaded by huge elms. The fence railings were white but the paint was dirty and peeling. The gate was made of curly iron bars and had peeled down to the rust.

It was Midge's responsibility, as they passed by, to make a note if the letterbox had mail sticking from it. There was no sign of rolled-up newspapers or any other evidence of life. But the mail looked fresh. Not yellowy or stuffed in the box as if uncollected for days.

'We need to find a hill or something to check it out,' said Shane.

The road was flat and any hills were behind the paddock fences.

They came to an intersection with gravel roads running off each way. The left road rose up towards a hill where black cattle grazed behind wire. Shane decided to take that road and drive at speed as if too busy going from A to B to be anyone suspicious. Midge hung his elbows out the window so his binoculars would stay steady enough to scan the property. Wheel dust blew across his line of vision but he saw no washing on the line. No vehicle. No people.

Shane turned the car around and headed back to the tarseal past the estate entrance.

This time Midge assessed the condition of the driveway. Small branches and leaves had blown across it. No tyre ruts in the gravel to indicate recent traffic. And there! A padlocked chain around the bottom of the gate.

'Padlocked chains are perfect for us, Rory. Have a think and tell me why.'

'Dunno.'

'Think.'

'Dunno.'

'The place is empty, that's why it's padlocked. It's a dead giveaway.'

They ate their sandwiches as they drove and headed south for half an hour looking for a clearing by the road to sleep the night. They found one beside a narrow bridge that had a thread of water trickling under it. They were screened from the road by a stand of willows.

Rock, paper, scissors for the right to be up the back of the wag with the seat down and more space, the rear door left down for breeze and more foot room. Shane won but gave the right to Midge because of his bad hip. They'd brought cardboard and bubble plastic for wrapping anything delicate and Midge used some for a mattress. They wanted more food but decided to keep incognito. Country shops have long memories for strangers.

Shane gave Rory the back seat and did his best to get comfortable cramped in front.

Sleeping was the last thing the boy wanted. He was so excited he had to get up twice within the hour to pee.

'We'll be leaving at 1 a.m. Go to sleep, Rory.'

Rory didn't think he had a chance of sleeping.

Next thing Shane was poking him. He didn't want to wake, confused by the darkness.

Shane poked him again—'Wake up and pay attention.'

139

He spoke close to Rory's face, finger to chest as if repri-
manding. He thought finger to chest made him teacherly. He
enjoyed having something to teach. A man of knowledge with a
sleepy-eyed student.

'First thing we do is lay bubble plastic along the back of the
wag. Second, we'll drive with the lights on until we get close and
then we stop and get our eyes adjusted to the starlight. Then we
drive with no lights. We need to be invisible. Third, we'll get to the
third in a minute. Now, up you get.'

They pulled onto the road, all three in the front, squinting
to follow the dim sheen of the bitumen and not talking in case it
broke Shane's concentration at the wheel. The road was all theirs.
Only two cars passed head-on as they travelled.

A mile from the estate gates they switched off the lights and
continued on.

'The third thing, Rory, is we only have till sunrise. We have to
hurry but we can't be rough as guts. That means we don't get greedy
and overstay into daylight. We only take what we can manage.'

They took gloves from the glove compartment and put them
on—gardening gloves thin as kid leather that let their fingers bend
natural. Shane told Rory not to take them off. 'They're your best
friend. Protects you against fingerprints and blisters.'

Midge took the bolt cutters and sliced the gate chain free. The
gate squeaked as it opened but there were no houses within half a
mile, no one to hear a gate creak or a voice speaking at ordinary
volume. There was swaying wind in the driveway's trees. 'That's
good,' said Shane. 'Wind and trees muffle hammer noise. We'll
have that on our side while we're busy.'

They eased up the narrow arc of darkness, the trailer rattling and the tyres crunching along. It got darker the further they went into the dense tree tunnel. They slowed almost to stopping where the black air left them blind. Midge got out and walked ahead for guidance, feeling his way with a tapped toe and tapping with his hand on the bonnet for the wag to keep left or veer to the right a bit. Then the stars shone again where trees were sparser. There was the homestead spread before them. Arms of many rooms held out each side of a steeple-shaped entrance. A verandah all the way around, pitched low and wide with overgrown briars for a fringe. And lawn let grow so long it encroached like a paddock needing cropping.

'Midge, give the front door a go,' Shane said.

He explained to Rory that by go he meant give the doorbell a ring. And if there was no bell give a knock to be sure the place was empty. 'If you've stuffed up by chance and someone answers the door then you say you're lost and please could you get directions into town and you get the hell out of there.'

Midge shuffled back to the car and said the place was all theirs.

'Let's get to work,' Shane said.

He took a crowbar from the tools wrapped in a blanket-quiver behind the front seat. He handed Rory a torch and showed him where the button was on the handle for turning on. He wasn't to turn it on yet, not until they were positioned at the back door ready for yanking the lock out. Even then it was important not to spray the beam around too much. Beams spray for miles at night and must be kept to a minimum.

The back door was two doors—tall oaken French doors that

closed together into one, wall-like. The kind you could sell for thousands if you could lift the bloody things and cart them. Shane had Rory turn the torch on and point it at the lock so he could work out the weak spot. He dug the blade end of the crowbar above the brass fitting, stabbed at the lock plate and wrenched it off. He dug again and got the blade deep in between the doors and all three of them heaved in time until the lock gave way with a splintering of wood.

A cool puff came at them, pent-up air rushing out of the place. It smelled of mould and the whiff of something dead, a possum or rat in the walls. Shane told Rory to point the torch around. The shaft of light flashed on curtains drawn across the windows. Long and velvet, red with gold ropes dangling beside. A lounge room perhaps, empty of furniture and rugs. 'The curtains can come. Midge, get the ladder.'

He told Rory to turn off the torch while he checked behind the curtains for viable windows. No good. They were a square kind, the kind he called standard and modern. Shane worried the whole trip was a waste of petrol if there was nothing vintage. But then he found a sunroom with chateau-style windows and little nooks of rooms with miniature arched windows. These rooms had small fireplaces, nugget-black with leaf designs in the iron's mould. Sailing ships on the flue flaps. Their mantelpieces were of dark wood.

In the largest room the fireplace took up half the wall. Much too big to consider taking. Except the carved timber sides of its mantelpiece. The top was a marble slab. Lovely but too weighty and out of the question.

The kitchen was empty except for the sink and an Aga stove in a tiled enclave. Aga stoves fetch a pretty penny. Shane tried rocking it but it was pure cast iron and didn't budge and never could be made to. Floorboards fumed with dust wherever the torch was pointed and creaked under every footfall. The staircase had a balustrade of liver-brown timber. Its anchor posts had been crafted as a series of bulbous cones. These Shane had never seen before and would dismantle. He noticed a hat rack of blackish wood on the hallway wall. He decided he'd take that and hoped it was walnut.

Upstairs rooms had nothing in them but more small fireplaces and some old-style light switches, round and porcelain with a brass nipple and worth having. Rory went to turn one on. Shane snapped, 'Don't be stupid. We only see by torch.' In a moment he would check the fuse box, he said. Make sure it was switched off so they could cut into electrics.

They went to work on the place with Shane explaining the tricks of the hammer and chisel. How you use the big chisel to chip out plaster and brick. A hammer to knock in wood wedges along the windows to help them be prised. Shane and Midge put thin torches in their mouths to light their work. Plaster spat into the room at the chisel blows. They levered the frames out and tipped them to the floor. Cobwebs tearing away like sinews. The tiny windows had leadlight glass, some of which was cracked or had sections missing. They smashed the glass out. Windows with leadlight intact got the better treatment: Shane cut cardboard shields to protect it for travelling. Midge taped bubble plastic over that and they carried the load to the trailer.

The chateau windows had normal glass. This they knocked out by laying the frame down and using a blanket to cover the glass for the hammer. The crook of the hammer was run around the edges to smooth off shardlets. They had no A-frame in the trailer to strap windows upright but in lieu of that they stacked them flat with cardboard and strips of plastic in between. The trailer was six strides long by three and half across and the chateau windows were almost as big. Five could be stacked, Shane decided. The light fittings, curtains, balustrade posts and hat rack would be tucked down the sides. Three more windows could go on the roof rack. A few of the little arch ones could be laid on top.

Three of the smaller fireplaces could fit in the wag. They used the same principle with them as with windows: biggest chisel and hammer for the brickwork. There was more chiselling to do than with windows because a fireplace went deep in. You had to smash well into the chimney base to get the thing free. Keep a watch for redback spiders. But it was easier to chip at because it was a fireplace—all iron and unbreakable to your blows. Shane looked at his watch as he handed the tools to Midge for a turn. It was 3.45 a.m. They had to work faster. He took the tools straight back from Midge and made Rory stand clear and hold the torch still.

By five o'clock they had two fireplaces pulled clear and loaded. The mantelpieces had come away too and though not particularly fine timber they were waist-high and narrow and fitted inside the car when jammed and twisted. A third fireplace was out of the question given that dawn was near. It was starting to glow like milky fire through the tree line.

What they had wasn't a bad load so they got ready to leave, flinging a sheet of black polythene over the top and a blue tarp over that. Then the ladder to hold the covering down. They threw a rope lengthways and criss-crossed it through the trailer rails until the swaddled heap was tightly bound.

A quick check through the place in case they'd left equipment. A shame they couldn't come back tomorrow for seconds.

Dawn was brightening the curtainless windows. You could see without a torch now.

Shane noticed something in the corner of the long room beside the kitchen. There poking out where red wallpaper had rotted from rain leaks and curled to the floor. He kicked the paper aside and gagged on the dust it made. A shininess beneath the thick peelings.

He bent and blew on his find. It was like an octopus with tendrils of glinting glass buckled under themselves. He counted four layers, each strung with glass stones cut in diamond shapes. Some legs had broken off from the main body. Some single stones had fallen from the limbs but were undamaged. He tried to hoist it off the ground and needed help to keep it tinkling in the air.

Midge and Rory got underneath and took some weight on their shoulders. 'What is it?' Rory asked.

'A chandelier.'

'What's a chandelier?'

'A fancy light,' said Shane.

They had to take this. This could be worth a small fortune.

They used the tool blanket like a sack to gather the chandelier up. It travelled in the front passenger side where feet would normally go. Midge and Rory had the dashboard for a footrest or could sit side-on with their knees up. They laughed that this was as good as fear can be, driving with a load behind them into the wakening day. The sky yawning open with a pink tongue as if they were life's breakfast.

16

Moira was worried when they hadn't got home by midday. She watched the sun edge across into afternoon and into evening and chewed her nails that something was wrong. An accident or police trouble. 'They should be here by now,' she said to Mathew. 'They would have left Mortlake at dawn—that means they should be home.'

Zara began swearing about inconvenience. If they were stuck some place or locked in a cell then how would she get to the interview? Rory's bike? Drenched in sweat and looking like crap?

'We'll think of something,' Moira said, to stop the girl panicking. She felt like telling her to shut up and think of the men. But what would that do? Worsen her manner. Instead she whispered to Mathew that the bad side of the family was also selfish.

Then they did arrive in the bright night, headlights growing as if descending from the stars. The wag was weighed down so heavily that its belly scraped over the road's ridges. Limpy ran out to meet them but shied off at the abrading noise. Moira put Mathew in the pram and wheeled him along as a greeting. Zara followed at a skipping pace, grinning and muttering how relieved she was.

Midge waved hello. He pointed at Rory asleep on his shoulder. 'Rory's knackered. But he did real good.'

Shane got out from behind the wheel and rubbed his eyes. 'Sorry we were so slow. Big load. Plus we got lost on the back roads. Midge and his navigating.'

Moira embraced him and said she'd put the kettle on but Shane wanted sleep more than coffee and food. Rory was so drunk with tiredness he could hardly stand. Midge had trouble standing but that was from so much sitting. He gripped Rory in a walking embrace and passed him over to Moira who steered him to bed. Shane drove the trailer up to the shed, uncoupled it, and Midge followed trying to stretch the kinks out of his bones. They unloaded the car. A few winks of sleep and they'd be sparking again, they said. Ready to go into Alfie's and inform him that things went well and organise a time and place to collect the truck.

Shane had a sleep for two hours and got up and ate, then slept till morning and was rested enough for action. Midge was deep asleep and Shane let him be. Moira decided to tag along into town and do chores. She wanted to bathe Mathew at a trotting track hose. And there was a particular matter to discuss while they drove. To do with Zara and her big Tuesday. Getting her made up properly with well-ironed clothes. Presentable in the shampooed-and-showered sense. They couldn't use the town's hotel. Hotels ban trants from going upstairs and using their showers—security reasons.

'Why don't I hire a motel room?' she said. 'Just for the Tuesday morning. That cheap-looking place near the bowls club. Offer them rent for a half-day and see if they'll take it.'

'Maybe.'

He bit his bottom lip and drove with his fingertips. He was proud of himself: a businessman with a stash of valuable goods he would soon drive to market. What a pleasing notion to know his family might indulge themselves in a little luxury. And on a sensible note, it was an investment.

'Go ahead and do it,' he said, puffing his chest out. 'You got to spend money to make money. If a motel room helps Zara get income, that's what I've heard called intelligent expenditure.'

Moira was in the back beside the little bed. She reached across and rubbed Mathew's cheek. 'Hear that, boy? Intelligent expenditure.'

She explained that intelligent was the opposite of stupid, and expenditure was the opposite of mean. She said that her trouble with reading words probably came from the bad side of the family. 'I hope you don't have that trouble, passed down from me.'

The motel wasn't too far from Alfie's so Shane dropped Moira off to wheel and deal. It was a khaki-brick place, single-storey and sliding-door office. Not a lot of rooms but they all looked vacant given no cars were parked in the spaces. She slid the door across and tipped the pram back to hurdle the floor rail. The air was chilled but still muggy. An air-conditioner rattled in the window and made the ground hum. She picked up the bell on the counter and gave a shake.

Through an archway hung with plastic beads for flies a hunched-forward fellow emerged, the beads pattering over his shoulder like dried rain. He had a thick bent nose and purple veins bruising his cheeks. He was clean-shaven but bushy white hairs sprouted from his T-shirt and wreathed his neck.

'What can I do for you?' he said in a thin nasally voice with phlegm in it.

'I'd like a room, please.'

Her neck stiffened into her 'lies' position, in case lies were needed. Her chin lowered over her throat till it almost touched her collarbone. She rested an elbow on the counter and studied the man's puce face for a moment. His eyes were bleary and green. She'd not seen him around town. Perhaps he was new. Perhaps he'd never had experience with trants. That would make it easier.

'This hot weather!' She smiled, and chatted some more about the weather. Then said she'd like a room to freshen up in on Tuesday, please. She and her daughter will be in town on business and this weather made freshening-up necessary. She leant on the counter with both elbows, a flirting leaning. Her smile twisting up on one side. 'How much for a freshening up on Tuesday? Not for the night. Just a few hours during the day?'

'Same rate as if you were staying,' the man said, shrugging. 'Seventy-five dollars.'

'But can't you just give us a few hours and a special deal?'

'Sorry. Can't. We still have to clean the room like you'd stayed.'

'Come on, you can break the rules.'

'I'd like to. But seventy-five is the rate.'

'You don't look like you're full.'

'True.'

'Then how about thirty for a freshen-up. That's thirty dollars you wouldn't otherwise get.'

They haggled for a few minutes. She kept smiling and got the man to play along. They settled on forty dollars for a three-hour booking. He wanted some money in advance and when Moira couldn't produce it he put his palms on the counter and cocked his head, doubting her.

'I'll be back in sec. My husband Shane's the money person.'

She bustled the pram out the door and headed towards Alfie's.

She got no further than the bowls club corner when the wag started coming her way. It pulled over on the opposite side of the road. Shane hung his arm out the window and smacked the car door.

'He's not bloody there. His shop's closed and there's a note stuck up saying *Till further notice*.'

He swung the wag around. He gripped and ungripped the steering wheel impatiently while Moira buckled the baby.

'It's Monday. He always opens sharp on Monday.'

'Maybe he's sick.'

They drove to Alfie's and got out and cupped their hands to the window for a glimpse of someone. Moira waited while Shane checked round the back. He jiggled the chain locking the mesh gate and called out. He looked into the neighbours' yard but it was a vacant building with only weeds around it. He returned to the front door and again cupped his hands. 'Till further notice. How long's further notice?' He put his hands on his hips and kicked at the cracked footpath. 'The pub. There's a phone there and a phone book with local numbers.'

They drove to the Barleyville Hotel and parked under the peppercorn near the bottle-shop entrance. Moira fanned Mathew with a newspaper she found on the ground. Shane went to do the phoning. He was only gone a few minutes.

'Phone's engaged.'

But the phone book did have his address: 5 Croke Crescent.

It was a no-through road with four newer-style houses of dark stucco and roller-door garages. Alfie's house stood out because it didn't have a preened garden. The lawn was sunburned bare and had a parched nasturtium border. There was a rusted horse sulky for decoration. And a pelican sculpture cut from tyre rubber. The surrounds were hazy with grey scrub low enough to see over into pale paddocks. The gutters of the horizon ran with their usual false waters. Moira made the comment that it might be new but not welcoming. Give her their place any day: much homelier.

She took Mathew and stood behind Shane while he tapped the front door knocker. They heard mumbling and cursing from inside and the door opened and there was Alfie with reading glasses on the end of his nose like wire eyes and his real eyes glaring. He pulled the door closed behind him. He was wearing check slippers.

'What's this about?' His voice was almost a whisper and he looked about to see if neighbours were watching. 'Why you coming to my house?'

He had his watch in his hands but didn't play with its lid. He squeezed it in his fist and pulled on its chain.

'You weren't at your shop.'

'I've closed the shop for now.'

'We got business.'

'As you know, I've had the authorities snooping. They've been round again. I've suspended trade until I'm free of them.'

'What about the truck you was hiring me?'

'Just be patient. And do you mind not coming to my house?'

'Come on, Alfie.'

'Don't *Come on, Alfie* me. First you start asking to use my computer. Then you want me for a character reference like we're best friends. Then you want to rent my jewellery. Now you come to my home. My place of residence.'

'You weren't at your shop and I got stuff ready for Melbourne.'

'I don't know what you're talking about.'

'What?'

'He's jerking you around, Shane.'

'I know. I know. Listen, Alfie. Don't play silly buggers.'

'Are you intimidating me?'

'What?'

'Are you trying to intimidate me? I'll have no business with you. Please leave my property.'

'I'm not trying to intimidate you. We had an arrangement.'

'Please leave.'

'What about the generator? We had a deal on a generator as well.'

Moira tugged Shane's shirt tail. 'Let's get out. He's turned on us.'

He pushed Moira's hand to let go of his shirt. 'I'm coming. I'm coming.'

Alfie went inside his house and closed the door.

They got in the car and sat arguing about whether to knock again and try reasoning. Moira said no, she had a bad feeling: if Alfie was having serious trouble with the authorities, best stay away in case the trouble jumped to them. She won because Shane was superstitious of her bad feelings. And this bad feeling came supported by crows. A few let out haggard squawks overhead as if warning him off.

He drove in the direction of the trotting track for Moira to do her baby bathing but she asked him to go to the motel first. She explained about the manager wanting a deposit. She was braced for Shane going back on his word and objecting to a motel now his dealings had fallen through. He did want to object. He was in that kind of temper.

Shane did the sums in his head and didn't like the balance. In his pocket he had eighty dollars cash. In their bank account they had not much more, though it was rotation money day on Thursday which meant a few hundred. As for his antique trove, he might have to burn the stuff or traipse off to dealers in other towns he'd worked with. No better than crooks, most of them, unreliable. But at least they didn't turn on you. Such an injustice, not being able to sell quality. If he went to Melbourne and tried to flog it where would he start without causing questions?

Shane felt a failure and put on a whistling act as he drove. If he didn't give Moira motel money it would look like he didn't support Zara. Truth was he didn't support her. He was embarrassed that a fifteen-year-old girl had more prospects than him. He hoped deep down she didn't get the job. Mind you, her money might be needed.

He was losing face and couldn't think how to bolster himself. He turned off the trotting track road and towards the motel. He unbuttoned his shirt pocket and gave Moira forty dollars from it.

'You sure?' she said.

'Course. Sorry about the generator.'

'Who needs a generator? Noisy things, generators.'

He changed from a whistling act to problem-solving hopefulness. 'Just a hiccup. All this is just a hiccup. I'm not going to be beaten. I'm working on a solution.'

He tapped his forehead as if he had ideas he was not yet ready to share.

By the time they got home he had enough bravado to put his hand on Rory's shoulder and lecture him about how this sort of thing happens in their trade. 'An occupational hazard. Nothing to worry about. Normal.'

'So what'll you do?' Rory said.

'I'll think of something.'

He winked at Rory. He kept his smiling up but it wasn't easy. His mouth muscles were heavy with worry. 'I'll tell you what we do. We'll keep it.'

He hadn't thought this through. It was more for the boy's sake.

'We'll keep it. We'll take the curtains and use them to doll this place up a bit. Treat ourselves. Get rid of that glad-wrap window and make one of the leadlights fit. We'll pick the eyes out of the rest for selling and I'll hop in the wag and try my old contacts. It means a lot of travel, but what a waste to dump anything.'

He waved his finger as he spoke and his voice got faster. He'd convinced himself he had a viable strategy.

'Come on,' he said, leading the way to the shed, clapping his hands and rubbing them together. 'Rory. Midge. Come on. Work to do.'

That's how they spent the day. Cleaning up a leadlight window to slot into the house wall. They'd have some chipping away at weatherboard to do to make a bigger hole for the frame. Two of the velvet curtains could be cut to size for the house. The longest would make a dramatic addition to the porch, draped across the front and sewn in place with twine. Their royally gold ropes would tie them back when needed.

Then Shane came to his senses. Gold ropes. Velvet curtains. Leadlight window. 'Someone drives past and these'd stick out like dog's balls.'

Yet one indulgence wouldn't hurt, would it? Just a temporary ornament that Moira would get a kick out of.

It was Midge's idea to hang the chandelier. Shane took the idea over and told Moira it was his. Midge didn't mind because he was used to that.

They carried the thing on a blanket from the shed to the L-shape. Moira was told to close her eyes and not look while they did the hanging. Shane leant his ladder against the tallest tree and climbed. A rope was tossed over a thick limb. He hitched one end through the chandelier's ring. Midge and Rory on the ground gripped the other end. They took the weight and pulled down in a winching fashion. Shane held the chandelier steady by hugging it against his stomach.

'Up. Keep going,' he called. 'Higher.'

He climbed the ladder further, the chandelier's tails tinkling against his body.

Two steps from the top he made Midge tie the rope off by hooking it around the trunk and doing a double knot. He let the chandelier go. It swung out and back. He reached to stop it hitting the tree. It swayed in smaller arcs until almost still, the faintest of wind chimes.

It was late afternoon and the air had stopped breathing for the day. The sun was sitting on a bronze tray. The dusk light filled the chandelier's braids and they looked like amber.

'Open your eyes, babe.'

Moira gasped.

Shane climbed down and stood beside her. Midge took a few steps back, mouth open at the beauty. Zara laughed at it and then stared and cocked her head, captivated. Rory watched it and said, 'I helped pinch it, Zara. I helped, eh, Shane?'

'Shh.'

As night fell, no one disturbed the crystal hush by speaking. Moira served a meal while above there was a meal for the eye: the Milky Way wore white gloves and brought its best silver service. The chandelier glistened as they dined.

17

Big Tuesday.

The motel's TV reception was poor but Rory didn't care. He had a bed to lie on and watch. Moira told him to turn down the sound or he could get out and go bother Shane and Midge who were in the wag waiting their turn for showering. Zara was taking forever and probably using up the water but Moira let her go on and get herself smelling pure and gleaming. When the girl did finally finish she dreamily dried her hair with the drier attached to the bathroom wall by a thin chain.

Moira had a bottle to feed Mathew, but there was no privacy to do it. She let him make his spluttering hunger cries. She placed him on the pillow end of the bed while she ironed Zara's jeans. The motel iron had a burning odour so she used a wet handkerchief to dampen the denim and prevent scorch marks. She made a cup of tea and ate the complimentary biscuit, saying to Mathew, 'This is the life.'

When Zara was ready to dress, Moira sent Rory outside. She

took Mathew into the bathroom and stripped naked and got under the water. It was a bath-style shower, which made the process easy. She sat and let the water rain on her back. She put the plug in and washed Mathew in the puddle between her knees. When the puddle was hip high she turned off the taps and leaned back and fed him using her nipple-to-bottle system. Such a drugging feeling to be reclined in wet warmth that she had to rouse herself with a shot of cold water—one blast of it across her shoulders with Mathew held at arm's length to escape the spray.

She let herself stay naked and damp to get the most benefit from the air-conditioning. Mathew was already asleep from his feeding. She put him on the bed and dressed him in a nappy and light cotton top. She ironed her best flower frock and painted her cracked toes red. Zara was at the mirror behind the front door, leaning close to it and painting her eyes and lips into shape. She kissed her lips back in on themselves to get the sheen right. She put the Salvos jewellery on. The necklace was a touch long but Moira adjusted it by putting a knot in the length, close to the clasps where it wouldn't be noticed. With that done the last task was the hair. Moira sat the girl down on the edge of the bed and brushed her cropped scalp into a neat part.

All ready to go. It was a three-minute walk to the supermarket. No decision was made about taking Mathew until the final minute. Midge maintained his view that having a baby accompany them helped their purpose: it bespoke maturity and a solid anchor. So Zara and Moira set off, baby in tow, and the boys took over the room for their showers.

The interview was held in the storeroom to the side of the meat and dairy section, amid cardboard boxes crushed and tied with tape for recycling. Mr Dixchit sat at a small foldout table. He wore the longest shirt they'd ever seen on a man. More tan nightgown than anything, way over his knees. He had on matching trousers and black sandals.

The whirr of the chillers was such that voices needed to be raised to be heard. This posed a problem for Zara because of the age issue. There were three other girls waiting to be interviewed. She knew them from school, not to speak to, but by sight. They were two years above her and from good families and would never give a trant the time of day. They might speak up if hearing her lie about her age. Let them go ahead in the line, Moira suggested. That way we'll have the last word and not have them listening.

When Zara's turn came it was Moira who did the talking. Mr Dixchit tried addressing Zara directly but Moira was nervous and couldn't help herself—she became a proxy Zara: Oh yes, the girl is a very honest young lady. That's the one thing she's had drilled into her—honesty. And hard work. And cleanliness. I had the pleasure of meeting your good wife the other day and I said to Zara there's a woman after our own heart: clean and well spoken. I can see you're the same, sir. It's written all over you.

He took the résumé and put it on the table, hardly reading it. He was more interested in viewing a school report, if they had one. A scholastic summary, in his view, was most valuable.

'Ah.' Moira sighed. She put her cunning hat on and touched Zara's shoulder and said, 'I knew we should of brought that. It's my fault, I'm sorry, Mr Dixchit. I thought to myself, they don't tell you much these days in school reports. Better to meet the person in person.'

To impress upon him Zara's cleverness she suggested he test her with a maths question. How much change from twenty dollars on a six-dollar purchase, that sort of thing. There was no need for that, he said. The tills perform such equations themselves.

It was clear he was not interested. 'Thank you for coming. I will telephone if we require Zara's services.'

'We're not connected up at the moment. We've been travelling, you see. When I say travelling, I mean for my husband's work. He's in antiques.'

He had paid no attention to the pram, as if presuming the baby was Moira's. She put her arm around Zara and had her step closer to the pram.

'In case you're wondering, the baby's Zara's. Isn't he, sweetie? His name's Mathew. You've never seen a girl blossom like Zara has now she's a mum. It's like she's leaps and bounds maturer in herself. Aren't you, sweetie?'

Mr Dixchit pushed back his chair to stand and conclude the interview.

It was here that a risk must be taken, Moira decided. 'The other girls you've interviewed, I'm sure they're very nice girls.'

She went up to him and spoke softer and quicker to create a confidential air.

'Nice on the surface, anyway. I hate to bad-mouth people. But sometimes it's part of doing right by someone like yourself. Truth is, they say things behind your back. Bad things. *Curry muncher* this and *curry muncher* that. Nasty. They were saying it just now while they were waiting their turn. Weren't they, Zara? It's the way some people are. You think they come from decent families and then they start bad-mouthing. If my Zara did that I'd clip her one, Mr Dixchit. I wouldn't stand for that kind of talk.'

'Thank you for coming,' Mr Dixchit replied. He had a face Moira couldn't read, stare as she might. Hardly a wrinkle in his brow to show his feelings. A black moustache so thick it covered any grimace of his lips. He's cool, this one, she thought. You can't put a thing over these Indians. She wanted to resent him but hadn't given up just yet.

'Mr Dixchit. Whatever you'd be paying, Zara will work for two-thirds, won't you, sweetie?'

Zara nodded.

'Oh no,' he shook his head. 'There are rules about that, I'm afraid.'

'Forget the rules. Let's do it all cash for two-thirds of what you'd pay those others. No one needs to know.'

'I am sorry.'

'Two-thirds.'

'I cannot do that.'

'Half, then.'

'Half?' His moustache stretched cheerfully and showed his front teeth. 'You are quite something, but no.'

'Half. In cash. Off the records.'

His moustache returned to normal. He sat down at the table, knocking its flimsy legs with his knees. He looked over at Zara. 'What do you say?'

'She says—'

'I wish to hear it from her.'

Zara put a finger to her mouth to bite its nail nervously but whipped it away, back to her side. 'Yes, please.'

'With a baby, you would not be available very much.'

'She will. I like to do the honours with Mathew, you see.'

'Available seven days would be of benefit to me.'

'She could be available seven days.'

'In my experience, with arrangements that are off the books, the important thing is...' He put his finger to his moustache to indicate discretion.

Moira responded with her finger on her lips. She pulled an imaginary zip across her mouth.

The world was giving her its full attention again. Granting her wishes and attending to her needs. She daren't scare it off by saying thank you too much. It might consider its job done and move on to others. Stay with me, she wanted to say, but it might turn on her for being so greedy. Better to keep her head down and believe the generous world was watching and taking pleasure in her pleasure and pride in her success. Admiring her for heading back to the motel not boastful but speechless with a straight-backed dignity. No smug smile, just the sweet knowledge in herself that she had done well.

Besides, to celebrate too much was likely to get on Shane's nerves. She let him take a measure of credit for the triumph.

'Cash, Moira. What did I tell you? Cash. Gets 'em every time.'

Midge suggested they buy fish and chips. And cold beers and take them home and sit under the chandelier. They each took a last turn using the motel toilet and washbasin. Drinking cool tap water and drying their hands on white towels.

18

The fish and chips were soggy so they ate the chips while driving along before they turned to mush. Shane sipped a beer and passed it to the back seat for Rory to share now that he was a working man.

'Cash. I wouldn't do business any other way. Know what I think I'll do? Think I'll take my load and become my *own* middle man, Rory.'

The more beer he swigged the more his opinion of his prospects rose. 'You can't rely on the Alfies of this world. You got to be your own middle man. That's the future.'

They saved their fish pieces for reheating over the cooker for dinner. Shane wanted to take the chandelier down because of the 'dog's balls factor'. He agreed to extend the treat for one more night, given the special occasion. He congratulated Zara, grudgingly. 'Good for you,' he said, then returned to his own plans. 'This Alfie letting me down, it's the best thing that's happened to me.'

Zara drank two beers and it made her garrulous and giggly.

She'd be getting a free blue smock and a nametag, she said. She repeated herself and Moira said, 'We know, sweetie. You've told us. We heard.'

As for getting her to work, Shane recommended bike riding. 'I can't have the wag tied up ferrying you in and out. When you're your own middle man you do double the driving.'

He said she owed it to the household to pinch things. A few items here and there.

When the beer was finished Shane moved on to bourbon. The reheated fish had rubbery batter but he couldn't care. Darkness didn't fall so much as rise to the stars and shimmer there. The chandelier flecked the ground where they sat like a shabby picnic party with crickets for their music, playing the one note, the only tune crickets know.

'A tree palace,' Shane said with a dreamy slurring.

'What'd you say?' asked Moira.

'What?'

'What you just said.'

'A tree palace?'

'That's perfect. That's what we'll name this place. Tree Palace.'

'That's great,' Midge said.

Rory and Zara agreed it was great too.

Shane reminded them that it was his idea. 'I'm a poet and I didn't know it.'

Moira slapped the ground. 'Done, then. Tree Palace.'

Midge decided to stay out under the tree for the night—he spread a jacket for a mattress and slept. Rory sneaked sips of Shane's drink and took himself, dizzy, to the caravan. Zara was so happy she needed to lie down in her tent because her legs had gone on her. That meant Shane and Moira were as good as alone together. There was Mathew but Shane had got used to him: the kid had his noisy moments but he slept as good as invisible.

'Come on, Shane. Let's go to bed,' Moira said.

Shane's eyes were shiny, his cheeks red. He was grinning, staring at the chandelier, more through it than observing its puppet light. 'Eh? What ya say?'

'Come on.'

She took his hand and made him stand and walk with her.

They didn't kiss much these days. Kiss in the proper way, with lips parted and a tongue on the tip of the other's tongue. Tonight they did and they pushed the bedroom door as closed as it would go. Shane's optimism wasn't faltering and he danced a few steps and slipped his hands inside Moira's panties. He held on to her buttocks and kissed and lifted her. He undid his trousers. Moira helped peel off his T-shirt. He helped her with her bra, in a hurry to lay her back. Too much of a hurry for her. That kissing was so wonderful. It made the smell of drink and smoke have no smell and the spit inside their mouths be as smooth as oil.

His habit was to pull himself out of her—pill or no pill he was always careful. Tonight she thought he was about to stay in. He held himself longer and it surprised her and she held him there, her knees pressing with the thrill of it. Then he bucked out as usual, even though she held him tight between her knees. He fell asleep that way, in his own mess, in the fork of her. She forgave him. When she tipped him off she tipped him gently so he wouldn't wake.

The trouble with sleep, she thought, was that a lucky day like this came to an end. She tried to keep awake. Mathew helped her. Then he took his feed and slept and Moira had no energy left and gave in.

She opened one eye and saw it was dark, everything still and silent. The kind of silence so pure that the air had an electric sound, a buzzing far off: the plains running their deep-buried engines of clay and stone. She closed her eye, listening.

A few hours later she did the honours with Mathew and walked him around the L-shape and he soon was asleep again. Shane turned on his back and snored. She pushed his shoulder and he coughed and sighed and snored more quietly. She could no longer hear that comforting earth-engine but she slept anyway.

Limpy's yap had such a shrill pitch she mistook it for birdsong. She tried not to be woken, her arm across her eyes to put off daylight. The yapping persisted. There was snarling to it. 'Shut up,' she called. She moved her arm from her eyes to her ears. 'Shut up.' The dog wouldn't stop. She got up to throw a shoe at him. The glare was fierce and she blinked to make the day visible.

A police car was driving up to the L-shape, veering at speed between ironbarks. A second car behind it had stopped down by the garage.

'Shane,' she yelled.

Two officers got out of the second car—the young blond fellow,

Dench. And a woman who looked like a skinny man in her blue uniform, with her stomping, arms-out gait.

'Shane. Shane.'

Fowler got out of the first car on the passenger side and an officer about the same age and size got out of the driver's. Moira ran into the bedroom and slapped Shane on his rump and pulled the sheet from him. Then threw the sheet back on him because he was naked. She put on her frock but didn't have time to zip it before Fowler had stepped through the door. He held up a forefinger and stood there, pointing. 'I want no trouble. You do as you're told.'

'There's two in here,' he called out. 'The Shane guy and his missus.'

Shane leapt from bed, wrapping the sheet around him and shaking his head for better comprehension. 'What the fuck's this?'

'You sit on that bed, mate. I want no trouble out of you. Missus, can you shut that bloody dog up.'

Moira ignored him. In the pram beside the bed Mathew was beginning to cry. She picked him up and whispered hush.

'Where you keep everything?' said Fowler. 'Where's all this heritage stuff kept?'

'Give us a minute. Jesus. I'm just waking up.'

Fowler called out, 'Search everything.'

Midge could be heard complaining, 'Fair go. Easy does it.' Through the glad-wrap window Moira saw him in his underwear, holding out his hands in waving surrender. Rory was in his underwear and bouncing on his toes, swearing *fuck* and *arsehole*.

'Rory, stop that,' she called, shouldering past Fowler. 'Take Limpy and quieten him. And don't *bounce*. How many times I got to say.'

There was a scream: Zara in the tent.

Fowler put his hand on the doorjamb and leant out to direct proceedings. 'What's your name again?' he said to Midge. He snapped his fingers. 'I want you to tell us where you hide things. Hurry up.'

'What you talking about?'

'I'll tell you all that,' Shane said. 'No need to hassle him. He's not involved. No one's involved but me.'

They were made to stand together in the L-shape. Zara was allowed to grab her dressing gown but the rest couldn't dress until a search was done. What Fowler called 'a precautionary poke around the dwellings'.

Shane was kept in bare feet and a sheet. Even when he led them to the shed he was made to walk without shoes and clothes. He complained the stones were hurting him. He was told to keep moving and not moan so much. At the shed he asked if he could go to the toilet. He was told to hold on to his bladder and tell them what in the shed came from where. When he hesitated, wondering if it was too late to play dumb, Fowler threatened to have all the family arrested and charged. Shane promised he was the only one involved. Midge had a buggered hip, he said. Poor bastard can hardly get out of bed. As for the missus, she was a homebody. Too scared off by all that licence business to say boo, let alone know anything about heritage. The other two are just children and the baby's a baby.

The police hadn't noticed the chandelier. Shane was arrested and Fowler and Dench accompanied him to the house to dress.

It wasn't until they were waiting on the step that they saw it. Fowler heard tinkling and thought it a problem in his ears. He dug out some wax with his little finger but the sound kept going and he looked up in the trees. He squinted and caught sight of sparkling among the branch-sprouting branches. He walked over to where the ropes were. He put his hands on his hips and laughed. 'Will you look at this!'

'I'll get it down,' Dench said.

Fowler held up a hand to stop him. 'Get a photograph first. It'll give the magistrate a giggle.' He kept looking up, agape. 'Now that is something to behold. Quite something.'

19

Shane was placed in a cell at the Barleyville police station and a solicitor, Elisha Kay, was called up from Stawell to give him advice. A woman young enough to make Shane question the point of having her. 'Can't I get someone older? I got rights to see a grown-up lawyer.'

She may have looked no more than fifteen but she stared him down through round red glasses and for one so young had a world-weary, cynical tone. She said if he didn't like her service free of charge, courtesy of Legal Aid, she'd be happy to get him a city Queen's Counsel. If he could afford it.

That set him back in his chair. They were in the station's inter-view room and he liked sitting at the table, the centre of attention. He was an important man. It made him formal in bearing: prefer-ring Miss Kay to saying Elisha.

She said 'miss' was not twenty-first century and she preferred Elisha. He said sorry but kept on with 'miss' anyway a few times not from rudeness so much as nerves.

He didn't like that she had a file opened concerning him. Files made a man feel followed. He asked to look at it. She spun it with her fingers to face his way. He nodded as if he understood the legal lingo and spun it back and crossed his arms, satisfied.

The police intended opposing bail. Being a trant, a man of no fixed address, Shane was a flight risk in their view. They wanted him remanded.

'I have a fixed address,' he said.

'You rent where you live? You own it?'

'Not in the strict sense.'

'You squat. In other words, no fixed address.' Her middle finger pushed her glasses beyond the bridge of her nose. 'There's evidence from an Alfie Tweedie, second-hand dealer. It's not helpful to us.'

Alfie had dobbed Shane in. The old man admitted 'selling on' antique house fittings for Shane but claimed ignorance that they were stolen. He thought they'd been scavenged from rubbish tips and small-town garage sales. He believed in the preservation of rural history and would not defile his country's cultural assets.

'That's bullshit,' Shane said, thumping the table, which made Constable Dench open the interview room door and ask, 'All good?'

'All good,' Elisha said.

'All good,' Shane said, lifting his hands and placing them softly on his knees. He bowed his head and moaned.

'Doesn't matter if it's bullshit or not. It's your word against his. And he's been in local business thirteen years. A member of Rotary. And his wife's an invalid.'

Alfie had written a statement that he was a victim of intimi-
dation. If not for Shane's threatening nature he would never
have done business with such a person. He was forced into it.
A vulnerable old man against a rough-and-ready trant and his
ragtag family.

'My family had nothing to do with this. How many times I
got to say?'

He made up his mind there and then not to put up a fight. He
would plead guilty and take the rap, the official sole offender. 'I
acted alone. That's the honest-to-God truth. I'll sign whatever I
got to sign.'

A guilty plea should keep the police happy, she said. 'Make an
example of someone. That's what they like.'

He'd never been to prison—he always skirted by. If he went
there now, so be it. There was pride in having a prison sentence.
The kudos of being a martyr for the family, or so he reasoned,
smirking at his moral bravery.

What he had going for him, said Elisha, was the absence of
violence on his record. He was no thug, just a thief. That she could
credibly argue.

'It's something I can work with. Get you assessed by a psychol-
ogist. Say you've got a disorder, a compulsive thief, that sort of
thing.'

'What disorder? I'm no mental case. No one's fiddling around
in my head. I'm no fruit loop.'

'It's a routine procedure to win the court over.'

'Nup. Never. I won't be made to look stupid.'

Elisha sighed loudly and wrote a note on his file. He craned to read it but couldn't with the writing upside down.

'Can you give me some mitigating circumstances?'

'What you mean?'

'To win favour with the court. Drink problem? Drugs?'

'Never touch that shit. Just a social drink.'

'Family troubles?'

'All good.'

'If you could have your partner...what's her name? Moira?'

'I said, she's not involved.'

'If you could have her write a statement to the court. What a good bloke you are. Good family man. That sort of thing.'

'Moira can't write. She can't read and write. It was like a thing wrong with her.'

'We can use that. It's a disability. She relies on you.'

'And make *her* look stupid?'

Another sigh and pushing up of her glasses. 'Your brother. Can he make a statement?'

'I don't want him roped in by making statements. He's got asthma and things stir it up.'

'We can use the asthma. He's a sick man.'

'Make him look pathetic?'

'Your stepdaughter has a baby? If she can come to court—'

'Not her. She's got a job now. Boss hears she's associated, what happens then? That fucks the job up.' He held up a hand: 'Sorry for the language.'

She looked at him with an eyebrow raised. She put down her pen and steepled her fingers together. A smile came to one side of her mouth.

'Very admirable. Not wise, but admirable. Okay then, Mr Admirable, here's the upshot. You'll probably get five or six months in jail to be served with the two months suspended sentence you've just blown. Seven, eight months in all.'

Shane took a deep breath and raised his chin, defiant. 'No worries. Piece of piss. Sooner I get it over with the better.'

The Barleyville court only sat fortnightly but St Arnaud was open the next day. Elisha said, 'I'll get the ball rolling,' and shook Shane's hand. Constable Dench took him into the lock-up. St Arnaud was an hour away, which was good for anonymity. There wouldn't be publicity in the *Barleyville Gazette*—letters to the editor calling for trants to be run out of town. Just in case, Shane decided he'd go to court alone. Mr Admirable, he said to himself. He enjoyed the title: like having a mission that made a hero of you. As for jail, if this lock-up was an example it wouldn't kill him. He had a flushing toilet to sit on and contemplate. It was cold steel and lidless but better than home's. There was a tap to drink from. The bed was narrow and smelled of disinfectant but you wouldn't have known it was summer from the cool temperature of the walls. A meal was due, he was told. Mr Admirable on holiday, he said out loud.

As the hours dragged on he wasn't so sure about the worth of his admirable status. The aloneness was a cut-off kind, a pure shunning from the world. He did not have the stomach he thought he did to endure it. He needed Moira to help. Her body to hold and her voice to banter with. He'd have to use her in court after all. And Midge with his asthma. Anything it took to shrink his jail sentence. The high-barred window hardly let in light—he could not see a skerrick of outside. The ceiling shone starkly. He could not sleep. A drunk was shut in next door and screamed and wept and vomited.

By morning Shane regained his nerve. Not all of it but enough to face the day. His cell door was unlocked and Sergeant Fowler said he had visitors. Given his co-operation he'd be allowed a few minutes with them in the interview room.

Moira steered the pram with one hand and carried his cellophaned suit in the other. Midge had his razor and foam and Zara his shaving mirror, which they wouldn't let him use because of the glass. Rory had his black lace-up shoes. 'I gave 'em a shine,' the boy said. They were all dressed neatly to be his entourage. They were sure he'd get off like usual. He'd just apologise and have a lawyer fix things in the way they do.

'Not this time,' said Shane. 'It's gone too far this time. I'm stuffed.'

Moira told him to stop being down in the mouth.

'Defeatist,' Midge called it.

'Yeah, defeatist,' she said. 'Stop being that.'

'I'm just saying what the lawyer said.'

'Then get another one. This one must be shoddy.'

'No, she's clued up. Alfie's dropped us in it. The good news is I've got the charges all on me. If you all fly under the radar, make no trouble, the coppers promised my lawyer they'd turn a blind eye to you staying on at Tree Palace. Midge, you got to look after things. Put yourself on the rotation. Rory, look out for your mum and don't give her crap.'

He didn't want the boy thinking he was frightened: he winked at him and, at the same time, made a clicking sound with his tongue. He hugged Moira and pecked her on the forehead. 'All I'm worried about is my beautiful Mortlake haul's gone.'

Then, 'What I want you to do is go home and let me face this without you lot there.'

'No,' said Moira.

'Yes. And Zara, if anyone asks you: Your stepdad, hasn't he gone to jail? You say, I have nothing to do with him. He's not my real father.'

'That'd be terrible to say that,' said Moira.

Even Zara agreed it would be wrong. But he kept insisting and extended the advice to Rory.

The boy said he'd never do such a thing. Shane loved him for that and put his arm around him. The hero feeling was back and flooding warmly under his skin.

Fowler came into the room and told them to finish their good-byes. They did so with Moira wiping her eyes and Midge and Rory shaking Shane's hand and embracing him briefly, patting his shoulder. Zara nodded her respect for his stubborn authority.

'I'll get Elisha to let you know everything. Where I am and all that. It's all right, Moira. Rory, help your mother wheel the pram.'

20

The sentence was only six months in total because of luck in getting Feather for a magistrate. The usual one was on sick leave and he was filling in. His real name was Finch but he was Feather for his judicial softness. He preferred fines to jail time. And a short amount of jail if jail was needed. 'I'm sceptical that prison deters the majority of non-violent miscreants.'

It was a favourite phrase of his and he used it in Shane's case. 'You're a public nuisance, there's no doubt. But the properties you entered for the purposes of stealing were abandoned, not functioning abodes. That's significant. The stolen goods are, however, estimated at more than five thousand dollars in retail value.'

Shane was sitting next to Elisha and whispered, 'Five thousand dollars! Jesus, more like eight thousand.'

'Shh.' She elbowed him. She stood up and said, 'As Your Honour pleases' and other formalities, and told Shane to count his blessings. Then he was handcuffed—he'd not been handcuffed in Barleyville but Elisha said it was for show for the court.

'Could you let my family know what's going on?'

She said she'd be happy to ring, but if there was no number they'd have to wait until she had time to write a letter.

Shane nodded his acceptance that she had dealt with him now. He was no longer her priority. It was not her job to run his errands.

She muttered, irritated, and turned his file over to write on the back of it. 'Listen. I'm going home via Barleyville to see a client. Give me directions to your place.'

She had to draw herself a squiggly map to get the Loop Road turnoff clear. Then the dirt road to Tree Palace.

Elisha stopped writing. 'Tree what?'

He explained the name and she gave a snorting laugh and said, 'Love it.'

'And could you take my coat and tie? Moira's fussy about keeping them nice.'

'I'm not your butler. *Jesus.*'

His handcuffs were slipped off for a second while he removed his coat and yanked his tie loose. Then Constable Dench put the handcuffs back on and held him by the top of the arm, a formal reminder that he was not free. They stood waiting up the back of the courtroom for a police car to be brought round. The handcuffs, their tight metal grip, caused Shane to tremble like he had in the pure loneliness of the lock-up. There were people all about but he was no longer among them. He was apart and disallowed.

'Shane,' he heard. 'Shane. Mate.'

It was Jim Tubbs among the minglers in the hall. He was

dressed in a suit, too tight around his arms and chest. He wore a tartan tie but the top button on his shirt was undone to let his neck swell out more comfortably.

'How you been?'

'Good.'

'Haven't seen you since that blue we had.'

'No.'

'Keeping out of trouble?'

'No.'

'Never mind.'

'Just got six months.'

'Shit. Ah, you'll do that on your ear, won't you?'

'Yeah.'

Tubbsy's ginger hair was combed neatly and wavy. His cheeks had a line of high whiskers where his shaving went to. His false teeth were in.

'What's all this?' Shane grinned.

Tubbsy patted his hair down. 'Nothing. *Urinating in public.* In the street after the St Arnaud races. I'll cop a fine. Nothing.'

With the aloneness sickening him Shane wanted to say, It's really good to see you, Tubbsy. How long should you stay fallen out with someone? There was a time when he'd have said, Keep an eye on things, will you? Make sure Moira's got money and Midge isn't crook with his breathing or his hip. He couldn't do that without Moira's say-so. And Moira hadn't shown signs yet of forgiveness for Tubbsy.

'Anything I can do, Shane?'

'Nah. All in order. Ta.'

Constable Dench got the signal that the car was ready. He tightened his hold on Shane and pointed for him to walk.

'Look after yourself, Tubbsy.'

'You too.'

Shane puckered his lips to whistle blithely down the steps but his heart was so sunk there was only an air sound.

21

Moira took her fancy cup and saucer into the L-shape and threw them on the ground. She had a square of cardboard for placing on top. She used a brick from the barbeque for smashing on the cardboard and thereby smashing the crockery and the connection to Alfie Tweedie to pieces.

Midge didn't interfere. The anger in her made him wince with every blow but he didn't say anything. He helped her scoop the shards into a plastic bag. He offered to put them with the rubbish for disposal in town.

Moira grabbed the bag off him and said she'd deal with it. She intended standing in the doorway of Alfie's and shaking the contents out and spitting on them.

'That might cause trouble, Moira.'

'Good.'

'He'll say it's us being threatening to him. Could make it worse for us and worse for Shane.'

That made sense. Moira could have screamed her hatred of

Alfie. She would have if she thought it wouldn't scare Mathew from sleep. Instead she took the rattling bag of bits to their shanty toilet and flicked up the wooden lid and emptied the bag down the stinky hole. As close to justice as she had. She would have dealt with the Alfie pot plants that way but didn't need to—they'd died in the heat.

Late afternoon Elisha Kay arrived. Limpy met her with his scampering hysteria and hung back in his usual coward's arc. Moira expected it was police cataloguing more evidence but seeing it was a lone girl and the girl had glasses, she summed her up as a social worker and ordered Rory to go inside. She told Zara to get in the tent and be quiet.

Ideally Mathew would be out of sight for such a visit but he was in Moira's arms finishing feeding. At least he looked settled and not starved or neglected. She decided to make a performance of him by standing her ground and rocking side to side: this baby's as loved and spoilt as any baby. She made Midge hold up his hand and fuss that he was shielding the sun from him.

When Elisha said who she was and why she was there Moira didn't believe her. She thought it was a trick to win her over.

'Here's my card.'

Moira pretended to read it and grunted and let Midge take a look. He nodded that the girl appeared truthful.

'Why couldn't you get him off?' Moira's lips hardly parted from bitterness.

'I'm very sorry if you're not satisfied,' Elisha said, sarcastically. She looked at her wristwatch and turned to walk to her car, muttering, 'Wasting my fucking time coming here.'

She had red boots that went over her ankles. They were covered in dust and she cursed herself for not changing out of them.

'Wait a minute,' said Moira. 'I didn't mean to be smart. Midge, get a rag from the kitchen. And bring a glass of water for the girl.'

She asked her if she'd like to sit down, if she'd like a cup of tea. Elisha said no thank you, she was busy. She looked about the place and had to resist being disparaging: Tree *Palace*?

'Shane was keen for you to know his movements. He's in a cell at St Arnaud police station. A van's on its way up from Melbourne to get him. He'll go down to Melbourne to the assessment centre. They'll decide what to do with him from there. That can take a while, days, weeks. My guess is Marnaroo, the prison near Bendigo. It's lower security and he's not violent so they'll treat him less hardcore.'

Midge gave her water and she sniffed it and sipped. She waved her hand to stop flies landing in her mouth. She handed the glass back. 'Well, that's about it. It's all I can do. Oh, and I've got his coat and tie for you.'

She went and got them and handed them over.

'Give her the rag, Midge,' Moira said. 'For your nice boots.'

Elisha flicked the dust off each boot with the rag and wiped the heels clean, standing on one leg to do it. She almost toppled, and Moira held Mathew tighter and freed a hand and steadied her.

'You can arrange visits. Bendigo's a couple of hours. Not that far.'

Moira gave Elisha her card back.

'Keep it,' Elisha said.

'Thanks. You can keep the rag.'

Elisha was holding the rag away from herself. She thought Moira was mocking her.

'For your nice boots,' Moira said.

'Listen, ring my office and we'll let you know Shane's movements. They still got public phones in Barleyville?'

'They got two,' said Midge.

'There you go, then.'

As Elisha drove off Midge reached over and took the card from Moira for safekeeping as he could read it.

Moira snatched it from him. 'I'll look after it. It's a link to Shane.'

Midge straightened his back. 'He's my brother. That's my link too.'

'I'm not going to argue about a card. We'll both look after it.'

They put it in the kitchen, under the table lid with Midge's memorabilia.

No sooner was the lid closed than Moira opened it and took the card out. Mathew was asleep and she let him have the big bed to himself, lying on Shane's side. He might as well have that now it was empty. She sat on her side with the card and tried to read it.

A letter such as *o* looked just as it sounded. It provided little problem in understanding. Same with *s*. *E* and *k* were not readable. Nor were *r* and *h*. Clumped together into words they were impossible.

'Midge. Come here. Sit down, here beside me. Read this out.'

He read the card aloud. *Elisha Kay. Solicitor.*

'All of it.'

He read out the address.

'So, that says Stawell there?' Moira asked.

'No. That says Stawell *there*.'

'And the word there that begins with *So*. That must be Solicitor?'

'Yeah. Solicitor.'

'Point all the words out and read them.'

He did.

She took Midge's Swan Hill write-up from under the table lid and asked him to read out the first line slowly, read it over and over. 'If you do it over and over I might have a crack at remembering what words sound like to look at. I can work out a trick for myself and match the shapes the words make with the sounds the words make. Will you help me do that?'

'I suppose.'

'I don't mean just *now*. I mean, make it a regular thing. I've had a gutful of always pretending. Let's give this a go. Maybe I'll be able to pretend less.'

'I'm no teacher,' Midge said. 'I'm no great reader myself.'

He was flattered that Moira thought him teacher material.

Moira said he'd be teacher enough for her. Good enough for her to get a driver's licence, maybe, one day. What kind of woman was it who couldn't write a love letter to Shane when he most needed it! Something in her own handwriting saying personal things. Things she'd never dictate to Midge.

They agreed on it: lessons for half an hour or a bit longer every day.

The headline in Midge's Swan Hill write-up was 'Battler Breaks Drought'. They started with that for the first lesson.

Moira looked at the *B* and thought: a boob and belly shape

189

combined. The *t*s were fishhooks. She connected the hook shape with *trout* to remember the *t* sounds.

She worked her way through the three words until each had a shape and a sound. An *r* was road with a dead end turn at the end of it. A *k* was a door key. She set herself homework: she must get the shapes and sounds remembered for instant recall.

22

There was no fixed time when the lessons took place. It depended on Midge. He had duties now beyond being normal Midge. He'd volunteered to be Zara's transport—to get her to work on time and pick her up when she'd finished. On her first day he was as nervous as she was. He bit a fingernail to the quick as they drove along. At one stage Zara demanded he stop the wag, turn around and take her back home. She couldn't go through with the job—she wasn't smart enough. Midge told her that was nonsense. 'You're smart and you're pretty. You'll show 'em all.'

He drove her to the front entrance and said he'd be right outside if she needed him.

She waited outside Mr Dixchit's office-storeroom and all she could think of was that she should get out, go. It was a stupid idea, her having a real job. She wanted to pee and clenched her muscles against the feeling. Then Mrs Dixchit arrived, her thick, shiny drapery like a brown wedding dress trailing down. She shook Zara's hand—more a touching of the fingertips than gripping.

'Welcome,' she said. No one had ever used that word to Zara before. A word that said: you're expected and deserve formal wording. 'Come this way and we'll try on a smock.'

The smock was pink, the trainee colour until she was ready for blue. Zara changed in the toilet, then followed Mrs Dixchit past the display shelves, getting a lecture about stacking products—keeping the labels facing forward, oldest used-by dates in front. There was a box of name tags—lots of Biancas and Kaylas, but no Zaras. Mrs Dixchit wrote a tag out by hand, which would do until her trial period, a fortnight, was over.

The cash register was the complicated part. Zara was told to watch how Ivari did it. She was the Dixchits' niece, taking a year off from uni, and didn't look right with a blue smock on: what a waste of her dark skin not to have jewels and long flowing clothes, Zara thought. She was un-Indian in her speaking, normal Australian, greeting customers with 'How's your day been?' in a bored, automatic way as she scanned purchases across the beeping red beam.

The register's screen was like a computer. The keyboard had tiny writing on it, saying *Day's Specials* and *Receipt Yes, Receipt No*. The eftpos and credit gadget had a groove where customers swiped their cards. You weren't to watch as they entered their secret code.

'Categories,' Ivari explained. 'When you pack purchases you pack meat and vegetables separately. As you do for cleaning products and frozen goods. Categories.'

Zara took up position at Checkout 2 where there was a cardboard sign that read *Attendant in Training*. Mrs Dixchit swiped her security tag against the side of the cash register. The screen lit up: *Welcome*. The till sprung open. She stood behind Zara and said, 'I will be here if you have questions.'

There weren't many customers at this time of day. Zara folded her arms to stop her hands shaking from the wait. Then a trolley arrived, filled to the top. A chubby red-haired woman was pushing it.

'How's your day been?'

The woman nodded, uninterested in chat.

Beep by beep, Zara scanned and packed the load. She accidentally beeped some things twice. Mrs Dixchit leant over and showed her how to *Delete*. The balance came to $153. The woman paid by eftpos and wanted one hundred dollars cash out in the transaction. Zara had never held one hundred dollars in her hands. She had to take a deep breath to control the thrill.

By the end of the shift her fingers smelled of money. She licked her fingertips to savour the taste of it. Money had no taste, but the smell was like leather.

How's your day been? She said it so many times she started to experiment with, 'Your day been fine?' 'Busy day for you?' 'You got much on?'

Because Mr Dixchit started Zara out on slower morning shifts, Midge stayed in town rather than make the trip home and back. That allowed him to take care of business matters: he organised his turn on the rotation and rang Elisha's office every day until they could tell him Shane's fate.

Marnaroo was indeed the appointed prison. Midge was told to apply to visit—it was not a lawyer's job to broker visits. He bought good writing paper from the newsagent and wrote a request. Moira stared over his shoulder, watching the words. He also wrote a letter to Shane and put on the top left of the envelope: *Private, from family.* The letter only went for half a page and all it said was all's well at home. Moira sent her love with a whole line of kisses. She had a vigil now, apart from Mathew's neediness. She had the postman to wait for, delivering Shane's reply in his little white van.

Two weeks went by. Three weeks. A month. No white van bearing news from him.

Zara started working more than just mornings. She was efficient enough to serve the busier afternoons and evenings. Midge drove home in that case and did odd chores and tutored Moira. He bought the *Barleyville Gazette* and read the front page to her and she did her best to apply her shapes-and-sounds method. It wasn't easy and she clenched her fists and cursed her bonehead.

When Midge drove back to town she did her homework and included it in her conversations with Mathew, as if she was the teacher and he the student. She joked as much to him as she recited a syllable. She placed her finger beneath a word and said, 'Let's try this again, Mathew.'

She was embarrassed if Rory came in and saw her learning words that even he knew. She distracted him with a chip treat. Or a request to feed Limpy or ride into town with a bag of rubbish for the trotting track bin. She kept a bag ready so he would ride and burn off steam. It was a chore he'd never have agreed to before. He was more co-operative than he'd ever been, as if Shane's representative now. Except over school.

The new term was starting and Rory refused to go.

'That's what Shane promised. He promised I didn't have to go no more.'

Moira wanted to snap at him to do as she ordered but her cunning hat decided it was better to say, 'Fair enough' and 'I'm glad if you don't go,' which made him sit quietly in victory. She had no sympathy for complaints about his uselessness in classes: she was the boneheaded one and he at least could read and write and should be grateful. She worried he might turn boneheaded himself if he didn't do more schooling. She did not want Mathew having a boneheaded older brother and decided on guilt as a strategy.

'I just hope they don't come after us,' she said.

'What?'

'The school people. The government. With Shane gone they might ask, Where's young Rory? I don't think that'd make Shane happy. But if you don't want to go to school, that's up to you.'

Rory's didn't respond. He wandered off into the trees with his head down, thinking and scratching his hair. He leant against trunks and swiped his foot across the ground.

He decided to go to school. He'd grown enough through summer that his khaki shorts rode high on him. Moira let them down to the absolute ends of the material. Barleyville High wasn't a stickler for perfect attire. There were hand-me-down uniforms for free at their fetes but Rory got away with a pair of Shane's black socks instead of grey. He wore a T-shirt instead of a school shirt because he said school shirts chafe. He had the slit-eyed look of someone determined to endure a hardship. He rode his bike slowly but got to the playground by bell time and went to his classes and sat sullen and silent.

Being trapped there, having to learn things was bad enough—the gobbledegook mathematics and lockjaw language of books. The word about Shane was circulating somehow, the way gossip does. Rory had to put up with sneering taunts, mockery he couldn't rage at and avenge because of fear the trouble would follow him home and Shane would be so mad at him and disappointed.

His old man's in jail. Hey, shithead, is it true your old man's in jail? What's it like having an old man in the slammer?

'He's not my dad. He's not my real dad.'

He was ashamed he said it but he said it anyway. Not that it made much difference. The taunts changed to mockery about how trants have sluts for mothers. Rory went cold in his blood imagining violence. He didn't get violent. He wanted to but didn't, and prayed to Shane for strength not to cry. He prayed for forgiveness for saying he wasn't his real dad. He felt so bad about saying it that he couldn't keep it up. He tried hard but couldn't and changed his tone to one of attack. He held up his index finger and middle finger and crossed them and boasted about Shane being as close to him as *that*. 'Yeah, he's in jail and when he gets out he'll come after you. He'll come after you and your families and burn your fucking houses down.'

He said it with a low-growl voice and meant every word, though he knew it wasn't true. He only had to say it twice to his playtime tormenters and they backed away and called him insane. He knew to deny everything if the teachers quizzed him. They didn't bother. The playground went hushed when he was around.

The word must have reached Mr Dixchit as well. He stared at Zara all the time and made regular counts of her till. She sensed him hanging about and thought he either had the hots for her or was suspicious. He wasn't the hots kind with his hands-behind-his-back way of addressing her. He counted other girls' tills during shifts but not as often as he counted hers. When he paid her her cash, doing it secretly as if they were shaking hands, he was fond of saying, 'You know what I have? I have eyes in the back of my head.' She expected he regretted hiring her and was ready to pounce at the slightest discrepancy.

She hated Midge coming into her work because he looked seedy. He looked the sort of man who had a brother in jail. She pretended he was just another customer. Under her breath she said, 'Go away. Don't speak to me.'

'I got to do the shopping for Moira,' Midge said.

She made a show of not recognising him—'Just these items, sir?'—then resumed her whispering. 'Get the other girl to serve you. And wait for me down the street. How many times I got to tell you. Don't hang around.'

He gave in and did as she asked and had another girl serve him. He parked the car down the street from the supermarket. He was hurt that she was ashamed to have him near but hoped it was just a passing rejection.

Driving home Midge said he wished she was friendlier. They had always been civil and friendly. Given he was driving her back and forth she should be respectful. Zara just shrugged.

Truth was, Zara looked upon them as inferiors now, Midge and Moira, Shane and Rory. She was young but felt like a woman of the world with proper employment. She didn't know what to feel about Mathew. He'd come out of her and therefore couldn't be inferior. Best thing was not to think of him at all. Best way to do that was put in lots of hours at the supermarket.

It didn't always work. One time she stood waiting for customers and had a terrible empty sensation along her arms. As if she'd been holding something heavy and put that something down and an aching emptiness filled her muscles. She had to shake her arms and blink the sensation from her mind.

She dug a hole under a corner of the tent and kept her money there. She wrapped the wad in cellophane for protection and made a lid for the hole by removing the top of her cosmetics box. She covered this with dirt and smoothed the plastic floor across it, checking the hole every evening and counting its contents. She was damned if she was going to share a cent.

One day she got home and looked at Rory and Moira bickering and thought, How can we even be related!

'What have you done?' Moira was demanding.

'Nothing.'

'What have you done, Rory?'

'Nothing. Nothing.'

'Then how come the school's writing to me?'

'Wish I hadn't given it to you. I only gave it cause I done nothing.'

Zara went into the tent and changed out of her work smock to keep it clean. She knelt and lifted the plastic and the dirty lid and counted her money. She almost had enough to get a mobile. There was a tower in Barleyville now and everyone talked about the good reception. She didn't know who she'd call. But she'd have it in her hand, a statement of progress. A solid promise of possibilities. She put on her dressing gown and went to the house to get a bowl of water and soak a flannel and take it back to the tent to birdbath herself. She closed her eyes to block out Rory's complaining.

'*She's* meant to go to school and doesn't.'

'That's different. She's older.'

'She's not the leaving age.'

'She's got a job.'

'I can get one too.'

'We'll see when Shane gets home. Midge, read me this from school. What's it say?'

Midge unfolded the neatly creased white page.

'It says.' He sat down to read. 'It says it's from the student development co-ordinator. It says, *We suggest as part of improving Rory's school participation and his overall studies that he undertake an activity program.* They want him to learn the recorder for the school orchestra.' He looked up from the page. 'What's a recorder?'

'It's a music thing,' Rory said. 'I don't want to learn a music thing.'

Moira told him to shush and let Midge finish.

'It says for you come in to the school, Moira. *We welcome your participation in a parent and teacher meet-and-greet evening.*'

199

'I'm not going into any school. I'd feel two inches tall. Where's it say that?'

'There.'

She took the note from Midge and put her finger to the line trying to decipher it.

Zara thought, I want to un-relate myself. She got her water and kept her back to them as if backs were protection against being related.

Next payday she bought the cheapest phone from the news-agent. At work she showed it off and got tips from the girls on its use. She gave her number to them and asked to be rung for the fun of answering. Beyond that she had no expectations of receiving a social call. It didn't matter. The phone was more a symbol: she was ready for the world. The world was her family, not the Tree Palace people.

23

Zara caked more make-up to her face to make it look older and cover her spots. She wanted to mix with older people and needed to look the part. When girls from school saw her working they'd say, 'That can't be Zara the trant.' She had no wish to be dragged back into classrooms. She made herself more forthright to win Mr Dixchit's favour. Instead of being timid when around him she made conversation and suggested small things like putting chocolate and lollies at the checkout so kids nagged their mothers to buy them. Her mood became different in the car, which thrilled Midge. She chatterboxed to him about how cluey she was.

One evening they arrived home and Rory had a plastic recorder to his lips. He was blowing a pitiful tune and complaining. It was meant to be the national anthem but amounted to a screech.

'I don't want to do this,' he whined. 'I hate this. I don't want to do it.'

'Do it,' said Moira.

'I feel dumb.'

'Do as you're told.'

'No.'

'I'll tell Shane when I see him.'

'I don't want to be in no orchestra. It's dumb.'

Midge scratched his head and smiled, not because of Rory but because of Zara. He had a copy of the local paper and took it to the porch where Moira was supervising the music session. 'You see this? This is all Zara's thinking. Tell them what you did here, Zara.'

The butterfly clip on Zara's ear studs had come loose. They were decent ear studs she'd bought from Barleyville Gifts and Apparel. Tiny silver parrots in a circle of silver leaves. 'Someone check in my collar,' she said, bending to have Moira look. The clip was caught down her neck. She didn't say thanks to Moira for fishing it out, so Moira said it for her, sarcastic.

Zara made Midge lower the paper so Moira could see.

'Mr Dixchit does all the advertising. I just said to him why not put pictures of meat and vegetables alongside the prices to high-light them. And take out the Colgate and shampoo photos which everyone knows look the same as last week.'

'She'll run that place,' Midge said.

'And that line there: *There's only one standard—the best.* That used to be at the bottom of the page. I said to him, "Put it higher. Put it higher."'

She gave a dismissive wave as if wasting her breath showing Moira a printed line. Moira pretended not to notice and prodded Rory to keep playing. He played two notes and had to look at the directions: a sheet with finger holes inked in for him to follow. The phone in Zara's pocket rang and he thought the chiming sound was his recorder.

'Hello,' Zara answered, excited. She walked with a skip in her stride towards the tent, then veered to the trees where they striped the L-shape dirt with late shadow. 'No worries,' she said. 'Great. See you then. Yip. See you.'

When she got off the phone they were all staring at her. She wiggled the device in her fingers. 'Cool, eh?' She reached behind herself to unzip her smock. 'Brent's picking me up down at the crossroads. Don't want him—' She stopped herself saying *coming here.*

'Who's Brent?' said Midge.

'He's from town. Brent Romano. His dad owns the refrigerator truck and him and Brent bring in the milk and the frozen foods.'

Midge had a suck on his asthma spray. 'And he's picking you up?'

'Yeah. We're going out tonight.'

'Where?'

'None of your business.'

She went into the tent to get ready.

He stood at the door flap. 'This Brent fella know you're a mother? I mean, you should spend your free time with Mathew. All day at work and now out at night.'

There was no answer. Moira told him to let Zara go where she wants. Mathew wasn't missing out. 'You saying he's missing out?'

'I'm not saying that.'

She thought, why mention Zara and Mathew in the same

breath? How dare those words be used together: Mathew, Zara, mother. The girl thinks she's too good for us now. Waving her hand in that smart-aleck way. Serves her right if I give up having feelings for her. Think of her not as a daughter but a roommate of Tree Palace. In fact, that had already happened.

Sometimes you have to force yourself to love people. There was no forcing with Mathew. With Zara she had to force herself these days. She had to force out remembering that Zara tried to kill Mathew, then in its place force in love for the girl, and she failed at it. There was no real forcing with Rory. Oh, she was short-tempered with him and always had been. Yet forcing herself with Zara made her want to force Rory away, as if they came as a pair, brother and sister. She felt herself doing it and tried to stop. Even now, as he was trying his best blowing and following the finger holes, she was doing it.

'Can I finish now?' he said.

'You hardly started.'

'School won't know.'

'They will 'cause I'll tell. I'll say Rory won't practise and do his studies and they'll say we wipe our hands of him.'

'Good.'

'You know what then?'

'What?'

'They'll send you to a place for simpletons.'

'No.'

'Yip.'

'No way.'

'Yip.'

'I'm no spastic-face.'

'I know you're not, but they'll think so and they'll send you away. I bet that's why they want me to go visit the teachers.'

'Bullshit.'

'Mouth!'

'Sorry.'

'I'll do my best to stop them sending you.'

'Promise?'

'I promise. Just do the things they tell you.'

Being God with her affections—giving them and taking them back and giving again—was the wrong thing to do but she did it anyway and it made her love Rory again, him sitting there, recorder in hand, worried and grateful to her.

Out Zara came freshened with make-up and jeans. A yellow T-shirt from the supermarket sale tray. Her good black shoes slung from her fingers and from her shoulder a shiny red bag on a long strap. She trod softly to avoid the hurt from stones.

'Anyone got smokes? Left mine at work.'

'My rollies if you like,' Midge offered.

'Yuk, no.' She cocked her head at Moira, 'You?'

'If you want. I'm off ciggies.'

She got Zara her last ten and said, 'Have the lot.' There was a strange moment where, instead of Zara being rude as usual, instead of her self-centred air and not saying thanks, the girl apologised for having been off-handed before. 'You know, when I was showing you the paper. I mean, I wasn't being nasty.'

'I didn't notice.'

Zara put the cigarettes in her bag, pressing them down to the bottom to keep them safe from falling out. There was a stranger moment from the girl. She asked, 'How's the baby?'

'Eh?'

'Mathew?'

'Why?'

'Just wondering.'

'Fed and watered. I got him under control.'

'It's good he's got you, I guess. You being here all the time.'

'Things are fine.'

'And he don't cry much?'

'No, he's easy. He's happy. You said you're going out?'

'Yeah.'

'Have a nice time of it.'

Moira moved backwards into the house and closed the door. Then opened it straight away to order Rory inside for more practice. She closed the door again once he'd obeyed.

Zara didn't like that, making pleasant conversation about a topic she had a right to and having the door closed to snub her. A return snub of Moira would be a good quick avenging but she had no time to think one up, not even a petty put-down. The crossroads were ten minutes away on flat heels. Twenty minutes at least if hobbling on her dress shoes. If she was late for Brent he might drive up to the dwellings or turn his ute around and leave without her.

'Midge. Can you do me a teeny-weeny favour?'

She granny-stepped over to him and hooked her hand under his elbow. He was standing with a foot on the barbeque to rest his hip and was so surprised by her affection that he lost balance and listed.

'Just a teeny-weeny favour, please?'

'Course.'

She smelled of deodorant or perfume—oranges and roses.

'Run me down to the crossroads in the wag. Pretty please?'

He had no wish to deliver her to some Brent fella on time, but also no wish to say no to her and have her let go of his elbow. He nodded and she let go anyway and raced ahead to the garage, a granny-step sprinting.

24

Midge dropped Zara where she wanted and she waved for him to go and not wait and gawk. She wrestled her shoes on with her finger and shimmied herself to shake off wag dust. There was no sign of lover boy. Midge took his time turning the wag around. 'You're too young for the pub, you know,' he said.

'I know.'

'You'd get sprung.'

'I know.'

'Lover boy must be old if he's got a car.'

'Not *old* old.'

Zara shooed him off as if drying her fingernails. She adjusted the bag over her shoulder like a sash to pose with.

Midge drove off slowly, made no dust tail and kept her in view. When the red ute appeared he stopped and watched Zara get in and leave. Wouldn't it be perfection, he thought, if she'd have held his elbow for real instead of merely wanting something from him? Like a father is held by a loving daughter. But you cannot be a father by appointing yourself. He could not recall so lonely a feeling.

His forearm was resting along the open window and a wet plop landed on it, too clear a droplet for bird mess. Another plop, coin-round and cool, dribbled off his skin and caused the hairs to prickle. He looked up through the windscreen to where the west sky had gone bruisy. The sun was covered over and the road was crawling with shadow. The autumn break should be starting about now but two drops didn't prove it. On the plains the summer could change to autumn in a night and do it with wild rainstorms and then days of quiet mist. Or there'd be false starts and plops like this and then nothing but more burning summer.

Midge drove on and the windscreen became dotted and smeared. Thunder grumbled but the sky was too thick with black cloud to let through lightning. The wipers needed new rubber for their blades—they couldn't keep up with the sudden quantity of rain. A sheet of it with hail pellets inside bounced across the road and he couldn't see ahead. He was driving by memory, swerving left towards the house. He stopped and wound the window up to sit out the fury and hope to God that Zara's lover boy had done the same if he had any brains.

Moira felt the house rattle and she hushed Rory's playing. The glad-wrap window was sucked out and cold wind and spray sucked in. Through it she saw the porch canvas start tearing. Rain spears were landing by the thousands, stuck at an angle. They pummelled the roof. The outdoor chairs flipped and slid in the thin lake that formed instantly across the L-shape. She slammed the door and there was water in her hair from the ceiling. Leaks everywhere through the house. They splashed on the table and soon turned one wall to liquid.

She picked up Mathew and he cried. Rory wasn't crying but he was scared and hugged Moira's waist and stayed there though she told him to go to Mathew's little bed and turn it upside down to keep it dry. She had to do it herself with a kick of her toe. The bedding already looked soaked.

It lasted for only ten minutes but what a performance! Nature crazy and flailing about, and then it fizzled. Like a muscle going slack and a final deep sigh of wind and calmness, but the damage was already done. Roof iron had been flung around. There were water puddles on the kitchen floor and more water in the bedroom, on the mattress. The caravan had shifted on its blocks but mercifully not slid off them. Water had leaked through its window frame and got under the lino. Clothes were wet in the cupboard. Zara's tent had stayed on its ropes but there was a definite lean and the L-shape's little brown lake was lapping near the entrance. You'd think nature was feeling guilty the way the drip-heavy trees hung their heads in apology and the sun brought the heat back as if to make things right. Cockatoos high above laughed off the incident.

Moira was not in the mood to accept apologies or see the good side of weather over the bad. Mathew needed the honours done and she couldn't lie on the bed as she normally would and let him nuzzle her. She did it standing. She had nowhere dry to set him down so she kept him in her arms while cleaning the place, using one hand and Rory's help to tip the mattress upright to be aired. The sun was bright despite the lateness of the day. It could shine all it liked, a special dusk-yellow effort of amends, but she was still furious.

Rory's music page was sodden. 'This means no more music,' he said.

'It does not.'

'Page is all mushy.'

'So?'

'I can't read it.'

Moira said nonsense. Her page of practice writing was mushy also but that wouldn't stop her practising. She told him to hang it somewhere. 'Or spread it outside on a rock. It'll unstick.'

She had him spread her page beside his and made him take the end of the broom. He swept water from the house and she used a towel to sop what remained. It was tiring holding Mathew and mopping but the wet wood and dirt were already smelling rotten.

'Why you bothering learning anyway?' Rory asked.

'What?'

'You got by so far.'

'I don't want to just *get by*.'

Rory said he didn't understand.

'I need to get a licence, for one thing. And if I could write I'd be able to write to Shane and say hurry up and write to me and say I miss him. Sweep harder. You're leaving water behind.'

25

Midge stuck a new glad-wrap window in place and then began hammering on the roof. The sunlight was fading but he took a kero lantern up with him and could see well enough to put nails where iron had lifted and let the storm through. He dragged strips of spare iron once used for the shed and laid them over the rust areas which hail had penetrated. He banged and bent them into shape. Chances were there'd be more rain through the night so he worked quickly, a patch job. He knocked the rain tank with his knee and it was like knocking something solid instead of hollow.

'Moira!' he yelled. 'The tank. It's full. It's chockers.'

He ran his fingers down the corrugated sides and felt the chill of water through the metal. The tank's overflow pipe was dripping. Through the aeration hole at the top he breathed in rain's aroma. A cross between no smell at all and clean cotton.

Mud oozed between Moira's toes. It tickled and she giggled, slipped and slid to show Mathew what rain looks like when it was captured. She knelt, turned on the tank's wing tap and held his tiny fingers under it and said, 'Rain water.' He smiled showing his pink gums, and wiggled his legs. 'This means showers and washing, Mathew. No trotting track for ages and none of them laundromat fur balls.'

She drank a palmful and so did Rory. Midge climbed down to have a turn. Limpy wanted some as well. They filled a bucket to wash their feet and topped up the jerry cans for the kitchen.

Night settled starless and cold. You could hear water draining among the trees and in the ruts of the road. Midge set up lamps at the house door and reattached the porch with a double amount of nails. The canvas was mud-caked but still in one piece. The poles were buckled—he stood on them and yanked and they straightened. He re-roped the tent so Zara wouldn't have skewed walls to contend with. He wanted to sweep her floor dry before she got home and check her clothes and bed weren't muddied but he was loath to go into her private place and touch her private things. He'd best let Moira do it, though she was busy with cooking cans of stockpot for their dinner. He mentioned it to her but she said, 'In a minute.'

The minute never came. After dinner and wiping the house floor again with rags and a towel she was so tired she lay on the bed to sleep without the mattress. She put a blanket over the springs, eased herself onto the coils with Mathew there on top of her and told Rory to leave her in peace and pull the door closed.

She woke when Mathew woke and ached where the springs dug into her skin. She sat at the table in the dark and did the honours. Kept falling forward in half-sleep and shook her head to rouse. When Zara got home she heard Midge greet her and explain the storm damage. He had stayed up waiting for her. 'I couldn't sleep till you was safe home.'

She'd been dropped at the crossroads and walked from there and was exhausted but chatty, not the slightest bit interested in discussing storms. She said Brent's car doesn't leak. You hardly know it's raining in Brent's car. He can afford a decent car. They got a proper family business. Not a shitty trant life.

When she got into the tent and lit a lamp she saw brown sludge on the floor and it stuck to her feet and she swore, *fucking shit*. It had got into things under the bed. Her linen was dry but half her clothes were affected. Her pop posters were ruined but she didn't care about them anymore, only the clothes and cosmetics. And her money hole. Especially her money hole. She pulled back the plastic and scooped away mud. She dug the lid off with her fingers. The hole had water in it but the wad was fine. The plastic-bag wallet had not let a drop through.

She called to Midge, 'Why didn't you do something?'

He stood at the tent door. She hid the wad behind her back.

'Why didn't you move my stuff off the ground?'

'I didn't want to touch your things.'

She swore at him and made him get a shovel and broom and help clean. 'You are *so* useless.' It was one in the morning and she had to start work at eleven. No way was she going to sleep knowing she had mud for carpet.

'Fucking hate living here.'

26

Midge only got a few hours sleep because cleaning for Zara took a while and Moira woke him at dawn and said today was going to be a washing day due to the full tank. Could he rig up a shower screen to the back of the house, please? Could he organise attaching a hose to the tank tap? And while he was at it, could he put something sensible down for a shower mat?

He got a sheet of iron for that purpose, snipped it square and blunted the jagged edges for safety. He had a think and remembered the trailer tarp which would do for a screen. He found two short branches with forked ends to work as hooks. He wedged the branches' other ends into the house wall by chipping two holes in the crumbly weatherboard. He hung the tarp to the forks and tied its gaps together with packing tape. He nailed its ends to the weatherboard. You entered the shower by ducking under the tarp's hem. If anyone looked they saw your feet and nothing more. He wiggled an old hose onto the tap. The hose had splits in places and was bleached by being left unused in the sun, but for showering purposes it was effective. It ran the water at low pressure but not so low as merely to trickle. He poked it under the shower screen and said, 'Bingo. Tree Palace has a bathroom.'

Much of the hose was exposed to the morning sun. The water inside it heated up, which meant Moira had a brief warm stream for Mathew. She knelt on the iron mat and bathed him, then stood and dried him off and put him in the pram beside her while she had her turn. The water was cold by then but it was better than the trotting track. She had Midge standing at the tap. She called 'on' and 'off' to save water while she soaped up. When she was finished Rory had his go. He didn't like washing. Moira always stood with him and supervised his lathering—'Under your arms, Rory', 'A good lather-up between your legs'—but he'd got to an age when he didn't like being nude in front of her. She had to stand outside the screen and call instructions.

When he was finished and dressed and sent off to school, Moira went on tap duty so Midge could take a turn. A breeze had begun ruffling the trees. The storm left droplets hanging from the leaves. Nature's chandeliers, she thought, watching them sparkle and fall. They so entranced her she forgot about the water.

'You still there, Moira?' Midge called out. 'Water on, please. Water on.'

They even distracted her from Mathew. She didn't hear him coughing and gagging. He was only a foot away but she was lost among those tree chandeliers and hardly heard him until he was red in the face and hot in the skin. She lifted him from the pram and his brow was burning. The next second he was cold to touch. Then he got hot again.

'Moira. Water on.'

She blamed herself for bathing him at dawn, the air still damp from the storm. Autumn was close. The sun had warm hands but not as warm as pure summer.

'Water on.'

Better clothes. He needed better, thicker clothing. A flannelette blanket. And booties and mittens. She reprimanded herself: boneheaded Moira should have thought of these things.

'Water on. Water on.'

She reprimanded Mathew. 'Don't you go getting sick on me now. Are you saying I don't look after you good? I'm looking after you just fine. Don't you go making a liar of me.'

'Water on.'

27

Zara said, 'You got to be joking. *That's* better than the trotting track?'

Midge said, 'Course it is. I rigged it up.'

He showed her a nail where she could hang her dressing gown and went on tap duty for her. She moaned about the water being cold, but she stayed in a long time. She was using so much scented soap and fruity shampoo Midge could sniff it wafting in the breeze.

When she finally got out and clip-clopped to her tent in thongs, she didn't say thank you, yet she didn't complain either, which Midge considered as good as a compliment. He smiled to himself and sat under the porch rolling a cigarette, waiting for her to be ready to drive to work.

She took an hour to get made up. So many layers of tan tint for her skin and black pencil around the eyes that she looked plastic in complexion. Not aged fifteen but twenty or more. He didn't like the look but didn't tell her so.

As they walked to the wag Moira called after them, 'We're coming too. Midge, carry the little bed, please.'

The day had misted up. The sky was no longer visible. A light drizzle fell, glazing the bitumen. The night's rain lay in strips by the side of the road and already a greenish tinge had appeared among the grey grasses. It was too cold now to have the windows down. Midge turned the heater on. Only the two front vents worked.

In the back Moira put her cardigan over Mathew and tucked it around him. He coughed and looked feverish again. Moira reprimanded him in silence. You could do that to a loved one, she reckoned, speak in silence and the other person heard. *Don't you get sick on me, young fella. Are you saying I don't look after you? I think I look after you perfect.*

He coughed and spluttered.

Zara reached up and turned the rear-vision mirror to see him. 'He all right?'

'Yip.'

'Sure?'

Here we go again, Moira said to herself. The baby hater's asking questions. 'He needs some warm clothes, that's all.'

Zara turned the mirror back.

When they got into Barleyville, Midge dropped Zara off. She told him not to bother collecting her later. Brent and her were going driving. She'd probably stay the night in town with him and had a change of dress in her shoulder bag. She would not need Midge till further notice.

She got out of the wag before he had a chance to argue.

He turned to Moira—'Zara shouldn't be staying out with this Brent.'

Moira shrugged. 'You going to stop her? Take me to the Salvos.'

He pulled the gear stick into first with an angry action. The wag spun its wheels on the slippery road and screeched. He said sorry to Moira and made sure he went slowly down the main street. You could smell the rain, a sewer smell through the town. Not the clean cotton water of home. More the colour of port wine someone was quitting under sufferance, bottle after bottle being emptied out upstream.

He waited in the car park while Moira took Mathew in, but it was too much for him, sitting there thinking about Zara, so he got out and walked around for a smoke. Then went up the ramp for Moira's company.

She'd put Mathew on his back on the floor and was holding jumpsuits along his body to get the right fit. Two were already chosen though she was uncertain about a pink one. The baby clothes pile smelled faintly of bleach and sick. Some clothes were too off-smelling to consider. She found a cap and mittens. Green booties and blankets faded to the point of having no colour.

There was a time she'd have stolen some of it and paid only for a little. She worried that may be bad luck for a baby. Wearing stolen clothing might taint his innocence, even affect his health. Midge's rotation money didn't go into the bank till next week but she had cash left over from the food kitty because of no Shane to feed and Zara hardly around.

She gave Midge the clothes to carry and went to the counter.

There was a different attendant from the last time. This lady was younger and thin with black hair tied in a bob. She wore a sling-type arrangement across her body, like you do for broken arms. It was long and wide. An infant was hunkered down in the pod of the material.

'I like that thingummy you got on.'

'This? Oh yes, it's very practical.'

'Can I look?'

Moira leaned across and liked how the sling wrapped the infant without shutting it away.

'I just knot it behind my neck here and my hands are free to do things and still carry my Tess.'

Moira had to have one. Was there a piece of cloth in the shop that could do? The lady left the counter and she and Moira picked through old rugs and sheets. The best option was a sarong-style length of cloth, silken in texture and patterned with white circle shapes and gold squiggles. It fitted her well enough if knotted high to have the sling hang over her belly. Like a pouch between her arms. She had the lady hold the ends open and lifted Mathew and tested him in the pouch.

She walked around the shop. It cradled him just fine. A baby hammock that was snug against her and gave the sense of being pregnant on the outside of her body. There was no way a cough or fever could withstand that connection. He was looking better already. His cough rate had fallen to hardly any coughs for several minutes. Better than medicines and doctors—a simple sling.

28

When they got home they could hear Limpy going crazy long before they reached the garage's branches. He was spinning himself around in a barking frenzy. It was the mail van backing off the road so the mailman could get his arm within reach of the letterbox. With that done he beeped the horn to tell Limpy to clear away so he could leave. He gave a wave as they moved to the road edge to let him by. Midge eased up to the box and got two letters out.

'One from Shane.'

'Let me look,' said Moira. 'Give it. Give it.'

She took the letter and attempted to read the envelope's hand-writing. She could tell it was Shane's writing—the way the words sloped to the right and had an awkward buckle in the middle because he wrote so slow and with his tongue out. She knew what her name looked like and it was only third on the top line. Midge was number one and Rory second. She only made third and that caused her heart to miss a beat in disappointment. Third, not first.

She muttered this to Mathew and closed her eyes, squeezing the lids tight to rid the hurt. She ripped the letter open and her name wasn't there at the start either. She put her finger on the first word and used her sound-and-shape method to decipher *Dear All*. She handed Midge the letter. Correct? Correct.

He offered to sit with her and have her go through the whole two pages but she was too impatient to know what the letter said. This was no time for lessons. 'Read it to me.'

He turned the ignition off and cleared his throat. 'It says, "Dear All. How are you? I am fine. Midge, how is your hip? There is a bloke here with bad hips. He takes fish oil. I am not much of a letter writer. Rory, how are you? I hope you are well. Are you keeping your nose clean? I am trying, ha ha. There is a nice bloke in here who is a Rory. He does the garden. The garden here is good as there is water. They let us do gardening. It is a nice garden and there is lots to do. I wear a green tracksuit. I was a deputy cook in the kitchen yesterday. It was bad but good fun. They pay us! There is pay of $30 a week if you are lucky! We can buy cigarettes and Mars bars. There is games and TV. Some say they don't want to go home, ha ha. They say it is a good holiday. I reckon I will put on a few pounds. Three meals a day!"'

Moira ground her teeth. 'Well, that's just lovely. Here we are and there he is on holiday.'

'He probably don't mean it,' said Midge. 'You know, he's just trying to have us not worry. You know Shane. All talk.'

'He hasn't said a word to me. No *Hello, Moira*. No nothing.'

Midge turned to page two and read: 'There are clever sorts in here. I met a bank manager. He cleans. The floors are very clean.

I hope this letter finds you all well. Midge, say hello to Moira for me. Shane.'

'That's it?'

'No. He says we can visit.'

'But that's it.'

He looked again at the pages. 'Yeah. But it's good he's well.'

'I hardly rate a mention?'

'Yes, you do.'

'Like he tacked it on.'

'I wouldn't say that.'

'Read that bit again. Where it says me.'

'Midge, say hello to Moira—'

'*Midge, say hello to Moira.* Can't even say it to me straight. It's through you.'

'He knows I'd read it to you.'

'Tacked on the end. And no *Love, Shane.* Just plain *Shane.*'

Midge opened the second letter. It was from the prison people advising of visiting times. 'They say we don't need an appointment. They've put us on the visitor list and we just turn up and they go get Shane. Saturdays, Sundays or Mondays.'

Moira lifted Mathew from the little bed and put him in the sling. She slid from the wag and headed for the house, muttering to the baby about being tacked on the end. Even if she gave Shane the benefit of the doubt, even if he was trying to ease their worry, what he'd done for her was the very opposite. He'd tacked her on the end like she was nothing to him. She'd never forced herself to feel strongly about Shane. She simply felt strong and it came natural. Was *he* forcing himself to feel strong about her? Was he done with her and using the letter as a sign, tacking her on the end as polite duty?

'I'm going to ask him straight,' she said to Mathew. She nodded as if he'd answered and was egging her on. 'Treating me like that. Tacking me on the end.'

She slapped a piece of paper on the kitchen table and took a pen in her right hand. It must be possible to will the words to come. When you really need them to say how you feel the pen surely can make them happen. There! *Dear* was no bother. *Dear Shane*. Shakily printed but legible.

It was as far as she got. No amount of will could get her past the opening. She threw the pen down and it bounced off the table. She swept the paper to the ground. She had a better idea than stupid writing. 'He said for us to visit? Well, Mathew, I'll visit all right. I'll visit with my face done up, and my hair done up as well. I'll let him see what he's missing.'

Her eyes welled. She didn't want Mathew to sense her sniffling. She turned to face the wall and sobbed to it. The mattress was leaning there, the rain stains on it lighter in colour. She patted them and they'd dried, except at their darker, dirty edges. She took a hold and lifted the spongy thing upright. Dragged it. Aimed it at the bedsprings and let it fall. She gave it a shove into place with her knees and picked Mathew up and lay with him on top of her. He rose up and down on the tide of her breathing. They breathed in time, slow and deep.

Moira slipped into sleep. Just a moment's doze, but full of dreams: of her breasts making a dripping sound as if filling, and hurting from the process.

She woke. She'd had these same dreams for four sleeps now and the hurting stayed with her on waking. This was the worst episode. She bent forward to get relief, let her breasts hang. She rubbed them with her palms and could feel they had a bulging shape. A prickle of heat stung her forehead. Fear that the bulge might be growths. Who would look after Mathew if there were growths in her? She tilted him so he slid off her belly. She stood and braced herself. She got Shane's shaving mirror and closed her eyes and unzipped her dress.

She opened her eyes. Both breasts were definitely bigger. Especially her left. It was bulging and heavier than normal. Much heavier. But it did not feel hard as a growth might feel hard. Her nipples were darker and thicker and tingled. She squeezed them and a tearing sensation rippled through her breastbone and into her nipples. On the tip of her left breast a creamy droplet had formed. She put her finger on it. The droplet stuck to her touch. She licked it. It tasted sugary and watery. She squeezed again and another droplet came. A bead of them fell into her hand. Milk of herself. 'Look what we done, Mathew.' The beads became a trickle. 'Look what we done. Look what we done.'

She lifted him, cradled him. 'Wanna try some? Wanna try?' She held him closer until he was milk to mouth. He gave a suck. He stopped sucking and Moira felt a shiver go through his body. He took the nipple again and sucked. He fed and the trickle became a flow.

29

When Mathew finished feeding Moira was so hungry she filled up on bread and honey. A gleam was in her eyes like two spots of light on the mirror's glass. Her skin shone; she had rosy cheeks and smoothness where usually there were sun cracks and blotches.

She thought the milk would go away as quick as it happened but it stayed all day. And the next day. Should she go to a doctor? She decided not to. Why involve doctors if she felt so good? Mathew got diarrhoea, yellow and rank and squirting everywhere, but that only lasted a day and his insides adjusted.

She intended to see Shane and show him that she had become a special woman. We all think ourselves special but not everyone can be miraculous and have the proof beneath their clothing. 'Me, boneheaded Moira, has the proof on her.'

She did worry, though. Shane might think she was a freak. It might frighten him off. Be too much for him, too weird. She swung between showing him and keeping it secret. She did not know what to do.

Midge wanted to know if he should ready the wag, get the ball rolling on visiting Shane. She kept the door locked on him, protecting her secret. She served up meals but was unsocial, which he couldn't understand. 'Shouldn't we be getting the ball rolling?' he kept saying, annoyed. 'Don't you want to visit Shane?'

Her first reaction was to say yes. Then the swinging took over and she changed her mind. Not just because she was worried about weirdness. She was not above playing a game with Shane: why not make *him* feel tacked on the end? Why not make him wait a while before she visits?

She was jealous of Midge for being mentioned in the letter first, and there was pleasure in seeing him frustrated by her swinging. 'Don't you want to see Shane?' he asked again, bewildered. He had a downcast look on his face, which she enjoyed. He was being hurt on Shane's behalf, which was as good as hurting Shane, and Shane deserved it.

She was bursting to tell her secret to Midge. See his old jaw drop. But if she did then the pleasure of having a secret would be gone. And he might think her a freak too, so what would she gain? Instead she allowed herself to gleam. 'Do you see anything different about me?'

Midge looked at her and took a few seconds to answer. 'Yeah, there is something.'

'I wonder what it is?'

'Dunno.'

'Do you reckon I look, you know, terrific?'

He lowered his eyes, embarrassed. 'You look fine.'

'A bit of a bloom about me?'

'You look fine.'

He stood up and left the house. She laughed to Mathew that seeing Midge blush was priceless.

She was also jealous of Rory and when he got home she made him suffer a little. 'Do you see anything different about me?'

'Nah.'

'Look harder.'

'I am.'

'You're not. You're eating.'

'Yeah, you look different.'

'Bit of a bloom about me?'

He slurped on his tub of noodles and nodded.

'You don't want to waste it when you feel a bit of bloom. When is it they've got that school business, that parent-and-teacher thing? Next week? I think a nice outing is called for, Mathew, don't you? A parent-and-teacher outing will have to do. Show 'em all what a bit of bloom looks like.'

Rory halted his chewing and stared at Moira, a cud of noodles on his tongue, trying to decide if she was joking.

'You're joking, right?'

'Nope.'

'You going into my school?'

'Yip.'

'No.'

'You ashamed to have your mother seen with you?'

'No. They'll tell you I'm stupid.'

'I don't mind that. I know that already. I'll have to get myself something new to wear. Not your Salvos rubbish. Something nicer.

We'll try Barleyville Gifts and Apparel, shall we, Mathew?'

'You never go to stuff like school meetings.'

'You can always complain to Shane, I suppose. You and him being such good buddies.'

30

Zara didn't come home for three nights. Midge drove to the super-market to check on her, not going in past the sliding doors. He hung back, peering, trying not to trigger the sensor.

Eventually she saw him and ignored him. He went to her counter on the pretence of buying chewing gum. 'I was worried,' he said.

'I've been at Brent's house. He rents a place with mates. Now go. *Go.*' She spoke with the fake smile used for customers.

In the car park he saw a truck being unloaded—milk crates, boxes of butter and orange juice. The truck door had a sign: Romano Cartage. The lad doing the lifting, was he lover boy Brent? Midge hid behind fence palings and called out *Brent*, ducking down as the boy turned. So, it was him. Midge took a deep breath of Ventolin. Too old for her, must be in his early twenties. Black hair long and swept behind his ears. Skin of the continental kind, off-white with an oiliness in it. Curly tattoos, green-black blade shapes down the forearms. Midge wouldn't have liked him if he was Jesus.

There was no point discussing Zara with Moira. Moira's view was quite plain: if the girl wants her own life, to hell with her. Besides, the house door was closed when he walked by. It was closed a lot recently, which made him feel shut out. Which was exactly what Moira was doing—keeping things private for doing the honours. He thought it was Shane's letter still bothering her.

When Zara finally did show up she assumed the closed door meant Moira had not finished snubbing her. The late sun was flaring on the caravan. The L-shape and the house were watery blue and might have looked welcoming if not for the sight of the closed door. She'd hiked from the crossroads with cool breeze on her all the way. She was yawning, tired from her nights away, but the breeze was a tonic and she was excited and smiling to herself, thinking, Do I knock or do I have some fun?

She didn't knock. She took a small toy from her bag, a pair of mechanical boots no bigger than her palm. It had a knob you wound up to activate the spring. She wound it and the boots marched off her hand and she had to catch them. She placed the toy on the top step and stood back while it marched with a rasping noise.

She laughed and Rory jumped from the caravan and laughed too. Midge looked through the caravan window. He laughed. Moira opened the door, sling and baby across her.

Zara kept laughing but this time it was at the sling, working out what it was and what it contained. She stopped laughing and went to the step and wound the toy again. It marched on.

'I got this from work, for Mathew. They got other toys but this looked clever and stuff.'

Moira said nothing.

'And it's, like, plastic and stuff. Won't smash if he chucks it about.'

'Mathew don't chuck things about,' said Moira. She patted the sling and was about to close the door.

'Can I give him a demo?'

'Don't bother him.'

'Just for a sec. See what he does.'

'He's sleeping.'

She saw Midge cocking his head to one side, making his way across the L-shape, frowning with disapproval. She held out her hand, palm up, to Zara. 'I'll give it to him later.'

'Promise?'

She handed Moira the toy. The thing sprung to life with a burst of weak marching. Moira dropped it. Zara picked it up and thought, You're not going to show him, are you? The first word babies speak is meant to be 'mumma'. He'll call Moira that. She, Zara, will just be another name in general circulation.

She went into the tent and sat on her bed. The empty-arms feeling had come back. Stronger than ever. Holding Brent helped make the feeling go. If he was with her now she would hold him and ask him to hold her tightly, please. Just hold without meaning to go to bed.

Sometimes in bed, lying awake, she held herself around the tummy, and there, below her ribs, was the shape of Mathew, of where he had been in her. The remembered weight. Then the empty-arms feeling would start and she hugged herself. Then she hugged Brent, but he wasn't what the emptiness meant.

Those plastic boots haunted Moira all night. She put them in the rubbish but they marched through her dreams. Good dreams such as reliving breastfeeding Mathew, lots of glow and tenderness in their vivid cinema. They were invaded by the mechanical rasp and stomp. A terrible sense of being alone and lost to the world. She dreamt about Shane being happy without her, not languishing but lounging in his prison cell. She woke up and did the breastfeeding for real, yet she resented those boots for spoiling the gentle perfection.

Her remedy was to head into town in the morning and find a new dress that would go with her blooming. Zara had met lover boy at the crossroads during the night. Midge had also gone out around the same time for reasons he wouldn't say. He was home now and that left him free to do some chauffeuring.

She had him perform on-off duties at the shower hose for her first and she cut Rory's sandwiches and got him pedalling away to school. She put on make-up, cut her toenails and found some old nail polish she thought might be dried and useless. After shaking the bottle there was enough red to paint her fingers and feet. She brushed her hair into a ponytail held in her fist and threaded it through a rubber band. She had no jewellery but given her skin was shining there seemed no lack of adornment. Her eyes were natural greenstone. Along the shoulder straps of her bra sunburn was more gold in colour than raw skin. Same for her neck and the gold V of her cleavage.

31

Summer was definitely retreating and letting the autumn mists in. The sky was higher and you no longer drove into it and through it; you drove under. You could not drive through the mist no matter how fast the car. The mist kept the same distance from you. It was a great judge of measurements. It contained surprises—kangaroos hopping out and up and over a drooped fence—but the distance gave you warning, about one hundred metres.

At the town silos the pigeons flashed out of nowhere because the mist obscured their air world. The silo tops were high in the new grey heavens. The plains wind seldom gave up its right to blow, but it was doing so now. Not a tree branch moved. The flag on the town hall was rag-limp.

Midge let Moira out at the gifts and clothing shop. From habit he went to help her extract the pram, then saw it wasn't there: she had that body-pram, that funny-looking sling.

'I'm thinking I'll go put petrol in the wag,' he said. 'I'll go visit Shane on my own. Maybe tomorrow or the day after.'

Moira knew she was expected to respond. She was tempted to, but she held out. Her swinging between seeing Shane and denying him the pleasure was not settled. The dream about him happily lounging as implied in his letter, though just a dream, did not help. It played on her as if true fact.

'I said, I'll visit on my own.'

'Go, then.'

'You're not interested?'

'I got better things to do than go visiting jails, thank you very much.'

Midge stood by the wag and watched Moira walk off. He wanted to call, 'You got no loyalty,' but that leap of anger was beyond him. The best he could do was slam the wag door, and even that made him apologise to the door. He lurched and hopped into stride and his hip made a click-lock sound. He was glad to be going in the opposite direction to someone not loyal. She could stick her reading and writing lessons till further notice.

The one person Moira could rely on was Mathew. That was her boast to herself. He put her first. He took her as his mother. Even the girl in the shop recognised it. She was a kid herself, Zara's age. She presumed them mother and child. 'Hello, little one. Aren't you cute, sleeping there against mummy.' She asked to part the sling for a better look and Moira proudly gave her permission.

The dresses were expensive. Exorbitant by Tree Palace standards—up to one hundred dollars, already marked down from one-fifty. The lowest they went was thirty-five. For that you still got good length and a carved-out fit at the waist, you just didn't get the best designs and better material. Which hardly bothered Moira because she didn't mind nylon. As long as the dress smelled new, never worn before, un-Salvos. A dress only she had put on since it left the factory. *Her* dress for once and not a cast-off.

There was one with cherry-blossom patterns that made her heart race. It was forty dollars. Moira said, 'How 'bout thirty-five?' The girl was filling in for an aunty and wasn't sure if she had haggle rights. Normally Moira would cheat her, given the girl's youth and uncertainty, but the worry of superstition, of tainting Mathew, made her force herself to dig out every cent she had.

She wore the dress from the shop and carried her old one in a shop bag. She felt light-footed and unable to stop grinning.

The street was becoming busy—Barleyville busy. The takeaway man unwound the canvas awning across his window and another shopkeeper swept a broom towards the gutter. The awning across Alfie's second-hand store was unwound. That bastard was back, business as usual, his sandwich board astride the footpath. To hell with him! She wanted to kick the board over and yell, 'Alfie is scum,' but wouldn't lower herself.

Lorries and utes were pulling into the garage for fuel. Dogs bark-coughed in ute trays and a carpenter climbed a ladder to repair the pub verandah. A smell of burnt onions was in the air. The mist was lifting and through an opening in it a spotlight of rain shone down. The sun and the rain were coming down together. The shower suddenly stopped to give way to the finer weather.

'That you, Moira? Christ, it is. How you going? Haven't seen you in bloody ages. Jesus, you look different. Hardly knew it was you.'

Jim Tubbs. He stood there in front of her, hands on hips like an inspector of the street, taking up half the footpath with his hairy bulk and his veiny arms. Grey stubble frosted his chin and dust and sweat had mixed to make thin mud in his wrinkles. You could smell he'd been working—you didn't need to get close. His body odour had a sniff of horse dung to it.

'Jesus, you look in good form, Moira. You had one of them facelift operations?'

He laughed from deep in his belly. It made his black singlet shake.

She wanted to step around him but his facelift comment had weakened her momentum. She couldn't help smiling and taking the compliment graciously. He kept staring at her and said nothing about the sling or the wriggling baby in it—men like him don't pay attention to children. But he did offer to carry her shopping bag, which was gentlemanly for him.

'Nice to see you doing good with Shane away. Must suit you.' He laughed again.

'I'm all right.'

She couldn't believe what she was doing—flirting with Jim Tubbs. She had no appetite for him and never had, the big bully who always wore the stink of horse. She should be spitting in his eye too given his recent history with Shane. Instead, she was meeting his eye with hers and getting hot in the face. She was tongue-tied, all because he had noticed her blooming.

'Been shoeing nags all morning, just finished. I'm heading for some vitamins.' He nodded in the direction of the pub. 'Tell you what, Moira. Why don't you join me? My shout.'

That was going too far, having him shout her drinks. But she did consider the idea. Just for a second. She wiped her palm over her forehead. 'Nah. Thanks anyway, Tubbsy.'

'Come on, just one.'

'Nah.'

'Come on.'

'Nah.'

'If there's anything I can do for you, Moira, just give a bell.'

'Ta.'

'I'm serious. Just give a bell. Maybe I'll call in one day. Check there's nothing I can do.'

'It's up to you.'

She suddenly felt sick that she was doing this. She was not being unfaithful, but it was unfaithful all the same. Flirting is the same as unfaithful. You don't need the body involved. All you need is the brain and you can feel guilty enough.

Tubbsy took a step away. His laugh had gone and his brow had risen higher into his scalp. He was looking at Moira's breasts and there was nothing discreet about his enjoying looking. He was ogling them. She felt dirty under his gaze. Then she felt what he was seeing. She was leaking milk. Her new dress was sticking to her and her right nipple was showing through it above the hang of the sling. She put her arm over herself and turned side-on but he stepped around to face her, still ogling. She turned further and uttered a rushed goodbye. She hurried up the street towards the wag.

Midge was crossing the road to meet her. He hopped to get his hip working faster. He was sneering. 'Why you speaking to him?'

'I wasn't.'

'I saw.'

'Just drive.'

He pointed at her wet front. 'What's wrong?'

'Nothing.'

'Drive.'

'I saw you talking.'

'So?'

'Has things blown over with Tubbsy?'

'No.'

'Then why the talking?'

'Just drive.'

'Things shouldn't blow over till Shane has the say. I'll ask *him* if things are officially blown over. If you want to go visit with me or not, that's your business.'

32

The new dress needed soaking and the sling had milk on it. She was resentful of Midge judging her and it made her more determined to choose *her* time to visit prison. Not be dictated to, nor scolded. Imagine, standing there on the street and having milk come out! 'Don't you think that's funny, Mathew? A bit creepy getting perved at by Jim Tubbs. But funny.'

She had him feeding in any position now. She could be standing up, sitting or lying down—he suckled. Doing it sitting in the kitchen she had to be careful where the chair was positioned in relation to the windows. Closing the front door was one thing, but the windows weren't exactly private. She pulled the chair to where she thought was a blind spot. She sat in her underpants, and no top on. There was a shuffling outside. A crunching upon the gritty ground at the windows. Mathew's suction was tight but she eased him off her breast and placed him on the table to cry while she got her dress and covered herself. A shadow moved across the glad-wrap pane.

She unbolted the door and opened it. Midge jumped from the bottom rung of the ladder, got off balance because of his hip and stumbled about. He thought momentarily of saying he'd put the ladder there for a maintenance purpose. But he didn't bother. He was spying and didn't care that Moira knew it.

'You was feeding him. I knew you was up to something. I didn't know what. Maybe hitting the grog, with the door always locked on us. You was feeding him off yourself.'

'Yeah.'

'That's not right, is it?'

'It happened natural.'

'Sucking on you, that's all wrong. Zara know you doing this?'

'She dried up ages ago. Hardly been near him since she came home from hospital. I'm his mother now. Don't you look at me like that.'

'You're not his mother. You gone silly in the head? Shane'd know what to do. He'd say this is all arse-about and he'd know what to do.'

'When Shane gets home he'll have to say: Well, look what's happened here, that's nature.'

'And Zara don't know?'

'She can stay away from Mathew. She tried to hurt him once. '

Moira went inside and Midge followed. She picked the baby up. He was crying and wanting more milk and would have to wait.

'It's like he was an orphan. Ain't that right, Mathew? Your bad mother didn't want you but you got yourself a new one, didn't you?'

'He's no orphan. His mum's Zara.'

'His mum's me.'

'What you mean Zara tried to hurt him?'

'You go ask her.'

'Ah, nonsense.'

'You ask.'

'That's crazy-woman talk. No mother would do that.'

'Ask her.'

'If she was home I might just do that. Just to show you up.'

His breath became lodged deep in his lungs. He had to cough and wheeze to get air going. 'Let's not have cross words, Moira, please.'

She put the baby in the sling and ignored Midge.

'You should pay more attention to Zara, that's what you should be doing. I think she's in with a bad crowd. I don't trust this Brent lover boy. You listening? I went into town last night, followed her and him. They ended up at the old railway station, you know, the old passenger shed. Music going and bonfire blazing. Whole mob of them yelling and drinking and dancing. There was this girl stretched out. Not Zara, thank Christ not Zara. This girl was stretched right out and she was letting boys take turns on her. Laughing and calling them onto herself. I didn't know what to do, Moira. Kids doing that. If they was forcing her I would have helped her, I swear, I would of helped somehow. And then Zara stumbled out of the shed, arms around lover boy and I think they saw me and I got spooked and I took off. I sat up all night in the car and made this bracelet for her.'

He took a bracelet of tan and white stones from his pocket. 'Those little quartz stones round here. I got a bunch of them and

I put holes through them with my littlest drill bit, and I thread some string through them, and there you go.'

Moira looked at the bracelet and made a grunting, dismissive sound. 'You know what I think? I think the best thing she can do is take her things and go away and not come back. That's what she's always wanted. That's what she should do. Leave us alone and never set eyes on Mathew again.'

'Now Moira, come on. Zara's family.'

'She shouldn't be around you no more either.'

'Me?'

'You jealous of that Brent boy? You take a lot of interest in Zara. She lead you on?'

'No. What you saying?'

'Zara this. Zara that. You fancy your chances?'

'No.'

'Making bracelets.'

'That's to say sorry for following her.'

'Fancying your chances.'

'No. I got no children in the world. That's what Zara is to me, as close as I got to having my own. I just want to take care of her.'

Midge worried Shane would think it was his fault: he should have spotted Moira was being abnormal and intervened. Long before she started behaving disloyal. Way before being a little too friendly with Jim Tubbs. Something joyful like visiting Shane was now something he was dreading. Something he decided he best delay until he sorted matters out.

He would start with Zara. What was she was doing mixing with a bad crowd? You don't just have a child and forget it. If you had time for a bad crowd then you had time to do the right thing by your baby.

He drove to the supermarket and loitered outside the sliding doors. Zara wasn't there—he watched for half an hour and there was no sign of her. He drove to the railway shed. Not all the way up to it: he kept a distance. He used his binoculars to see if the party was still going. The bonfire was smouldering but there was no one.

He drove around Barleyville's backstreets. There were only a couple of dozen streets and he was looking for lover boy's ute. Just what he'd do if he saw it he had no idea. He had a speech he was refining to say to Zara. He acted it out as though she were sitting beside him. I hope no one sees me, he thought—a man talking to himself. He might get arrested.

Midge went back to the supermarket and parked on the opposite side of the road under a half-dead peppercorn with ivy growing through it. He would give her two hours, he decided. If she didn't appear he would go home and check there. If she wasn't there he would return to this spot and keep a vigil.

33

She arrived for work half an hour into the wait. The Romano Cartage truck dropped her at the entrance. The sun was in Midge's eyes but he could see it was lover boy's tattooed arm resting out the window. He saw Zara kiss him goodbye on the cheek. There was no return kiss. Just a jerk of the shoulders and nonchalant finger-combing of his hair as he put the truck in gear and spun the steering wheel with the heel of his hand. Zara waved and the ignorant bastard didn't wave back. If Zara waved to Midge like that he'd wave until his arm ached. He gave her ten minutes to get settled into her shift, then made his way over.

He came right out and said it rather than give her time to perform her act of treating him like a customer instead of family. 'There's an emergency. We need you at home.'

'What emergency?'

'I can't tell you here. When's your shift over?'

'Four hours. Tell me now.'

'No. I'll pick you up in four hours.'

'Brent's expecting me.'

'Too bad. Ring him.'

'What emergency?'

'I'll pick you up.'

'Shit.'

She pretended to be fiddling with the receipt cartridge in the register, getting the paper unjammed. He pretended to be counting change in his hand. 'See you in four hours.'

He turned and walked away before she could argue. He was pleased with himself, his assertive tone. He'd kept his nerve and spoken without losing breath and coughing. Even his hip felt solid enough to stride to the car without needing a hop. He put his chest out and nodded his satisfaction. The trick would be to keep that attitude going and ready for using again in four hours.

He sat in the car rehearsing the speech he wanted Zara to hear. About bad crowds being no good for her. About his fatherly affection and Moira and her orphan nonsense. It was easy talking about those things to himself but as the deadline loomed he wasn't so confident. He put his hand across his mouth so passers-by didn't see his one-man conversation.

He kept starting the wag and edging it forward to stay under tree shade. When all the shade went he drove in search of more but the sun was too high for shadow casting. It needed more angle to work with. He stood in the supermarket car park under a ledge and picked up the cool air when the rear doors opened for a shopper.

When Zara's shift was due to end he made sure she couldn't slip past him. He went in and strolled around the aisles, making her eye catch his eye.

As soon as she got in the wag she said, 'What's the emergency?'

'Let me start the car first. Let's get out of town a bit.'

'Fuck.' She slid down in the seat, shook her head and puffed her cheeks. 'Bet this is bullshit.'

At the silo turnoff she said it again, 'All bullshit,' and Midge worried she might jump out when he stopped at the give-way sign. He better start explaining himself. He pulled off the road through slushy wheel ruts and halted. Out the corner of his eye he saw Zara turn to face him, arms folded and head to one side.

He was shaking and unclipped his seatbelt. He took his puffer from the gutter of the dashboard, sucked in a long breath of it and held the breath.

Zara snatched the inhaler. 'You get a buzz from this?' She gave herself a puff and grimaced.

The rehearsed speech was gone from his memory. 'Oh, darling,' he said, and he reached across and hugged Zara. 'Oh, darling.'

'Fuck off. What the fuck you doing! You smell. Get off.'

She opened the door and fell out backwards, giving Midge a kick as she went.

'Zara, come back, please. I was trying to say something. I'm trying to help you.'

Her palm was stinging from landing on gravel. She blew on it and swore at Midge and started walking towards town. He scrambled from the wag, saying, 'Don't run off, Zara. Don't go.'

He caught up with her and she yelled for him to keep away.

'Come back, please.'

'Don't fucking come near me.'

'You got it wrong. I was just hugging.'

'Fuck off.'

'I won't touch you.'

'When Shane comes back I'll tell him.'

'I wasn't doing nothing. I wanted to give you this.'

He took the bracelet of stones from his trouser pocket.

'I made it last night. To say sorry for snooping.'

'Brent said he'll bash you next time.'

'If he said that, you shouldn't bother with him. Bash-talk shows he's got meanness in him.'

'I like him.'

'You don't love him or anything?'

'I like him. Yeah, I love him.'

'You don't love him.'

He shuffled behind her, being sure not to get too close. He noticed blood on her arm. A smudge of it above her elbow, poking from under her smock's sleeve. She hurdled mud to get to the road edge. Midge told her not to walk on the road in case of vehicles.

'What vehicles?' she said. There were no vehicles, only crows that flapped like black cloaks into flight as she neared.

Then there was a vehicle. A sheep truck, its cages and chains rattling. It swayed past with a blast of wheel-wind and left the reek of sheep shit in the air. Zara turned her head away and pinched her nose. She jumped back across the mud onto grass.

'What's that on your arm there?' said Midge.

Zara wiped the blood with her finger. 'Tattoo. I crashed out last night and one of the boys did it, fancies himself, like, an artist. He had a bottle of ink and a pen or something. I don't know what.'

'That's terrible. Doing that while you're sleeping.'

'Brent was too wasted to stop him. It's supposed to be a rose. Lots of girls have roses.'

'That could go septic. I'll put some metho on it when we get home. Come on home.'

She lifted her sleeve and the rough rose was more scab-looking than flower. Weeping watery blood.

Midge shook his head and said, 'Oh, Zara.' He made a clicking sound with his tongue. 'That's ugly and sore. Might need a bandage.'

He took a step nearer. She let him cradle her arm while he shook his head more.

'Try the bracelet on. It's them stones you pick up around here. I can shorten it if it's too big.'

'Looks all right.'

'Good.'

He stood back and admired his handiwork on her thin wrist.

'You know I've always cared for you, Zara. That's the feeling I have for you. Not any other kind of feeling. But that's a big feeling. That's the biggest. I want nothing bad happening to you because I think of you as my daughter. Shane's got Rory, and they're like kin. And I want you in that kin way. Because when I die no one would ever think of me again. It's like I never existed. But a daughter would have to think of me once and a while. Just a little snippet of remembering that I was here and I was alive once.'

She didn't laugh at him and that made him smile. That sealed it for him: her silence was a kind of acceptance of him.

Then she said, 'Okay, *Dad.*'

He wanted her say that again, and almost asked her to. He said it to himself: *Dad.*

'How much money you got?' she said.

'Eh?'

'How much money you got?'

'What? On me?'

'No. Altogether. How much?'

'Why?'

'Just tell me how much.'

'I don't know. Not much.'

'A few hundred?'

'Why?'

'Brent's getting a new house in town to rent for himself. He hasn't asked me to move in with him. But that's what I'm working on.'

'No, Zara.'

'The more money I can put in—'

'Oh, darling.'

'I'm not lumping him if I bring my own money.'

'It won't work out with this Brent fella.'

'Will so.'

'No, it won't.'

'How would you know?'

'You don't want that. We're family. You got family.'

'You mean Mathew?'

'Him. Me. All of us.'

'I should be around him more. He's probably forgotten who I am. But I'm his mother. You know what? When I'm working I think about that. How I'm his mother and stuff. I want to be that and want to make things right. I used to think a baby'd be shit.

It'd be shit and I'd be shit at it. But I'm good at things, Midge. You ask anyone at the supermarket. If I moved in with Brent and I had Mathew, it'd be perfect. Brent and me and my baby, home together. Like normal people. I wouldn't work so much.'

'No. You're better off with us. You can't think of taking him away from Moira. Let's let things carry on as they are. Just until Shane gets back and he can sort out Moira.'

'What you mean, sort out Moira? I want Mathew with me in a new house. I got to work on Brent. He'll like the idea if he sees it can work. He gets good pay.'

She was jigging on the spot, happy and grinning at the sky as if it was sending down encouragement. Midge wished she wouldn't look at it that way, like faith lived there and all you did was make a wish and smile.

'Come down to earth,' he said.

She was too full of belief to obey. He didn't have the heart to meddle with her dreaming. For once she looked her age, not a woman but a girl. He was in awe of her innocence. How do you stop innocence? He felt he should but it was too big for a man to stop, and beyond reasoning with. He backed away and let her be in that state. It made her so beautiful he had to look down, ashamed to be old and ugly in such a presence. A cloud passed across the ground and there was a dimming, then a return to bright mud and green glimmers in among the sticks of grass.

Zara took a skip towards him and grabbed the sleeve of his shirt to make him follow her.

'Come on. Let's go and see Mathew. Come on. Don't make a face. Come on. Drive. Let's go.'

34

You had to hand it to Rory, thought Moira. He hated that recorder but he hated other things more. Being sent to a place for simpletons, for one. It was about time she told him the threat was just a bluff. She should withdraw the other bluff too: about her going to school for the parents-and-teachers session.

The boy sat in the caravan and played and played. He'd changed as a young man in such a short time. Developed, gone ahead. Not so wild in her opinion: not so foul-mouthed and the misfit of Tree Palace, running off lighting fires and belligerent. As though he had a purpose in life. He wasn't a mother's boy, he was a father's. Or as good as that: a Shane's.

She'd have gone to him and given a kiss in affection, but there was no point in disturbing the peaceful order, having him squirm and wriggle away. She put Mathew down in the kitchen in his little bed and went into the caravan. 'Good boy. Sounds nice. What is it you're playing?'

'It's called "Mull of Kintyre".'

'Whatever it is, it sounds lovely.'

It sounded terrible but he blinked at her, her smiling face, and was fooled into missing the lie. She lifted her hands in soft applause. She gave him his reward, saying, 'You're off the hook, honey.'

He asked her twice, double-checking: 'No place for mentals?'

'No, honey. You're off the hook.'

'No parents–teachers?'

'Off the hook.'

'Promise?

'Cross my heart.'

He said he'd play her the tune again. She wanted to say no. Instead she said, 'That'd be nice.'

He played and every time he made a mistake he said, 'No, wait. Hold it,' and started again. The wag arrived after six mistakes and restartings. Moira used the moment to say, 'That's real good, Rory. Play it for Midge.'

She saw Zara was with Midge. The girl was to her like a person you avoided due to a falling-out: ignoring she existed, not exchanging looks, but aware of her every movement. Zara called to her. Moira had got all the way to the house and was almost inside and able to close the door.

'How'd Mathew find the boots?'

Moira kept quiet and swept her foot across the door mat as if leaves and twigs had gathered.

'The wind-up boots. Did you show him?'

'He's just a baby.'

'You didn't show him?'

'He didn't like it.'

Zara's shoulders gave a slump of disappointment. She perked up again on remembering she had a present for Moira. She reached into her bag. 'Got some smokes for you. PJs are on special this week, so I got you three packs.'

'I don't want them. I've given up.'

The girl's shoulders slumped again and she reached into her bag. 'I been putting money away and here's twenty bucks to get him something. A warm top or something.'

'He's catered for.'

'Forty bucks, then? I'll buy him something. What you reckon I should get?'

'There's nothing he needs.'

'Must be something.'

'I don't think so.'

'Something.'

Midge said, 'Maybe just let it be, Zara.'

She put the money back in her bag. 'Can I see him?'

Moira ignored the question.

'Can I have a peep in?'

'No.'

'I think that's fair enough,' said Midge. 'A peep in.'

'I'll bring him out,' Moira said.

'I want to pick him up, myself.'

'I said I'll bring him out.'

'I got to pick him up sooner or later. I know I been a bad mother. But I been working and earning money. And when I go out at night it's more than for going out at night. I got this guy Brent and I'm getting closer and closer to him. So he'll want me to move in with him. Me and Mathew'll have a real home.'

Moira had her back to Zara and kept it that way. 'You and Mathew?'

'Brent knows I got a baby. We don't talk about it. But he knows.'

The bloom was gone now from Moira's cheeks. She'd chewed the lipstick off her bottom lips. Her eyes were clenched so narrow the skin was puckered around them. 'He's not yours.'

'He is so.'

The chewed bottom lip was bent down, baring her teeth. Moira had a fist raised as though ready to throw a punch. Zara stepped back quickly and trod on Midge and they made a clumsy dance of standing.

'Steady on, Moira,' he said. 'She's got a right.'

'Yeah, I got a right. I want to be in a real home and take care of my baby. I got a right.'

Moira raised her fist again. It was clear to her what side Midge was on, him standing with an arm on Zara's shoulder and stepping in front of the girl like an amateur policeman. He was up to something, she thought. He had no poker face for being cunning, not to his trant tribe. The cunning always came mixed with guilt and his eyes went wide and the skin on his chin twitched. It was twitching now. He, the man who hated cross words, was not giving way for once. 'Let her inside,' he was saying. 'She needs to get some metho for her arm. She had a nice tattoo done. A nice rose on her arm. You got to dab these things with metho, don't you, Zara? Come on, in we go. Out of the way, please, Moira. In we go, we got dabbing to do.'

He brushed past Moira and had Zara by the arm. 'Got to dab these things.'

Instead of going straight to where the metho was kept, he said, 'Now, Moira, I want you to stand aside, if you don't mind. Come on, let Zara have a pick up of the little fella. Come on, please.' He waved for Zara to slip around behind him and go to Mathew. Moira pushed Midge but he wasn't about to move easily. 'Fair go. The girl can pick up her own son, for Christ sake.'

She gave him another push, a harder one, and he almost lost his balance but was wild enough at her to stay up and put his arms in front of himself. He didn't want to push her in return. He leant against her instead, kept her from reaching out and grabbing Zara. The girl was peering at Mathew where he was lying in his little bed. She put her fingertips on his face and felt how spongy to the touch the skin was. She leant and breathed the pure and impure smells of baby breath and bowels. She said, 'Look at you. You came out of me.' She touched her stomach. 'You used be in here.'

Moira shouted, 'Get away from him,' white spit flecking her lip.

'She's his mother. You can't stop her having a pick up.'

'What she going to do, kill him? That's what she tried to do in the hospital. Don't let her touch him, Midge.'

Then Mathew hiccupped into crying. Zara lifted him and put his body against hers, his chin over her shoulder. He cried and a splash of pale vomit came with the cry. Moira shoved Midge hard enough that he held his hands in front of his face and expected to be knocked over. She wasn't interested in him, though. Zara was holding Mathew at arm's length, puke dripping from his mouth. 'Sorry,' she was saying. 'What'd I do wrong? Sorry, baby.' She was so worried that she'd taken the wrong kind of hold, she didn't feel Moira grab the baby from her. She kept her arms outstretched and her hands cupped as if he was still there.

'Get away from him. You go live with your boyfriend. No way you're taking this child.'

More vomit came out and Moira hushed Mathew with gentle patting and whispers. 'I fed you too much before, didn't I, boy.'

Midge said to her, 'What was all that *tried to kill him* talk?'

There was no reply.

'Ah, you really have gone bloody mad, Moira.'

Zara was looking about for something to wipe her shoulder with. She tore off a strip of paper towel. Midge tore off a strip too and helped clean her neck. 'What was all that about you trying to kill him, Zara? What's all that about? She's got so attached to the little fella she reckons he's hers. Even feeds like she is. You know, off herself, you know.'

'Off herself?'

'Yeah, you know, off her, you know.' He touched his chest and made a cradling motion with his arms. 'She's got milk there.'

Moira gave a satisfied smile.

'I seen it,' Midge said, in case the girl thought he'd gone loopy himself.

Her face was twisted in a sneer of disbelief. Her mind felt so bent out of shape she was dizzy and thought she too might vomit. Was this Moira's baby all along? No, this was not Moira's. It was hers. Here came the empty sensation again. No matter how much she shook her arms she couldn't shake it away.

'I'm sorry,' she said. Midge thought she was speaking to

264

him but she pushed past his comforting hand and said to Moira, 'I'm so sorry. Can't I try and be his mother again? Can't I do that? Please.'

'Too late.'

'Please.'

'You'll say sorry today, and tomorrow you'll try killing him again.'

'No.'

'Decide you got better things to do than be bothered with a baby.'

'Please.'

'You try and take him away and I'll to go the police and tell them what you did in that hospital.'

'I won't have you talking to Zara like that,' Midge said. 'Accusing her of horrible things.'

'You tell him—go on, tell him.'

'You didn't do nothing like she's saying, did you, Zara?'

The girl didn't answer.

'Did you?'

Just a sorrowful bow of the head and a silence.

'I don't believe you ever would do that. What I believe is, you got Moira convincing you of things 'cause it suits her to have Mathew to herself.'

Zara stumbled outside and Moira told Midge to get out as well. She bolted the door and ignored him standing outside, his finger pointing at her through the window. He was stamping his foot and accusing her of being double-banger disloyal. First to Shane by flirting with Tubbsy, and now to Zara by even suggesting a trant would go to police about family. Trants go to police *never*, full stop, let alone about family.

'Never heard the like,' he said, shaking his head and walking in stamping circles around the L-shape. 'It just don't happen. Trants don't go crazy neither, but you've gone crazy. I want to get drunk. Rory, shut up with that bloody recorder. Shut up and see if there's any bourbon under my bed, under the sleeping blanket, should be a bottle. Zara, I'll disinfect your tattoo with it too. Darling, can I come in?'

No. She told him to stay out and close the tent flap and let her be alone. He could hear her crying.

35

That was a victory, Moira decided. There were no secrets now between her and Zara and Midge. The secrets were in the open and Zara was shamed. It should settle the matter. Let's see the girl try it again, come in the house to touch Mathew, tricking her about metho.

Yet Midge was right about that disloyalty business. She would never go to police. It was just a thing you say. She wished she hadn't opened her mouth. Now she had the label of crazy, which put you lower than low. Worse than not reading or writing. Someone you don't trust. Someone suspicious.

If she'd have just let Zara hold the baby and kept close watch. She should go and say that, but she was too proud. The magic in her must have a bad side. Maybe the bad side of her family was affecting her. Trants are on the outside of everything. Now she was on the outside of them, her own people. She worried the bloom in her was fading. She looked in Shane's mirror and her face was less shiny and her eyes were normal-dull instead of glinting. Her breasts hadn't felt as full today. There was still milk in them but not the normal bursting amount.

The thing to do was pretend nothing had happened, there had been no flare-up. It wasn't dinner time yet but she unbolted the door and leant out and called to Midge in a cheery voice, 'You want a can of stockpot tonight or spaghetti?'

Rory called out, 'Stockpot.'

'Didn't ask you.'

'Sorry.' The boy was in the caravan and his sorry had a lazy, singsong lilt to it, as if he was lying down. He must have had a tipple from Midge's bourbon bottle.

Midge had drunk plenty and wasn't communicating. Usually when he drank neat spirits his insides turned watery and he had to sit on the toilet till he sobered up. He seldom drank himself drunk and when he did he was the sentimental kind of drunk, hugging people, even men, kissing them on the cheek and apologising with a belch. He was in a different state at the moment. He'd put on his racing helmet and was riding an imaginary horse to the finishing post. Whipping the air and hissing the horse on.

He grumbled to Moira that he didn't want to think about dinner. Stockpot, spaghetti, it was all rubbish to him. She could go feed Mathew off her titties and let everyone else starve. 'I won't eat food from a trant with no fucking loyalty. If I want food I'll drive to town.' He looked at the tree where the chandelier had hung and he pointed. 'That's what that tree needs, another chandelier. I'll fucking well find one. Pinch one somewhere. Got to be chandeliers worth pinching in Barleyville.'

She was frightened for him, stumbling about and angry. The

kind of Midge that Midge really wasn't. If he tripped he might do damage to himself and she'd be more than on the outer then. She'd be to blame for driving him to the bottle. She wanted to be the Moira she was once in his eyes. The Moira you respected and didn't swear in front of, as he was swearing now, or ever doubt was on your side. The way to do it was say they'd visit Shane. That'd calm Midge and start to win his trust back.

Moira put Mathew on the big bed to sleep and went to the chandelier tree. She stood beside Midge but he moved away from her. 'I want to visit Shane,' she said. 'I miss my Shane. Let's visit him. What's tomorrow? Sunday? Sunday's a visitor day.'

He grunted and shook his head. He farted and there was a wet sound to it.

'I think you might have done something in your pants,' she said.

His lips were puckered in sulky resentment of her. The chandelier tree was alive with breeze and leaf-chatter. He sought his companionship there and not with her. He didn't speak. Keeping his head tilted back to regard the tree made him dizzy but he fought against it for the sake of ignoring Moira.

'You better take your pants off and I'll wash them. Come on. Have a shower and I'll do the on-off for you. Come on. Or else you'll stink and your pants'll stick to you.'

'Let 'em stick.'

'You want to visit Shane.'

'Course I do.'

'Well, if I wash your pants you'll have clean pants for the visit. Come on, stop drinking or else you'll be hungover for days. I know you. You'll be laying about and groaning. In no shape to drive the wag and visit.'

She went to him and tugged on his collar. He pulled away and kept puckering and not looking at her. Then he nodded as if the tree had said something and he agreed with what was said. He farted again and that too had a wet sound to it. He said 'whoops' to the tree and shuffled his way to the toilet, keeping his legs tight together.

He was in the toilet for ages and when he emerged his face was grey and sweating. His belt was undone and he held his pants up and hobbled to the shower. There he took off his pants and threw them out for Moira to deal with. She did on-off duty until he yelled that he was done. She hosed his pants and soaked them in a bucket. Midge's insides were completely emptied out and his head was fog-tired from drink. He still wasn't speaking to Moira, though not for the sake of being rude to her so much as from the fogging spreading to his tongue.

He got into bed with his damp towel around him, his back not dry. It was late afternoon and the daylight was not yet dimming but he was asleep in seconds, snoring louder than his normal loud. Rory tried closing his mouth by tapping his jaw shut. It flopped open straight away. A piece of masking tape might work, attaching the jaw to the cheekbone. Moira said, Rory, we're not taping up faces. Let him breathe and snore. Put toilet paper in your ears or go for a wander.

Midge didn't wake when Zara's phone rang and she took off

for the crossroads in her going-out clothes and red bag, her shoes in her fingers. Moira watched her and said to herself, *Call to her. Call to her.* She said to Mathew, 'I should call her in. I should show her the proper baby grip to lift you and hold you, keeping that wee neck of yours from bending.' That would build a little bridge between them, she thought.

She couldn't bring herself to do it. Zara was the crazy one. The girl couldn't begin to feed a child, let alone set up house.

Rain was striding this way and that along the horizon, bendy stilts of it which the wind blew over. Back and forth went the showers, spraying the house and making the tank trickle with fresh filling. Perhaps the rain will make Zara turn around, Moira thought. It didn't.

Dusk arrived darker than usual. No stars or moon standing by. Clouds kept tearing apart and drifting further apart. They looked soft that way, and fleeting. Then they joined back together and darkened at the centre. Rain fell hard and at no angle. Under the porch the lanterns rocked on their hooks, flames spluttering. Inside the house the flames stood straight and glowed.

Rory sat and ate and was quiet, for Rory. He had definitely taken a swig too many. You could see it in the high colour of his face. Moira told him that she didn't blame him, she blamed Midge. She didn't want an argument with the boy. He was her only friend other than Mathew at the moment. It was better to fuss over him and have him eat and off to bed. She gave him a brief talking-to about swigging from adult bottles. 'You feeling sick?'

He shook his head.

He was feeling sick. His appetite was flagging; he was staring down at the table.

'Let's get you into bed.'

The boy said he was fine but let himself be led in Moira's arms. They dashed across the L-shape in the dying rain. The clouds had opened and there was a flash of sun which caught on the blue caravan. It turned them blue and they laughed at their skin.

36

Moira scrubbed Midge's pants in detergent, hosed them until they smelled better and hung them on the line. The legs moved back and forth in the airstream like empty walking. She pulled down on the cuffs to straighten out the creases and as she did she flinched at the sudden commotion of Limpy barking. He scrambled from under the house towards the dirt road. This must be Zara in her boyfriend's car. Were they coming to lay out the plans for taking Mathew? She was not prepared for this, had no plans of her own for this confrontation.

It was not Zara. It was a green one-tonner, battered and squeaky. Jim Tubbs's truck. You could hear his smithy tools clanging in the back. See the pointy, stumpy arm of an anvil strapped to the tray. His physical bulk was such that he took up half the cab; his huge head went right to the roof. He drove past the wag and the truck slid sideways in the slush. Stopped side-on as if about to turn around, then backed up to get the rear wheels onto firmer ground. He parked there and began the process of getting out, putting both hands on the door frame and heaving himself to his feet. He stretched, hands on hips, surveying the surroundings, reached into the tray and laid a cellophane wrap full of flowers across his arms. He crabbed his way across the slippery ground with Limpy taking lunges at his heels.

Moira thought of hiding behind the house. She would have if Mathew wasn't inside by himself. Flowers? If Midge was awake he'd be sneering at her: *Flowers!* Tubbsy caught sight of her and waved. She held up her hand but didn't wave.

He had a white short-sleeved shirt on, though his shoulders had been rained on and the material made transparent. You could see his shoulder hairs through it as he got closer to the porch. He'd recently shaved, going by the aftershave smell blowing off him.

'Gidday, Moira,' he said. 'I was out this way and thought it's time I dropped in.'

He looked about. 'No Midge?'

'He's resting.'

'Better be quiet, then.' His big hands gripped the flowers and squashed the cellophane. 'Thought I'd buy these for you. Brighten up the place.'

They were irises, their purple petals wilt-brown at the edges.

She took them and made sure not to admire them too much, though they were a pretty sight. 'Ta.'

'No worries.' He blinked and nodded, clearly expecting an invitation inside. He kept looking down at her breast region. He tried to conceal that he was looking by scratching his forehead, but Moira saw and folded her arms.

274

'How things going with Shane away?' he said, 'You coping good? Nothing you need?'

'All's going good, thanks, Tubbsy.'

He snapped his fingers. 'Tell you what I got in the truck. Wait there, I'll bring it.'

He went to the truck, almost falling backwards in the mud. He had his arms out tightrope-style for balance. He returned with a bottle. 'Made this myself. My little homemade still. It's a cross between a bourbon taste and I don't know what. She's got a fair kick.'

Moira realised he was not entirely sober. Steady enough on his feet but his speech was slurred. He looked at the sky and shook his head. 'Might rain again. How about we get inside and have a shot of this.'

'I got things to do, and I don't drink at the moment.'

'Ah, come on.'

'If you want a drinking partner I'll wake Midge up.'

'Nah, not Midge. I'd rather drink with you.'

'No, Tubbsy, can't.'

'After I bought those nice flowers and everything.'

'I'll wake Midge.'

'All right, then, I'll go.'

'Okay.'

He didn't move. 'You don't need nothing?'

'No, thanks.'

'Come on. One drink.'

'No.'

He pulled the cork from the bottle, drank and puffed his

cheeks in appreciation. 'Oh, that is nice.' He walked under the porch and sat on the sofa, cradling the bottle. 'Come on, sit down with your old mate Tubbsy.'

'I don't feel like sitting.'

'Come on.'

He drank from the bottle. He held it towards her.

She shook her head. 'I said I'm not interested.'

He swore under his breath.

'You have to mind your language around here.'

'That's right, you give yourself airs. I forgot.'

'It's just manners, that's all.'

'Get off your high horse, Moira. Fucking hell—you're a trant, not a fucking schoolmarm.'

'If that's the way you feel then leave now. Go on.'

'You don't mean that.'

'Leave or I'll get Midge.'

Tubbsy laughed. 'Midge? Now I'm frightened.'

'I'm serious. Leave. Come back one day when Shane's home and you're not drunk.'

He stared at her. 'What was all that about in town?'

'I don't know what you mean.'

'You were pleased to see me then. All nice and chatty, all lit up in the face. All nice and wet down your front too. You were quite something.'

She folded her arms tighter.

'Now all I get is a brush-off. Confuses a man, that does. Makes him confused and pissed off.'

'I don't know what you're talking about.'

'Oh, Moira, I got eyes. You know what I'm talking about. You're a fine-looking woman. You're still lit-up enough to suit me. I always fancied you. Always regretted the day I introduced you to Shane. Should have gone after you myself. I was being catered for in that department at the time. I'm not catered for now. And you're not catered for at the moment neither. Come on, have a drink. Relax.'

'No. Get out of here.'

She called out to Midge, and Tubbsy told her to shut up. He put his finger to his lips and whispered, 'We don't want no company, you and me. Have a drink. Jesus, you're difficult.'

She could hear the baby starting his hiccup-tears. She took a stride towards the house. Tubbsy reached out and just missed grabbing her arm. She got through the door and tried closing it and sliding the bolt but he pushed the door open before the bolt could catch.

'Get out,' she yelled.

He thumped the bottle on the kitchen table and the weight of the blow shuddered the floor and made Limpy bark in a lower, more curdling register. The house was dusk-dim inside. Two lamps were going and Tubbsy waved for Moira to step nearer to them so he could see her better.

'Come on, just light up for me again like you did in town. Just light up for me and let me have a feel of you.'

Moira shouted for him to get out.

'Just a feel. Shane'll never know.'

He lifted her dress with his left hand. She threw a punch and it skimmed his face but he didn't flinch. He held his forearm up and deflected another punch, shoved her and held her against the wall. She bit his arm and scratched at his eyes but he didn't care. He got his right hand down into her dress and onto her breast. She slid along the wall to stop him. She crossed her legs but his fingers started digging upwards past her underpants. It hurt and she squeezed her legs together against his hand and he pushed up harder.

Of a sudden he pulled his hand away and rolled across the floor swearing, both his hands clutching his thigh and his arse. Rory was standing there bouncing on his toes and panting, terrified, but not letting go of his throwing knives. He had one in each hand and no way was he letting go. He had them held up ready to stick into Tubbsy again.

Tubbsy rolled on his back from side to side and groaned. The only words he managed were 'Jesus' and 'fuck'. He slid closer to the lamp glow to inspect himself. He felt his backside. There was a whimper of panic when he saw blood starting to leak through his fingers. The floor was getting smeared with it as he rolled in his own bleeding. He called Rory a 'fucking little shit' and kept wiping the blood with his fingers and looking at it, not believing it was his. 'Look at that. Just look at that.'

He got to his feet, holding his backside with the blood dripping on the floor. His jeans were turning dark and wet. One stab mark at the top of his thigh had so torn the denim and his skin that a bubble of muscle had popped through. He walked, crouched over, watching his blood drip. He leant on the table and picked up his bottle and threw it, aiming at Rory, though it missed and smashed against the wall.

Moira took a swing at the back of Tubbsy's head, yelling for him to get out of her house. His head was hard and hurt her knuckles but she hit him anyway. *Pig. Fat, ugly pig.*

Rory was ready to stab him again but Moira stopped him in case the mongrel died. Tubbsy muttered that he was not about to die. Not this way, he wasn't. Not some shit of a kid doing this to him. He was going to get fixed up. And when he'd got fixed up he'd make every one of them pay. He'd make Rory pay most of all. Christ yes, that's exactly what he'd do.

He lurched towards the door and slipped on his blood. Midge was coming through the door, only his towel around him. Tubbsy pushed him aside and Midge fell down, trying to stop the towel from splaying.

'Stop bouncing, Rory,' Moira said. 'You can stop bouncing now. Good boy. Stop bouncing.'

She took the knives out of his hands, slowly. He had a fierce grip on them, too shocked by what had happened to let go. But he let go and Moira threw them on the floor. There was blood on his fingers. She thought it must be Tubbsy's blood and it disgusted her that that man's blood should be on her son. It wasn't his—it was Rory's. His hands had slid down the blade with the thrusting and cut him. Not badly, but enough to see the cuts opening and closing when she wiggled his fingertips. She told him to cup his hands while she figured out the right treatment.

'What's going on?' Midge said. He was still drunk, he was blinking and rubbing his eyes.

'Not now. I'll tell you later,' Moira replied.

A wash with metho and water for hygiene and a couple of

band-aids per cut should work. She made Rory sit down and think how brave he was, saving her from that pig of a man. If he could do that to such a monster then the sting of metho was nothing. He could laugh away metho pain and show his bravery was no one-off, rather in his nature.

37

Rory grimaced without complaining. He certainly did not cry. He kept saying to Moira, 'I don't feel nothing.' She called him her hero. She joked about him having had swigs from Midge's bottle—that probably had helped him: Dutch courage. He smiled. There were only two band-aids in the house and they went on the shallowest cut. The two deeper cuts required something more bandage-like. She took one of her sanitary pads and cut out squares.

Rory didn't like that—a women's thing they put between their legs—but he trusted Moira knew what she was doing. She pressed a square gently into place over each cut and snipped masking tape into strips with scissors. She bound the squares with the strips just tight enough so they wouldn't slip off if he gripped something.

Midge said sorry over and over, ashamed of being no hero himself. 'Drunk on duty,' he called it. 'Sober, I would have dealt with the situation. Promise you. My oath.'

Moira let him ramble on. She said, 'If you want to be useful then take those irises and chuck 'em down the dunny. And stop

Limpy licking the blood.' The dog was poking his nose in the door and sniffing and licking the red trail Tubbsy left. 'Making me sick the dog licking that fat pig's blood.'

Midge yelled at him and clapped his hands but Limpy wasn't scared away. There was blood under the porch and Limpy licked that too. No amount of dirt kicked over it worked. Midge scooped up thick mud and threw that on. That didn't work either and the bending down and the sight of the blood, even blood gone black with nightfall, made him throw up.

Of their worries payback was the first concern. Tubbsy had made a threat, especially to Rory, and he was the type to go through with it. Would police listen to Moira? They'd say trants trying to rape trants don't count as criminal. Shane's the man they needed to speak to. Shane would sum this up, cunning as cunning gets.

If Midge was too crook to drive tomorrow they'd have to wait till Monday and gamble on Tubbsy being too crook as well. Too many holes in him to start dishing out payback.

Morning worked like medicine on Midge. A cleansing nip to the air and utter stillness in the trees, no noise of leaves or grass. No bird racket, just the drip of wet silence. Steam rose out of that shallow scoop they called the dam as if the very water was standing up and wading in itself. His head hurt with each throb of his pulse but the peace and chilliness of the dawn eased his nausea and his fretting. You could almost be optimistic when the earth was so at rest and innocent. If it was like this all the time you'd be tempted to think people would follow suit and be quieter and decent, Tubbsy included.

He took a walk to breathe the wholesomeness in. The chill made him cough but he didn't mind. In his imagination he was coughing up last night and replacing it with fresh morning. He'd be ready to drive in an hour or so if this medicine kept working.

Which was fine by Moira. All that 'tacked on last' nonsense about Shane's letter was behind her. Not behind her completely but behind her for now. There'd be time to bitch about it when Shane was released and life was back to normal. She had Mathew to arrange for the car trip. She fed him off herself—there was milk enough still in her, but she was definitely not producing the same amount as before. She could see in the mirror her breasts had sagged and flattened. Mathew was powerful in his sucking and wore an impatient frown which she thought would bring more milk down. It didn't. She closed her eyes and begged her body. *You gave the miracle, please don't take it from me.*

She forced herself to eat a big breakfast—bread and biscuits. She drank cordial and held her bladder to bursting in case that forced more fluids into her milk system. All it did was hurt and made no difference. Whatever was going on in her she needed a back-up plan. If she dried up on the road how could she mix formula in any healthy way? She worried that panicking might bring on drying-up.

She wanted to look attractive for Shane. She put on her new dress and applied make-up in the Zara fashion—thick and shiny, blue around the eyes, silvery lipstick. It would half melt off by the time they reached the prison. She put her face kit in a bag for touch-ups. Make-up was as close as she could get to having that bloom back. One day she'd buy classy shoes to match the dress. For now she went into the tent and tried on Zara's meagre collection. She chose a pair more string than shoe. High heels that gave her trouble balancing.

Rory was so excited he kept forgetting about his hands. He was visiting Shane and having a couple of days off school and he couldn't help but clench his fingers and punch the air, which made his wounds sting. He had no fear of reprisals from Tubbsy. Any mention of Tubbsy made him jut out his jaw and bounce. 'I'll stick him again,' he said.

Moira told him he'd do no such thing. 'Remember Shane's rule about violence. It gets you extra jail time.'

That made Rory sit down, confused. One minute he was a hero for saving Moira. Next he was told not to use violence. What else would work on Tubbsy? Playing the recorder?

They left a note for Zara. Midge wrote it out in his neatest printing. It said they'd be gone a day or so and she should eat what food was in the house and look after herself and not do anything silly.

'Put my name up the top,' Moira said, tapping the page with her finger. 'Say I said to eat well and to look after herself.'

That was a start. She had to force the feeling but she was building a bridge. Like a wrong she had to right: be a mother to her daughter. 'That make sense to you?' she whispered to Mathew. 'Making things right. You want that, don't you?'

They drove east into the white sun and the mist. Moira covered herself with a blanket and massaged her breasts to give the milk a help along.

38

The journey took four hours but it was trouble-free. Only one stop for petrol and to fill the radiator. Moira fed Mathew without going dry. Rory stole a bar of chocolate from a roadhouse. Moira told him not to steal on this trip but he did and got away with it. He said sorry and shared half.

The prison was not what they expected—no vast stone walls like a castle. More a fancy motel with gardens clipped and colourful. A pastel tinge to the paintwork and sliding-door entrance of glimmering glass. There was razor wire on the mesh fences and that made it a prison, but the sign had a painterly flourish—Marnaroo written in red with gold outlining on the lettering. It didn't even say prison: it said 'correction centre'. Moira muttered, 'Holiday, all right. Shane wasn't joking.'

They knew they were in a jail once they tried to get in. They needed one hundred points of identification. Not Rory, he was fine, clearly a minor just to look at him. Midge had his driver's licence and other bits and pieces from his wallet and that gave him passage. Moira had no proof of herself expect her Medicare card. The officer stood behind a glass window and said, 'Didn't you get a letter from the department? It tells you: one hundred points.'

'We got a letter,' Midge said. 'But we forgot about the points.'

'I can't get in?' Moira asked.

No, said the officer, a short man in a blue uniform with a nicotine stain in the centre of his grey moustache.

Moira asked him for some understanding. She put her cunning hat on and talked about the long distance they'd travelled, with a baby in tow and a car that was old and uncomfortable.

The officer said he'd allow twenty-five points for the Medicare card. But that still left seventy-five points. He said he was sorry and asked her to step out of the line because other people were waiting. She did and then stepped back in, crying and confessing she had no hope of getting seventy-five points. 'I don't have a licence, sir. Never have. I can't read, can't write, sir. Sir, I just want to see my Shane and you're saying I can't.'

Mathew cried. She jiggled him in her arms and accused the officer of upsetting him. 'We had family die in wars for this country and you're saying I don't have enough points.'

'How about a birth certificate?' said the officer.

'I don't have one of those on me. Lost it years ago.'

People were staring at her. Midge and Rory had moved away, embarrassed, but Moira wouldn't be quiet. 'I don't amount to nothing more than points? I don't think I want to live no longer. Might just go jump under a truck if that's all I am to you. Please, sir, please let me see my Shane.'

Two guards came up behind her to shepherd her out of the

place but the officer behind the glass said hold it a minute. He said he'd call a supervisor. The guards backed off and Moira sniffled and said, 'Thank you, sir,' meekly.

There were rows of plastic chairs along the walls. She sat rocking Mathew and signalled with her eyebrows for Rory to sit beside her and put his arm around her shoulder. She signalled for Midge to sit on the other side of her and act worried for her health. 'You got that asthma thing. Give it to me, quick,' she whispered.

He took his puffer from his pocket and she snatched it from him and sucked on it as if struggling for breath. 'I said, act worried.'

'I am,' Midge whispered.

'Do more.'

He got into the swing. 'She's going to have a turn. Oh, Jesus, this is bad. Don't pass out, Moira. Oh, Jesus.'

A supervisor arrived behind the glass booth. Tall and dark-bearded, in a black suit instead of a uniform. He and the officer leant close together and spoke, keeping their eyes on Moira.

The supervisor came out of the booth and crouched in front of her. He said he had sympathy for her situation but they had rules about identity and rules were rules.

That sent Moira into a howling performance. She threw her head back and slid off the seat onto the floor, heaving as if choking.

Midge slid down with her. 'Don't have a turn, Moira.'

The supervisor said he was going to call an ambulance. Moira screamed—no, she wanted to be left to die.

This went on for ten minutes, the supervisor helping lift Moira onto the seat and telling a guard to fetch a glass of water. Moira decided it was time to go silent and quiver. She'd done her best but her antics hadn't worked. She sobbed genuinely at the failure.

Then the supervisor walked off for a moment, spoke on his mobile phone and came back and crouched again. He said he had powers of discretion in such matters. He was prepared to allow her half an hour with Shane on the condition they not touch except on greeting and departure. Just this once.

Moira almost kissed him. She gripped his arm in genuine gratitude. He said they could proceed to the search area.

39

When they finally got into the visiting room it wasn't what they expected. The place was full of people—prisoners in green track-suits, women sitting with them at plastic tables. Kids running around as if in a playground, dirty-faced from chocolate. There were two TVs with cartoons showing. No privacy, no nook where you could have an intimate talk.

They didn't recognise Shane at first. When a guard let him in the door he was so spruced-up in crisp-clean greens, hair short and combed tidy, his goatee gone and his face and physique fuller in shape, they had to look twice. Moira made Midge hold the baby and she ran up and held Shane tight. They kissed on the lips. Shane didn't want to stop and kissed her again and kept hugging her until a guard said enough. Midge and Rory got hugs. 'Been in the wars,' he said to Rory, pointing to the boy's bandages.

'Nah. Sort of,' Rory said.

'Bad?'

'Few cuts. Nothing much.'

Mathew got a rub on the forehead from Shane. They found a free table and they sat there and stared at each other.

'Everything all right?' Shane asked.

Yeah, fine, they nodded.

'All good with you?' Moira asked.

'All good. Look at me, I put on some weight. I've made mates in here. We got all sorts. Business people. Professional people. See the lawn out there?' He pointed through the window-wall beside them. 'I mowed that. And the bloke who helped me, he's a million-aire. We got all sorts in here.'

'Good for you,' Moira said. She couldn't tone down her sarcasm.

'What's that mean?' said Shane.

'Glad you're enjoying yourself.'

'Did I say that?'

'Good as.'

'I'm trying to make the most of it. I'm not free. I can't walk out the bloody door. I go mental thinking about it.'

'Sorry.'

'What took you so long coming to visit? I been here two months. You didn't get my letter?'

'We got it,' said Midge.

'I kept saying to myself, Why don't they visit?'

'No reason,' said Moira. 'Except, well, you didn't sound like you was missing me.'

Shane leant back, his bottom lip flopped down. 'What?'

'I mean, you tacked me on at the bottom and didn't say you missed me or sign off with *Love, Shane*.'

'Christ, Moira.'

'I'm just saying.'

'Of course I missed you. Christ.'

'You did?'

'Yes.'

'Really?'

She reached across the table and took his hands in her hands and kissed them. A guard looked and turned a blind eye.

'I'm no letter writer. You don't get mushy in letters.'

Moira shook her head: of course you don't get mushy in letters. 'Forget I said it.'

'Don't think I'm pissing away my days in here. Sorry, Moira.'

She nodded acceptance of the apology.

He lowered his voice and waved her to come closer. Midge and Rory too.

'Me, I'm making contacts here. One bloke, he's from South Australia and he pinches sheep and cattle. He says there's abandoned homesteads as far as the eye can see. He says there's more antique dealers in Adelaide than dog turds in the street. A whole new territory opening up for us.'

Midge rubbed his hands together and Rory went to do the same but it hurt him.

'And I tell you this. I'm moving up from just being a trant. One bloke here used to be a lawyer. He tells me about a law called adverse possession. Moira, this'll be of interest to you. This is a law that works in our favour.'

Midge lifted his head and considered. 'Adverse. Adverse. I thought that word means bad things.'

'No, no, no. Listen to me. This law says if there's a property and

291

this property has what's called a dormant title—if no one's lived there for a really long time because they died or something, and no one inherited it or cared about it and no rates have been paid and someone like us moves in and lives there and starts paying rates—then you know what?'

They all shook their heads.

'That property becomes ours after fifteen years. That's the law. It's like something for nothing. You own a property without buying it. Except a few rates. And I don't reckon the rates on our place would be more than a tank of fucking petrol. Sorry, Moira. Just think, you could be the queen of Tree Palace and us boys can go strip homesteads in South Australia and then come home and then back to South Australia for a load and then home again. Zara can do her thing at the supermarket.'

Shane didn't get the congratulations he expected. Moira didn't reach over to kiss him or pat him. Midge narrowed his eyes in thought. Rory shrugged, scratched his nose with a bandaged finger and asked, 'What's a title?'

After a moment Midge said, 'How do you know no one owns Tree Palace?'

'Look at the place. Been rotting there for years till we came by. That's a job for you. Go check.'

'How?'

'This lawyer guy says start at the shire council or the land registry. Get that girl-lawyer to help. The one that worked for me. Whatsaname. Elisha Kay. Ring her. Get the ball rolling.'

'Someone probably owns it,' said Moira.

'Maybe. Maybe not. If they do we find another Tree Palace.

This could be the future, I tell you. A new business venture for us. Maybe we search all the towns we can for dormant titles and make claims for them...I thought you'd be thrilled. Instead you're down in the mouth.'

He and Moira stared at each other and she forced a smile. He smiled at Midge and at Rory. They didn't smile widely in return.

'What's wrong?'

Midge bit his fingernails. 'Nothing's wrong, Shane. Not wrong so much as, there are things going on that aren't, you know, perfect.'

'What things?'

'Things, you know.'

'No, I don't know.'

Moira took a deep breath. 'Um, where do I start. You see, well, it goes back to when Zara had the baby.'

She set it out for him, straight and honest. About how the girl tried to smother wee Mathew and how she, herself, had become his mother and was breastfeeding him. The breastfeeding had made her bloom and be very happy. But Shane's letter had set her off and she went into town and (another deep breath) flirted with Jim Tubbs. (Shane's bottom lip flopped again.) It was stupid, meaningless flirting, but that mongrel scum got ideas in his head and he arrived at the house and was all over her and Rory stabbed him.

Shane lurched backwards in his chair, stood up suddenly and made a wounded sound. The guard walked up and asked what the problem was. Shane mumbled that there was no problem. The guard said sit down or he'd end the visit.

'I didn't mean nothing with the flirting. I was blooming and you wasn't there to see it and I was feeling good and at the same time bad about your letter. I'm sorry. It was all a stupid accident.'

He eased slowly down into his seat. 'You're not hurt?'

'No.'

'Did he get far?'

'You mean—'

'Yeah. Did he—?'

'No, Rory got him.'

'Good boy.'

Rory beamed. 'You're not mad?'

'Course not. Sometimes it's the right thing.'

'I stuck him good.'

'In the leg and bum region,' said Midge.

Shane laughed. 'In the bum region? He got more than one hole down there now?' He looked at Moira and said softly, 'You're not hurt? Promise?'

'No.'

'I want to hurt him, bad,' he said.

'Where would that get us? He said he's coming for payback,' Moira said. 'I'm scared.'

'What do we do?' Midge said. 'You reckon he's bluffing?'

Shane shrugged. He squeezed his chin in his fist. 'No. That'd be Tubbsy. He'd be wanting to give Rory a hiding.'

'Let him try it,' said Rory, bobbing in his chair.

Shane said shoosh. He crooked his finger for Midge to crane closer and listen. 'You got to go bluff him. A bloke like Jim Tubbs don't want a soul ever hearing he got stabbed in the clacker by a fourteen-year-old. You got to go to him and say, Here's a message from Shane. He tries payback and what's left of the trant grape-vine'll go ape-shit with the news—a *boy* got the better of Jim Tubbs. I'll put a sign up in the hotel and write it in white paint on the main road. He'll be the laughing stock of Barleyville.'

Midge squirmed. 'You sure, Shane?'

'Sure.'

'I don't think I'm the one to do that.'

'I'll do it,' Rory said, bobbing in his chair.

'You will not,' Moira said.

Midge shook his head. 'Normally I'd jump at it, but I think it'd be better coming from you.'

'I'm in prison.'

'We can wait till you get out. Only two months off.'

'He won't wait two months,' Shane said. 'You stand in for me. Soon as you get home you go say that to him, that you're standing in for me. And you tell him this. If he goes anywhere near Moira again I'll finish the job Rory started.'

The Zara problem didn't get further mention. Moira was about to ask, What do I do? How do I stop her taking Mathew? But it suddenly didn't seem his business. It was hers, between mother and daughter. Shane had never been to Zara what he was to Rory and this was no time to include him.

He looked down at her breasts and said, 'You really got milk or just joking?'

Midge said, 'No joke, Shane. She's got milk all right.'

'Don't talk about me like I'm not here.' Her teeth were clenched ready to hiss him into silence. Shane had a quizzical look as if about to laugh at her. She said, 'So what if I got milk?

You think someone like me can't work miracles?' She reached over her neck as though to unzip her dress. 'I can work miracles. I'll show you.'

'Jesus, Moira. Stop,' whispered Shane.

'You want me to go into all the ins and outs of it with you? All the women's bit and pieces of how these things happen?'

'No.'

'Sure? I can just flop everything out and give the run-down?'

'No, no, no.'

He looked at the wall clock. The half-hour was nearly gone and the guard had given a nod to finish their session.

Shane's eyes went narrow and he sighed as if in pain. 'You'll come again, won't you?'

'They want me to have more points than I've got.'

'Get more points.'

'I'll come, I promise. I'll find a way.'

Midge and Rory promised they'd see him again too.

'You do as I said, Midge. Walk right up to Tubbsy and say what I told you.'

Midge nodded. He shook Shane's hand and hugged him. Then it was Rory's turn for a hug. Then Moira's. The guard said she and Shane could kiss and hug longer. They could keep going till the big hand got to twelve.

'How could you think I didn't miss you?' Shane whispered.

'I'm sorry.'

'I'll tell you something. I think about how you go on about having a baby with me. I know I always ducked it. I've been doing some serious thinking. I like being a dad to Rory a lot. It feels good. If you still want to, let's you and me make a little Rory of our own. No joking. Let's do that.'

'You mean it this time?'

'I mean it.'

'Promise?'

'Promise.'

'Not carried away?'

'No.'

'You might change your mind when you get out.'

'I'm not changing my mind.'

They kissed and the guard said that'll do.

40

The Barleyville wind greeted them in the usual way—pushed the wag from side to side, whistled through the open windows. Paddocks threw bits of dead grass at the windscreen. The sky had two clouds but they drifted off without rain. The wag reached home with only one downpour to manage, near the town silos, which was just as well because Midge had forgotten to get new wiper rubbers.

Limpy gave them his jumping welcome and looked like he'd rolled in mud, though it was a carcass going by the smell of him. Moira told Rory to tempt him to the water tank for a hose down.

Zara hadn't been home. No dirty clothes on the tent floor or bed slept in. The house was as they'd left it—note on the table, weighted down by a stone. Food was still in its packaging.

It was late afternoon and getting cold. They lit the lamps and ate and Moira got Mathew to sleep. She let him cry himself to exhaustion: she thought his wailing might trigger extra milk stimulation. Perhaps it did—she had enough in her to keep him happy. Only just. Tomorrow was no certainty.

Midge ate one mouthful of canned stockpot and no more. He was nervous about facing Tubbsy and had no appetite. The fork shook in his hands. He passed his portion to Rory and the boy lined it up behind his own plate. Zara was also on his mind. His instinct was to go into town and find her. Yet if she was going to set up house with lover boy he'd have to stop doing that—following her, being her protective father figure. Might as well start now, he thought.

But you can't turn feelings off like you can the tank hose. He wished he'd never let Zara into his bloodstream. He felt jealousy. He felt pain in his stomach from no food and fear of Jim Tubbs. The jealousy caused an even sharper pain: an icy ache higher up near his heart.

He began rehearsing his Tubbsy speech: 'I'm standing in for Shane and I got a thing or two to say to you.' He rolled a cigarette. His shaking tore two papers. He paced around the chandelier tree to perfect his lines.

Moira asked, 'When you going to do it, Midge?'

He muttered, 'Tomorrow maybe. Or the next day.'

The wind dropped and the sun went red and fell away. The moonlight and the stars when they came were like a spare world to go on with. Strong enough to cast shadows. It was so quiet that Limpy let out a bark and it echoed. He kept barking and the echoes ricocheted.

There was a vehicle coming. The headlights were on dim and Midge could see clear as day that it was Brent Romano's. It was going fast and had rock music blaring. 'It's lover boy, Moira.'

She came out of the house. *If you're going to take him let me train you first, girl. Please.* She curled her fists for fighting.

The vehicle stopped near the sugar-gum garage. The passenger side door opened and Zara got out as if pushed—fell on her knees, stood up and tried getting back in. She was begging to be let in.

The door was pulled shut. She banged on it and tried running around the front to the driver's side but the ute went into reverse and sped backwards down the road, the reverse gear whining on high rev.

Zara threw her bag down and knelt, swearing and sobbing. The ute used some width in the roadside to turn around.

She crossed her legs and sat in the dirt. When Midge went to touch her shoulder she elbowed his arm away and hung her head. He was puffing from the effort of running to her and had to step back and cough.

Moira moved close and knelt down. Zara was wearing her work smock and there was mud on it from sitting there. 'You'll get this all filthy for work.'

'I don't give a shit. I don't work no more. They sacked me.'

The girl punched the ground and put her hand under her armpit to quell the pain of the punch.

'What'd you do that they sacked you?' said Moira.

'Nothing. I didn't do nothing. It was Brent's dad. He said to Mr Dixchit, I don't want that girl hanging round my son. Get rid of her or I'll call the tax department and say you got two sets of books, whatever that means.'

She was shivering from the cold and the crying and Moira

tried standing her up but she was not about to move. 'Midge, get a jumper or something. Go on, don't fidget and gawk.'

Zara sniffed and wiped her nose with her finger. Moira didn't have a handkerchief, so she used her frock instead. Lifted the hem and told Zara to blow into it. The ute had reached bitumen by the sound of it: in the acoustics of the night the engine grabbed a low gear and the tyres yelped.

Zara looked down the road and said, 'Brent dumped me. Laughed about me moving in. He said, "Have your kid move in? You're joking." His dad said to him if he gets tied up with a trant he's out of the family business. An underage trant. His old man went mental.'

Moira spat on the ground. 'Family business? That's what I think of their family business. I'll tell you about family business. Shane says he's got ideas in South Australia. He's met people inside and they told him about adver-something possession and how you get houses for nothing. We'll be looking down on the Brents of this world one day, not the other way round.'

Midge arrived with a jumper. It was one of his because going through Zara's things to find one still didn't seem right. The jumper smelled of mould.

'It'll have to do,' said Moira, giving it a shake.

She put it over Zara's shoulders and the girl thanked her. Midge asked her if he could get her something else. She said no thanks, and no thanks again when he said she only had to ask and he'd get something.

Moira snapped at him and told him to leave them be, they had things they had to talk about, just her and Zara. 'Where's Rory?'

'Still gutsing himself,' Midge said.

'Get his food and take it in to the caravan and you go sit there with him. I need the house. I need it private.'

He nodded. He starting walking to the house, calling to Rory. He rubbed his hands together assertively. 'Pick your plate up and head in to the caravan. Come on. Move.'

Dew was falling. You couldn't see it but you could feel it on your skin. It was in Zara's hair when Moira touched it, damp and soft. 'I got something to show you. Come to the house with me. Stand up. I want to show you something.'

Zara shook her head that she wasn't going anywhere. Took her knees in her arms and would not stand, would not talk.

'Don't, then,' said Moira. 'I got something very special to show you, that's all. But if you want to sit there in the dirty road and not be shown, then sit there.'

They both sat in the road. The dirt was sticky-wet and slippery and Moira lifted the bottoms of her dress into her lap to keep it cleaner, though so she wasn't too fussy as it wasn't her good dress.

'We'll have to wash our hands first before I show you. You think that Brent boy means a thing to you? In a week, he'll mean nothin'. What I'll show you—it'll mean something all your life.'

She stood and cradled Zara's elbows and gently raised her. 'Come on. Get up. Come on, sweetie.'

41

Zara hung her head and walked, letting Moira usher her by the elbows. When they got to the house Moira told her to sit on the step while she filled a bucket from the hose. She put a cake of soap in the bucket and had Zara wash her hands and arms and knees. She got the girl's dressing gown from the tent and had her get out of the muddy smock and put the gown on. Then Moira washed herself, took off her dress and they both used that for a towel and then for a mat to wipe their feet on.

They went into the house and Moira positioned a lamp on the kitchen table close to the edge so it spread a brighter glow where she told Zara to sit.

'Let's put things right, girl,' she said. 'You might not want to just now. You might not care about it at the moment. But you will care one day, I bet you that. You'll care and Mathew'll care and I'll care. Because if things don't get set right between you and him, and you and me, then it's like we done wrong by nature. We don't fit into the world right.'

She went into the bedroom and lifted Mathew. He gurgled and wriggled. She sniffed him and his nappy was not clean but not bad. She folded a blanket around him and brought him out into the glow. 'When you pick him up, you don't pick him up like he's a bag of shopping. See how I got a hand behind his neck and I'm holding him with my fingers spread. All gentle but not too gentle. He's got to feel he's against you but can still move and breathe and be natural around you.'

She lowered the baby for Zara to take. The girl didn't lift her hands. Moira kept holding him there. 'Take him and feel him against you like it's for the first time. The very first. Like you're starting from the very first day. Close your eyes and do it. Close your eyes. Take him.'

Zara did.

'Lay him down along your arm. That's good. That's perfect. See? You're doing it perfect.'

They stayed like that for a while, till Zara's arm became tired and Moira helped shift Mathew to the other one. She heated up some stockpot but the girl wasn't interested.

'You got to eat.' She held a spoonful up and made her sip it. 'That's a start.' Another spoonful. Another. Moira helped switch the baby back to the other arm.

She said they'd keep doing that until Mathew woke.

When he did wake, bawling hungry, Moira said, 'Take him into my bedroom and lie down on your back and let him lie on you and cry.'

Zara was tired and was glad to go to bed, but this was no ordinary lying down. Moira told her to place Mathew stomach down between her breasts. Such small breasts—but Moira said leave him there anyway, crying. She lifted Zara's hand and had it rest on the baby's back and stroke. Don't worry about him crying, just leave him there.

Moira sat on the bed and watched Zara's stroking. As the crying went on she said, 'Move him closer onto you. On a nipple. That's the way. Let him have a suck.' She explained that this was what she herself had done. It might take weeks but milk would surely come. 'If I can do it, you can. I can pass the bloom on to you.'

When they finally fed him that night Moira boiled the baby bottle clean and mixed milk powder. She had milk in herself but she would not feed him—it was no longer for her to do. She gave the bottle to Zara and showed her the nipple-to-bottle system.

Mathew cried and would not take the bottle's teat. Moira craved to give in and place him on her own breast and have him drink what he could. She did not give in. If it was cruel to him, then cruel she had to be. *Suck on Zara. She's your mumma, go on. Now suck on the bottle. Don't spit it out. Go back and suck mumma. Now back to the bottle. Come on, little man. That's the way.*

He stopped crying and hunger made him drink from the bottle. The change of milk might make him ill, she thought. She had to trust in his trant constitution.

In the morning she passed the sling on to Zara. The material was too long for the girl and needed the knot made shorter. The baby's weight caused her to tip forward. Moira tied the sling higher and that helped her balance. 'Talk to him,' she said. 'Let him hear

307

your voice real close. I talked to him about our family. Tell him about you. Anything you like. Tell him about yourself. I won't listen. Let's go outside and you walk around with him and I'll hang back and not listen. It's a nice clear day and not too hot so take him up the road and I'll hang back.'

She hung back and couldn't tell if Zara was talking to Mathew or not. The girl was cradling him correctly, and that was something. She had her left hand against his back and was joggling him in the sling.

Rory wanted to bound up and make conversation but Moira said not to disturb his sister until further notice. He had another day off school because of the Tubbsy threat. Until the Tubbsy business was settled he was to stay out of town. 'Midge, if you don't do your job and get this trouble settled, I'll do it myself,' Moira said. She did not know how she would do it herself, but she said she'd try.

Midge vowed he would do it. He was so happy watching Zara walking the baby that he was angry to have Tubbsy in his thoughts, dirtying the moment. Resentful of Moira for presuming he would shirk his duty. And he was angry at himself that he wanted to shirk it.

'I'll do it today,' he said.

'We'll see.'

'I will.'

'Good. Off you go, then.'

'In a while.'

She refused to say another word to him until he did his duty. 'That's the last word from me.'

308

He followed her as she followed Zara and said there was no need to give him the cold shoulder.

Moira called for Zara to come wash Mathew and put some talc on him and a fresh change. 'Why you following us like a lost sheep?' she said to Midge.

'Could you pass out Shane's coat and tie, please?' he said. 'I'd like a lend of Shane's coat and tie.'

42

Wearing Shane's clothes gave Midge more heart, or so he imagined, as if taking on extra power. Mimicking his brother's pose, arms away from his sides, feet apart and springy on the spot. Head back in readiness for argument. The knot of the tie went tight up to his throat. It helped him speak with Shane's raspy temper.

He stepped down from the caravan with a forthright jump and jarred his hip. That was the end of his Shane-act. He was just plain Midge and hobbled to the wag, flicking his leg out to loosen it.

Rory got on his bike to ride with him to the crossroads. Moira whistled for him to stay on Tree Palace land, where she could see him. She wanted to whistle for Midge to come back too. One of Shane's crackpot notions—sending a half-cripple to settle their scores! She realised she should never have gone along with it. Should have gone to the police. Or put her cunning hat on and rung a radio or newspaper. No, that's not the trant way. Too late now. She wished she'd told Midge she loved him like a brother.

She told Zara to use the word 'love' to Mathew, to tell him over and over that she loved him. She went outside to leave them alone. Sat on the porch couch, where she could keep one ear on Zara's mothering.

The girl did as she was told and said she loved him. Said it loud, as if for Moira's benefit. As long as the girl was saying it, loud or soft, forcing love to come, it didn't matter to Moira. The sound of the word around the baby was better than not having it in his earshot.

Midge drove slowly and acted being Shane. 'Well, Mr Jim Tubbs. Got your comeuppance from a fourteen-year-old boy. Ha ha ha. Well, I'll tell you this, Mr Jim fucking Tubbs. You try payback on us and it'll go hard on you. Won't be a single town won't know it: Jim Tubbs got his comeuppance from a fourteen-year-old boy. Ha ha.' He experimented with threats but they all sounded lame: 'You'll have me to answer to, Midge Flynn. I'll...I'll...' His voice trailed away. 'I'll write on the hotel chalkboard what you tried to do to Moira.'

He put his asthma puffer in his mouth and bit on it and took a breath. It steadied his nerves. He drove slower the closer he got to town, putting off the inevitable.

The place to go was the Barleyville Arms. He could be bleeding to death, Tubbsy, but wouldn't miss happy hour. There'd be people there too, witnesses—safer. Yes, there was his green truck parked in a paperbark's shade. There were two other vehicles and a van with a trailer of beer kegs.

Midge found some shade cast by the bottle-shop sign and sat there trying to whip up a temper and get a snarl about him. All fake and unconvincing. His natural approach, politeness and a smile, kept coming out in his voice.

He rolled a cigarette to give his hands an activity and didn't smoke it. He stood beside the wag, did up the coat at the middle button and said, 'Get it over with, Midge,' and off he went.

Tubbsy was at the tall table by the window by himself. A half-empty pot of beer sat on a coaster. There were a few regulars watching the TV wall but Tubbsy had his back to them. He wasn't sitting on a stool. He was standing and leaning on a wooden crutch. When Midge said hello he twisted awkwardly on the spot, his teeth gritted in pain and brow sweaty. He was wearing shorts. His thighs were bandaged and his legs were swollen above the knee.

This gave Midge confidence to move up closer, say his speech and not fear Tubbsy being too physical. 'I'll keep this simple. A message from Shane. You hurt us and—' He snapped his fingers. 'You'll be a laughing stock by the time we've finished with you. Got your comeuppance from a fourteen-year-old boy. Ha!'

Tubbsy didn't look him in the face and that made Midge bolder. He got carried away. He started bouncing on his toes, Rory-style. 'Moira spits on the ground when she thinks of you.' Midge pretended to spit on the carpet. 'What trant tries interfering with another's missus? You're no friend of Shane's, mine or anyone decent. We don't want you in this town around us. Piss off and find another town.'

He pretended to spit again and looked around and saw drinkers were watching. He knew he'd gone too far, too loudly. But Tubbsy didn't argue with Midge. His eyes were downcast, glassy from drink, and sunken. You'd have thought life's spark had gone out in him. It made Midge back away and think, Tubbsy's got that curse men have when their meanness turns on them. You see them in pubs, the cursed men of meanness. When they've screwed up so bad, betrayed all they can around them, the only thing left to do was to drink themselves down into lesser men.

It made Midge shiver to see it. He was scared of Tubbsy all right, but not the old Tubbsy. He was scared of this new shrunken one: half man, half dead. He went out of the hotel as fast as his hip could go. He didn't believe in ghosts but he'd just left one behind.

He didn't tell about this ghost-Tubbsy when he got home. He enjoyed the accolades for having done his duty.

Rory couldn't believe it. '*You* took on *the* Tubbsy?' The boy didn't feel so brave anymore.

Moira sat Midge down under the porch and poured him bourbon in celebration. She topped it up with Coke as he drank. And as he drank he exaggerated the story. 'I stood toe to toe and he was ready to hit me.'

'Thought you said he was on a crutch.' Moira grinned.

'Well, yeah, but a crutch is a weapon in the hands of a Tubbsy. I poked my finger in his chest and I said—'

'Thought you said he had his back to you.'

'The point is, I dealt with the threat.'

He wanted Zara to come out and listen to him but Moira said the girl had duties of her own. The house door was ajar and he could see her wiping Mathew's naked bum. The baby was on his back on the kitchen table and gurgling and flicking his legs. Zara was talking to him but Midge couldn't read her lips.

Moira told him not to spy.

'I'm not.'

'Yes, you are. Let her be private.'

'I am letting her.'

'You saw more than you bargained for when you spied on me.'

His eyes went wide. 'Is she doing it now, feeding him off herself?'

'No. We're trying. Now come away from the window. Tell us the story again.'

He put down his drink and buttoned Shane's coat. 'I wasn't going to be bullied. That's what I promised myself. I looked him in eye and I spat in his eye.'

Moira wasn't really listening. She nodded as if taking in every word but her ear was cocked for any sound in the house. That's the way trust works, she figured. You trust someone but you keep an ear cocked. The girl was past harming Mathew now. Have faith. Have faith. Keep your ear cocked.

She stood and congratulated Midge. Like a man congratulates: handshake, tight-gripped, arm shuddery. 'You did your duty. Good on you. Tomorrow we start our duty to Shane.'

'What duty?'

'Business.'

She knocked on the door with a soft knuckle, pushed it further open and went inside. 'Just getting something,' she said. She lifted the kitchen table top and took out Elisha Kay's business card.

Zara had tied Mathew's nappy too loose. Moira saw it was going to ride down when he was lifted. She said, 'I'd take that off and go tighter next time. You're doing good, though. Let him nuzzle you and put his hands under your top. That's the way. That's the girl.'

Midge wanted to glimpse through the gap in the door. 'How's she doing, Moira?'

'She's doing perfect. Don't peep and pry.'

She put her hand on his chest and with a light push moved him back a step and gave him the card. 'That law Shane was going on about. You know, where you get land for nothing.'

'The adverse one?'

'Let's see if Shane's really on to something.'

43

Next day Midge drove them to town. Zara with Mathew in the back in his little bed. Moira beside her saying, 'I'm not interfering, sweetie, but put another blanket on him. When he wakes up shove that bottle in his mouth. He'll get skinny if he don't feed better.' Rory was in the front—Moira had let him off school again. 'Shane would want you to learn the tricks to it, this law,' she said. He could stay off school till further notice. This was a law Rory liked.

They parked at the phone box near the lawn-bowls corner. Midge put the coins in and dialled and gave the receiver to Moira.

'I'm sorry, who am I speaking to?' asked the receptionist.

'Moira. Moira Duggan.'

'Who?'

'Shane Whittaker's de facto. I need to speak to Miss Kay about adverse possession.'

There was silence on the line. Then: 'Hello. Elisha Kay speaking.'

'It's Moira from Tree Palace. You visited us. You dealt with

Shane. Remember? Barleyville. You gave us your card? We're hoping you'll help us with this thing called adverse possession.'

The money ran out and the phone clicked off. They scratched around for more coins and called and called. The receptionist said Elisha Kay was busy.

They drove to the supermarket and Midge went in to buy supplies. It upset Zara and angered Moira to be so near the supermarket but Mathew needed formula. Midge took an empty can with him so he got the right brand. They tried ringing Elisha again later in the day but even Moira's crying act got her nowhere.

It took two more days of calling to speak to her again. Elisha Kay was irritable when she answered, sharp in the voice and crude: 'You're giving the receptionist the shits, all your calling. Anyway, adverse possession, you reckon. I've never done any adverse possession. I'll give it to you people, you're a crafty lot.' She said she'd be in Barleyville next week on Wednesday. Meet her at the council offices at 11 a.m.

A crafty lot. Moira wanted that to go in a letter to Shane. It was a compliment: crafty means you use your brains. This business would probably come to nothing but at least they had a compliment out of it. And from a smart person like a lawyer. She made Midge write that in the opening lines. 'Tell Shane I said I think he's very, very clever.'

Rory said, 'Tell him I'm toughening up my hands for heavy lifting. I'm using Limpy's tennis ball. I'm squeezing it.'

Midge was more interested in boasting about his dealing with Tubbsy. 'I think Shane'll want to know *that* instead of tennis balls.'

The letter took a few days to write because Moira kept wanting to add things and have Midge rewrite it so there was the right amount of missing Shane in it and the right amount of *we're doing fine*. She wanted him to know that Zara was trying hard at mothering. A bit quiet and withdrawn but you couldn't fault her otherwise. She hoped that might warm him towards the girl and they might get along better when he was out.

On the final day of rewriting there was wonderful news involving Zara to tell him. 'You know how I didn't have points enough to say I was me at the prison? Well, I got enough points now,' she dictated to Midge. 'Zara and me was going through all my years of stuff, old bags and bundles, little boxes of photos and rubbish, and Zara said, "What's this?" And I said, "I don't know. Just a piece of paper." She said, "No, it's not. It's your birth certificate, Mum." What about that! I got points enough now to have identity. Thanks to Zara I can waltz into prison like I belong.'

They posted the letter on the way to the Wednesday meeting. Or as Moira preferred to put it, 'The meeting with our lawyer.' She'd dressed in her cherry-blossom purchase, washed her hair and put on a dignified dab or two of make-up. Zara was in her best jeans and white lacy blouse. The tattoo on her arm had healed into a cheap-looking scrawl. Moira made her wear a cardigan to hide it. Midge wore Shane's coat and tie. Rory wanted to wear them but had to settle for his cleanest board shorts.

Moira was pleased they'd made the effort because Elisha turned up in a red tartan skirt and red stockings. A cream top with black leather waistcoat. She had a red band across her hair and those red fancy boots on her feet. 'Now *that's* what I call class,' Moira said with a flourish of her hand.

Elisha didn't respond, didn't want to waste time with chit-chat, going by her bossy manner. She was carrying a silvery metal briefcase and put it on the council office's counter and flicked it open. She took her business card from a pocket in the case and gave it to the woman who served her. 'These are my clients,' she said.

Moira lifted herself on her toes and smiled and nodded to Midge. 'Clients. Like the sound of that.'

'We want to check a land-registry title. If you bring a local map, we'll show you the place we mean.'

The woman hesitated and mumbled something about not being authorised and not having those records at hand. Elisha interrupted her and told her to fetch someone who *was* authorised. 'These are public records which you can access electronically and we want to see them.' She spoke as if in a filthy bad temper but it was more professional than real, Moira realised—at one stage Elisha winked at her and said, 'Bureaucrats! You've got to hassle them or they fuck you about.'

Such a classy girl, such a foul mouth. Moira decided it must be a trick to sound tough and not too classy.

It took half an hour to organise but a local map was eventually spread on the counter and the location of Tree Palace was circled in black ink. An office assistant was sent to search for the title on a backroom computer.

'And neighbouring titles too,' Elisha called out. 'In case a neighbour owns the place.'

Rory wandered off down the corridor and into the library and poked around. Elisha Kay went outside for a cigarette and to check her phone messages. When she came back in she impatiently tapped her fingernail on the wood counter, saying, 'They're taking their time. I got a divorce to sign off on at 12.30. A client's, not mine.' She said at 1 p.m. she had a drunk-and-disorderly. At 1.30 a dispute over child support.

The title information arrived. Five pages. Elisha Kay studied them a minute. 'Parish of Barleyville, Loop Road, Lot 902.' She put her elbows on the counter and studied the pages again, flicking them back and forth. 'Shit.'

'What's wrong?' said Moira.

'Nothing's wrong. Your bloke Shane might be on to something. There's been no movement on this title for fifty-seven years. Nearest neighbours don't own it. No rates paid for yonks by the looks of it. To all intents and purposes, dormant and up for grabs.'

Moira gripped Midge's arm and jigged on the spot. Midge almost cried from pride in Shane.

Elisha Kay asked for the title to be photocopied so she and Moira could have one. She said it was up to them now—if they wanted to live there for fifteen years they might well become the owners. 'What I'll need to do is organise a statutory declaration from you all to say you squat there, or whatever you call it. We'll have to survey the land at some stage. Get its measurements done. There'll be a small cost to that. Make sure you put a decent fence up around the boundary.'

'We'll take a drive and we'll get some posts and rails some-where,' said Midge.

Elisha advised them to put money down as a gesture towards paying rates. Not much money. 'Rates on a place like that? We're talking small.'

Midge reached into his pocket and produced a crumpled twenty-dollar bill and some coins. 'That's all I got until rotation on Thursday. How much we got to pay you?'

'Nothing. Pro bono. I'm amused they've got this law.' She laughed and shook her head. 'You crafty bastards. Good luck with it.'

Zara stepped beside Midge and said, 'I got money. I got a hundred and sixty. I got it buried in my tent. I saved it.'

44

They paid twenty dollars and planned to top that up with some of Zara's funds next time they were in town. When asked what name to put on the receipt for the twenty dollars, Moira said, 'Everyone.' She told Midge to oversee that everyone was written down. Shane's name at the top, because it was all Shane's idea, this adverse business. Her name second. 'Make sure they spell me right, Midge.'

He leant over the counter to watch the office assistant tap their names into the computer. He pointed, 'Shane Whittaker. With two *t*s. That's right. Moira's got two *g*s in Duggan.'

He nodded, satisfied. 'Who goes third on the list?'

Moira said, 'You go.'

He smiled and said, 'Midge Flynn has two *n*s.'

Fourth should be Zara because of her putting in money for rates. Mathew should go next, right under Zara. Midge scratched his chin. 'What's Mathew's last name?'

'Um. Ah. I think,' said Moira. 'I think it should be the same as Zara's.'

Midge nodded. So did Zara.

'That's Bunce with a *c*, not an *s*.'

Last of all, Rory. 'That's Rory Spinks. With a *k* in it.'

'We're all there?' said Moira.

'All there.'

The office assistant swivelled the screen so they could see. 'Come here, Zara. Have a look. Rory, come have a look. Where's Rory? Rory!'

Midge skipped into a slow jog to find the boy in case he was off being trouble. He found him coming out of the library, shoving open the heavy glass door.

'What you been up to?'

'Nothin'.'

'Rory.'

'Nothin'.'

'Come and see your name. Come on.'

Moira had a feeling of floating instead of walking. It blurred her eyes and made her think she was missing a step every second stride. Getting in the wag, sliding in beside Zara, she worried she might miss the seat and land in the gutter. Everything was different now. Driving out of town—past the silos, the pigeons, the brown flat plains speckled with green—was driving to a real home. The sky was like water, blue and foamy. *That* wasn't different. How many times had she yelled at the sky for being too hot or too wild with its wind. She could still yell at it and still it wouldn't listen. She could yell for fifteen years and it wouldn't. Fifteen years. She hadn't lived anywhere that long. Not even five years. Not even one. It was frightening to be that connected suddenly. She wasn't sure she liked it. A responsibility you didn't have to take on. Not like people where you can kiss them and hold them or give them a wash and they listen to you. The land won't even know it's owned. It'll hear Midge saying, '*Our* Tree Palace'—he was saying it now as he drove—and it wouldn't even listen. More selfish than people.

But she couldn't wait to tell Shane. She held a copy of the title on her knees and folded it carefully. 'I want to see his face when we tell him. I want to show him this title and see his face.'

Rory turned and said to her, 'Look at this.' It was a book, a hardback with a picture of chandeliers on the front. 'Pinched it from the library. I don't have to go back to school ever, I reckon. This is what I should be learning. Antiques. There's pages and pages of antiques in here and I should be learning them.'

As they reached the crossroads and turned onto the Tree Palace road Moira told Midge to slow down and enjoy the moment. 'Stop here. I want to walk up to *our* front door.'

She got out and invited Zara to do the same. The girl accepted, though she said she was feeling funny—must be carsick or the excitement of the day. She was glad to be walking along, the breeze on her face, carrying Mathew who was waking and gurgling.

The wag shuddered over a ridge in the dirt, making magpies flap up from the road onto the leafless limbs of a dead gum. Magpies and every other bird would be like guests now. If they were flying on our land, Moira joked, they'd have to ask for permission to fly.

Too right, said Midge. And people better ask permission to

visit. 'We can put up a sign,' he said. 'No trespassers.' He chuckled. 'That's a laugh coming from us.'

Moira and Zara walked ahead. Midge followed them in first gear. He was nodding but not really listening to Rory read out bits of his book. *'Mahogany is a des…desi…*What's that word?'

'Desirable.'

*'Desirable wood bec…because…of its…*What's that word?'

'Hue.'

'What's a hue?'

Just then, Zara appeared to lose her balance and almost fell. Moira held her up. 'What's wrong?'

'Feel funny.'

'What kind of funny?'

'Sort of sore?'

'Where?'

'Here.'

'Breasts?'

'Yeah.'

'They feel funny?'

'Yeah. Different. An ache.'

'Kind of a full feeling?'

'Yeah.'

She told the girl to sit down on a clump of rye grass. She waved to Midge. 'You and Rory drive on. We'll see you later.'

'Something wrong, Moira?'

'No. Do as I say. Go. We want to be private for a while.'

'Sure?'

'I said, we want it private.'

Midge drove past them and changed into second gear. Rory said, 'What's a hue?'

'I don't know. A hue is a hue.'

Mathew was awake and crying. Zara put her hand across her front. 'You think it's happening?'

'I don't know.'

Moira told her to loosen her top.

'Let me look.'

'You think it's happening?'

Her right breast, small and white, had a larger look.

Moira touched it. 'I think it might be.'

'You think?'

'I think it's happening.'

She touched Zara's face. She saw it in her face. Eyes gleaming. Skin gleaming.

The bloom.